THE INTERGALACTIC GUIDE TO HUMANS: VOLUME 1

BOOKS 1-3

SKYE MACKINNON

Peryton Press

ALIEN ABDUCTION FOR BEGINNERS

THE INTERGALACTIC GUIDE TO HUMANS #1

LESSON 1

INTRODUCTION TO ABDUCTIONS

XIL

This had been a mistake. A big one. Judging from their groans, Havel and Matar thought the same thing. When I'd signed us up for this course, I hadn't expected there to be assignments, let alone exams. It was supposed to be a bit of fun, not an entire degree.

"Is it refundable?" Matar asked with an irritated flick of his tail.

I studied the terms and conditions. Klat. No such luck. And we'd paid way too many credits to just give up before we'd even started.

I grit my teeth. "We're going to do this. Exams be damned. We don't even have to do well in them. There are some planets that accept abductors without qualifications."

Havel flashed his fangs in annoyance. "We know. And look how that's worked out. We're the laughingstock of the entire galaxy."

"Just this sector," I quipped. "And we can still change that. We just need to get it right the one time and everything will be forgotten."

Matar groaned again. "We've tried six times. I can still see the last female waving at us as she stole our escape pod. Do you really think we'll be successful after taking this course?"

"The Intergalactic University has an excellent reputation. Their classes must be good. And if we fail, we can always choose a different path. I hear space pirating pays quite nicely."

"Kardarians don't become *pirates,*" Havel spat. "They abduct females. It's what we do. What our people have done ever since they discovered spaceflight. We have to do this. There's no other way."

"Yeah, I don't plan on staying a bachelor forever." Matar licked his lips. "I can't wait to have a female of my own. Soft and succulent, ready to worship me."

Havel snickered. "I think you got something wrong there. You're supposed to worship the female, not the other way round. Make her feel like the only woman in the universe. Even I know that. Maybe it's good that we're doing this course after all."

I left them to their bickering and select the first lecture. We were on autopilot and wouldn't get to Kepler Two for another seven intergalactic hours, so we had got time on our hands. I threw it at our main screen, hiding the view of the Scorpion Nebula flying past.

"Now?" Havel groaned. "Don't we have better things to do?"

I shot him a glare. "It was you she ran away from. Sit down and watch this klatting lecture."

He grovelled but both him and Matar took their seats. I was already in my captain's chair. The only difference between my seat and theirs was that mine was a little elevated, giving me a better view of the bridge. It wasn't any comfier and the thick skin on my arse told of the many hours I'd spent in this chair. Autopilot was all well and good, but I was a traditionalist at heart and liked to fly Jade, my ship, manually.

After the logo of the Intergalactic University vanished, a Karangi female appeared on the screen. The third eye on her forehead sparkled with enthusiasm as she introduced herself as Professor Katila welcomed us as her new students. Not that she was actually aware of us. This was a recorded lecture, just like all of them. We'd only get to talk to our professors face to face in seminars and in preparation for our exams. I shuddered. I hated exams.

"Abductions are one of the galaxy's most sacred traditions," she said in her smooth, delicate voice. They'd done well to choose a Karangi to hold these lectures. They were known for their intelligence and benevolence. If a Karangi was able to do an abduction despite their deeply ingrained morals, anyone could.

"Ever since the first species discovered space flight, abductions of lesser beings have taken place. It's a universal urge that cannot be ignored. Whether it's for companionship, research or simply to get a new pet, abductions are your cheap and easy way to get what you need. The rules of the University require me to say at this point that we do not condone slavery in any shape or form."

She smiled, all three eyes full of warmth. I almost felt loved simply by looking at the video of her. "We shall begin this course with the four Ls. Learn. Locate. Lure. Leave."

The four words appeared on the screen. Matar snorted. "She left indeed."

"I don't think that's what Professor Katila meant," I whispered before realising I didn't need to keep my voice down.

"We're currently at the learning stage. You need to know everything you can about how best to abduct. It's not enough to simply know how to take someone from their planet. You have to be prepared for the aftermath."

Matar chuckled again but both Havel and I ignored him.

"Once you've completed the basic modules of this course, you can start thinking about locating your target. There is a lot to consider even if you already know the species and planet you prefer. Knowledge is key for a successful abduction. As soon as you've done your research and have set your eyes on your target, it's time for the luring stage. Some might simply use a tractor beam to get their target aboard, but in my opinion, that lacks finesse. Abducting is an art form and it should be treated as such."

"She's a little over the top, right?" I asked the guys. "How is it art?"

"Maybe that's where we've gone wrong," Havel muttered.

"Finally, leaving the planet. This isn't just a physical task. Your target will feel lost and alone so far from their home. It's your responsibility to make them comfortable and prepare them for their new life. Even if that life means being probed and researched until they expire."

Interesting. Katila was against slavery but didn't mind subjects being experimented on. I didn't know much about probing, but I was pretty certain that it didn't always happen with the consent of the being on the lab table. I supposed we'd cover that later in the course.

"Today, we shall talk about the motivations for your planned abduction," the Professor continued. "You can do this as a solo or group project, although we do recommend beginners to cooperate with other students for their first abduction. It will help you achieve the top grades possible while also assuring a safe and rewarding experience."

A set of questions appeared on the screen, all of them ridiculous. I regretted signing up for this class even more now. Group work. I hated it. I'd never been much of a team player. The raisers in the hatchery had despaired over my desire to sit in a corner on my own, tinkering with some project I'd come across. I only worked with Matar and Havel because they were good friends and excellent at their jobs. Unless it came to abductions. That's where all three of us sucked. Hence this klatting course.

"Do we write down our answers?" Havel asked. "Do we need to submit them?"

"This project is not graded," the Professor's voice replied immediately. It had to be an automatic, recorded message. "But we would like you to send us your answers anyway. My assistants and I will be happy to help you and provide feedback."

Matar rolled his eyes. "Great. Yet more work. I've still got the booster engine to fix. Does this really take priority?"

"Do you want to get our reputation back or not?!" I snapped. "We need to abduct a female and quickly. If this is the only way to achieve that, so be it. The engine can wait until we're done with the first module."

I flicked open my wrist communicator and projected a large piece of virtual paper in front of me. Real paper was way too expensive to use for something like this. I synced it with the guys' comms so that whatever one of us wrote would appear on everyone's paper. It was a great way to avoid having to sit in a circle.

1) Why do you want to conduct an abduction?

"It's part of our culture," Matar said and his words appeared on the paper. "If we don't get this right, we'll be laughed at for the rest of our lives."

"Without respect, we won't get good tariffs on our products," Havel added. "And we need the money."

I sighed. "My father will never let me inherit his wealth unless I can prove to him that I'm not useless and an embarrassment to our species."

Havel snickered. "You don't have to rub it in, we know your family's loaded. Once he dies, you'll be able to buy an entire fleet of ships, not just this one."

As much as I hated my father, I didn't want him to die. I didn't respond to Havel's comment and took a look at the second question instead.

2) How do you imagine your perfect abduction target?

"Soft, beautiful, female, sexy, willing," Havel said with enthusiasm, the words blending into each other. "Fertile. And compatible with our physiology."

Matar laughed. "Don't worry, she doesn't need much to be *compatible* with your tiny cock."

Havel snarled, flashing his fangs. "If you don't watch your tongue, I'm going to make sure to add something poisonous to your next vaccination. How do boils around your balls sound?"

"Cut it, you two," I growled. "Of course we're going to take our target from a species that's similar to our own. We want a mate, not a servant, and certainly not a lab rat.'

"And a breeder." Havel smiled. "Can you imagine, us becoming fathers?"

No, I couldn't. None of us was ready for that kind of responsibility. I was sure he knew that, but for now, I'd leave him to his fantasy.

"Clever, funny, courageous," I added to the list.

My friends rolled their eyes but I ignored them. It wasn't all about looks. Especially because I wasn't the most desirable Kardarian that had ever lived. Havel and Matar were lucky, their colouring was what Kardarian females wanted. Deep blues and greens, while I'd been born yellow, the colour of my disgraced great-grandfather. It had only added to the disappointment my father felt whenever he looked at me. I bet that he'd pushed me out of the family long ago if I hadn't been his only child. My mother and he had tried again and again, but I was the only result of their union. They despised me for it.

3) What will you do with your abductee? Will you keep them permanently?

Yes, all three of us wrote as one. I smiled. We'd been unsuccessful so far, which meant that we'd never let our female go once we'd finally captured her. She was going to be ours for the rest of our lives.

"She'll be our mate," I said and the words appeared below the three Yeses. "Our companion. Our friend. And eventually, the mother to our offspring." I shot a look at Havel. "Mother sounds better than breeder."

He nodded. "Right. Unless she prefers to be called our breeder. Depending on her species, that may be the correct term."

I checked the screen and realised with relief that we'd answered the final question. I quickly compiled our replies and submitted them to Professor Katila. We'd have to wait for her to send us the next lecture, but the university had provided us with several textbooks on abductions. I forwarded them to the others. It was time to do some hardcore reading.

LESSON 2

PREPARE OR FAIL

I stared at the galaxy map, my tail twitching with nervosity. I wrapped it around my leg to keep it out of the way. The other guys were used to it by now, rarely stepping on it, but I'd been self-conscious of it all my life.

Four planets were blinking fast, giving us our possible destinations. The Intergalactic University had sent us a database of abduction-ready planets this morning and now we were trying to find the perfect one.

"What's the green one?" I asked, pointing at the largest dot.

Xil checked the database entry on his comms. "Laranus. Sparsely inhabited. Females are compatible with us but...oh."

"What?"

"They don't have breasts."

I gaped at him. "No breasts? How do they feed their offspring?"

He scrolled through the information, then started to laugh. "They have tubes extending from their pussy that the younglings feed on for several years. Like straws. I doubt the females would be agreeable to sex during that time. It might squash the tubes."

I cringed at the thought of plunging into a female while weird fleshy bits were hanging out of her. No thanks. I wasn't speciest, but that was a little too exotic.

"The red planet is Riva Four," Havel muttered, checking his own comms. "They're very underdeveloped. No spaceflight yet. They still use animals for transportation. I suppose it might make it easier to abduct a female from there. They may even see us as gods. Wouldn't that be fun, being worshipped as a deity? Yes, you can suck my godly cock and receive my holy seed."

I elbowed him. "Don't talk like that. Females don't like vulgar language."

"Who says that?"

"I read it in one of the books," I admitted. "I was bored last night."

"Teacher's pet," Havel snickered. "Did it say anything else that might come in handy?"

I nodded. "Lots. But why would I tell you? I'll use my new knowledge to make our female love me the most."

Havel flashed his fangs at me. Most of our kind had lost them in the process of evolution, but some of us still had the features that told of our predatory heritage. Havel complained about them all the time, saying they got in the way while eating, but he'd refused any offers from dentists to have them filed down. I thought that secretly, he was quite fond of them.

"That one," Xil said and pointed at a blue planet at the very edge of the galaxy. "Peritus, but the natives call it Earth in most of their languages, not sure why. It seems to have several oceans, but maybe they worship the ground they live on? Maybe they're scared of the water."

"Do they have vaginal tubes?" I asked with trepidation.

"Not that I can see. And they have breasts of all sizes. Some are almost udders. Wow. Imagine burying your head between them, like soft pillows."

Havel laughed. "I'd bury something else between them."

"They only have one truly sentient species on their planet called humans. They've discovered spaceflight and are slowly spreading across the galaxy."

I dimly remembered coming across their kind before. It had to have been on some space station, but all I could recall was the name of their species, nothing more.

"Do they have tails?" I asked carefully.

Xil shot me a knowing look. "No, not that I can see. No fangs, either, but they do have beautiful manes." His eyes widened. "And fur in other places. I like it."

I couldn't resist any longer. I opened my own comms and searched for the IGU's database entry on humans. Several images appeared before my eyes. I was the only one of us who had the implant that connected my comms to my optic nerve. It was handy for looking at information that I didn't want anyone else to see. And porn.

I ignored the image of a male and scrolled to one of a female. She had a long, black mane full of curls, dark skin that reminded me of the pap tree beans we had at home, and yes, there was hair under her arms, between her legs and on her lower legs. Beautiful. My mouth watered. I could get used to having one like her around.

I quickly skimmed the section on human biology. They were compatible with us physically, although there was no information on successful breeding between our species. That worried me a little. Had nobody abducted a human before? Unlikely. The planet was part of the university's database, which meant it had been studied by scientists.

Still, I liked the look of these humans. So much so that I didn't even feel the need to explore the fourth blinking planet on the map.

"How long until we get there?" Havel asked. He seemed just as eager as me to get there quickly."

I frowned. "Two galactic weeks, faster if I get the booster engine sorted. We should have enough fuel for a round trip; no need to stop at a space station on the way."

Xil switched off the holomap and sat back in his captain's chair, a smile curving his ochre lips. "That gives us enough time to complete all the other lectures before we reach the planet. Matar, get that engine fixed as soon as possible. Havel and I can complete the next module without you."

"No way," I protested. "I don't want to miss anything. I'll work on the engine later."

The captain sighed but didn't argue. All of a sudden, the IGU course had become less of a pain in the arse. We needed all the help we could get if we wanted to abduct one of those precious humans.

Human. I let my tongue taste the word. Human. It didn't sound too bad. Not quite as pretty as Kardarian, but that didn't matter. Our female would have her own name.

Something beautiful, I was sure of it. If not, we'd give her a new name. Maybe we couldn't even pronounce hers.

"We need to get a translator," I said into the silent room. "Or do we have one on board? I'm not sure she'll speak anything but...whatever humans speak."

"They have hundreds of languages on their planet," Havel said without looking up from the text he was reading. "But it seems all of them have been catalogued, so a standard interstellar translating device will work. I think we have a couple of them in the med bay, they came with the Jade. I'll check later."

I nodded and got back to reading the chapter about Earth's geography that I'd just started before I got distracted once again. I didn't think I needed to know any of this. We weren't planning to settle on our abductee's planet. We'd land, find a suitable female, abduct her, and leave. I couldn't care less how many continents they had, but Professor Katila said there would be a test, so it was better to be prepared. Failing wasn't an option.

Four continents. There had been another, but it had disappeared when ocean levels rose. Humans seemed to be a very destructive species. They'd almost torn their planet to pieces before just about managing to turn it around, becoming more aware of the environment they depended on. Still, I understood why they'd started exploring the stars. It didn't look like a planet I'd like to live on. Pollution was ripe. I flicked forward a few pages until I found information about air quality. Thank A'Ta, we'd be able to breathe their air.

"Look at those breasts," Xil groaned and sent a picture to all our comms.

I sucked in a breath when the naked female appeared in front of my eyes, projected into my optic nerve. She was hot. Scorching hot. Her breasts were full and tempted me to reach out and squeeze them. She had strange rubbery shafts in their centre, probably to let the milk flow into her offspring's mouth. Kardarian breasts didn't have those, they had pores through which the milk diffused into the open. What would it feel like to suck on those fleshy knobs?

"What do you call those...appendages?" Havel asked breathlessly.

"Nipples," Xil answered, his face turning slightly orange. He was aroused. And not just him. My cocks strained against my uniform bottoms. How could an alien female make me feel this turned on? It was just a 3D image, nothing more. This wasn't our abductee and I shouldn't feel this way about a random female.

I pushed the image away together with the boring text about geography. "Let's listen to her lecture," I proposed. "We can continue reading tonight once we've done our other tasks."

Our captain nodded and turned on the main screen, touching his comms until Professor Katila appeared in front of us. Her third eye blinked a couple of times while her other two eyes stayed wide open.

"Welcome to our second lecture," she said with a wide smile. "Today we are talking about how to prepare for an abduction. If you've looked at the recommended reading, you'll see that there's a lot of ground to cover. If you don't prepare, you will fail. Some of you may have already tried your first abduction. If you're taking this course, I assume it didn't go well."

"You could say that," I scoffed. "Not at all."

"Preparation is key. Remember the four Ls. Learn and Locate are far more important than Lure and Leave. Without the first step, you will fail at the subsequent three." She smiled again, some of her seriousness washing away. "If you haven't decided on a planet and species yet, now is the time. Once you have, please watch the next part of this lecture."

She froze for a moment until Xil pressed the play button again and the recording resumed.

"Now that you have decided on a species, it's time to do as much research as you can manage. If you're working as a group, you can split up these topics, but I do recommend that all of you learn the basics. Remember, it is your duty to care for your abductee. They will have to get the right food, the right sleeping arrangements, even medical care."

"I'll do her medical care," Havel interrupted. "And I'll do any necessary probing too."

Xil shushed him so we could continue listening to the professor talking.

"You will also have to know about the planet's defences. Some species don't take kindly to having members of their own abducted, while others may even pay you to take some of their undesirables. Either way, you need to make sure that you won't be shot down or pursued by their military. This is why we often recommend planets with no space-faring capabilities for abduction beginners."

"Too late," I muttered. "We're definitely getting a human."

"A human with breasts," Havel reiterated. "Big ones."

"I will send you all a list of areas to research. Since all of you are likely focusing on a different planet, you don't need to send me your results, but please contact me if you have any questions or can't find enough material about a particular species."

Her lecture was followed by the logo of the IGU, a strange animal that I'd never been able to identify. It had to be from a planet I'd not been to yet.

"Let's split the list in three," Xil said, already sending Havel and me our parts. "Research your topics and then we'll get together tomorrow and share our results. Put anything that everyone should know into a separate document, that way we can compile a guide to our future human."

I scanned the list he'd sent me. Food. Technology. A few other things that aligned with my interests. I shot Xil an appreciative look and left the room, still thinking about breasts.

It turned out that humans ate a lot of strange things. Most of the animals they ate didn't mean anything to me, but it would be hard to replicate those. We had a food replicator, of course, but it needed blueprints and ingredients for anything we wanted it to make. We'd fed it the genetic code of the livestock we were used to from our home planet, but we couldn't exactly probe every single Earth animal just on the off-chance that our female might like their meat. Many of the vegetables humans ate weren't too different from what we were used to, especially the various kinds of roots they grew in the ground. Again, a connection to the earth. I hadn't found any explanation for their planet's strange name yet, but their religions weren't on my list. Maybe one of the others would discover the answer.

They drank something called water, which was the base of most of their drinks. A fairly simple mix of hydrogen and oxygen. Hydrogen wasn't a common element in this part of the galaxy, but we could easily synthesise it to make that drink for her.

After I read through everything I could find on their various dishes - very confusing since every single tiny village had their own foods, which meant we'd never be able to know what our abductee liked until we knew where she came from - I continued on to exploring Earth's technological advances. They were about five hundred rotations behind Kardar, with their spacefaring technology still in its infancy. Humans seemed excellent at exploiting other species' technology though, which meant they had access to spacecraft that they hadn't developed themselves. Cheeky. They were scavengers, in a way. Not unlike the three of us. We called ourselves traders, but we got a lot of our goods by entering abandoned space stations and crashed ships.

Earth's defences were negligible, at least the tech they'd created on their own. Without knowing whose technology they may have borrowed, we would have to be careful, just in case. If they'd got their hands on Lurian weaponry, we'd never leave the planet in one piece.

I made a note to take enough weapons with us to the surface. We wouldn't use them on our female, of course, but on anyone who would try to stop us. We deserved a female and we would take her no matter how much resistance we had to fight against. All three of us had served in the Kardar military, although as a healer, Havel hadn't been on the front lines. His fighting skills were rudimentary at best, but Xil made up for that. He could have risen high in the military if he hadn't decided to leave with us.

I blinked, tiredness making itself known. I still had to fix that booster engine. I sighed, but then remembered that the faster I fixed it, the quicker we'd get to our female and her voluptuous breasts. I grinned at the thought. Yes, I could get used to seeing a female like that every single day until the end of my life.

LESSON 3

HOW TO CHOOSE THE RIGHT FEMALE

Earth looked rather pretty from space. Its atmosphere cloaked it in a blue sheen, a similar colour to the oceans below. We'd taken our position in orbit, ready to take the shuttle to the surface. The tractor beam wasn't strong enough to cover this distance, and besides, I always loved travelling on the shuttle. Steering it through space was exhilarating.

"What are you going to wear?" Matar asked, looking uncharacteristically insecure. He wouldn't usually care what other people thought of him, but he did seem to care about our female. To be fair, I felt the same. I wanted to impress her. Show off the muscles I'd worked so hard to achieve. I wasn't a warrior, not like Xil and Matar, but that didn't mean I didn't have abs to die for. That's what my ex had said, anyway, before complaining that she didn't find the rest of me to die for. I'd show our human that I was irresistible. She'd fall in love with me.

"We're going to have to use disguises," Xil interrupted before I could reply. "We don't know what humans' reactions to us will be. We don't want to stand out and attract unwarranted attention. Our abductee might flee if she sees how different we are from her."

I sighed. "I don't like those holosuits. They're itchy."

"You'll wear yours," the captain snapped. "And if you complain again, I'll make sure you look as ugly as the Black Oboto himself."

I flashed my fangs at him but didn't protest. He was right. The holosuits would make us appear human, letting us blend in.

"I'll download some templates," I sighed and opened the holosuit catalogue on my comm. They didn't have a lot of choice when it came to human costumes, but I quickly chose the three best looking ones. Mine was the one most similar to the sexy big-boobed female we'd seen on the photograph. Dark skin, long black hair that was braided in a strange but fascinating way, and an outfit that left little to the imagination. His dark green shirt was open, revealing his smooth chest. I ran my tongue along my fangs like I always did when I was confused. His skin was so...bare. No scales, no spots, not even tribal tattoos. How very boring.

My own torso was covered in dark spots that resembled the Earth leopard I'd read about during my research. It was a leftover from our evolution, a camouflage feature that wasn't of any use to me now. Still, I loved my spots. They were nice and smooth to touch, unlike Xil's scales. I hoped our female would like us despite all our differences.

"Before we get dressed, we need to decide on where to land," Xil said. "We've agreed on what kind of female we want to abduct, but someone like her could be anywhere on that planet. There are billions of humans crawling in their precious earth and we need to figure out how to find *the one*."

"Maybe we should ask the Professor," I suggested. "She keeps saying that she wants us to get in touch if we have questions. It might make a good impression on her if we ask for advice."

"Or it might make us look like idiots," Matar muttered darkly. "I say we should simply choose a continent at random and let A'Ta's divine tail guide us."

I sighed. "You're the only one here who believes in A'Ta. I'd much prefer our research to guide us. Or our teacher."

"We shall call her," Xil said in his best captain's voice. He always sounded older when he did that. It was hard to resist a command given in that dominant tone and he took advantage of that whenever he needed to.

Before Matar could protest again, Xil had already opened a communication channel to the IGU. Their logo appeared on the screen, followed by a hairy furball with tentacles instead of arms. A dentril, a rare and exotic species. I'd never met one in person. It was said that their fur was poisonous to the touch and their cuteness a natural weapon.

"State your business," the dentril squeaked. I had to suppress a grin. It was adorable.

"We'd like to speak with Professor Katila. We're her students."

The creature's tiny orange eyes blinked a couple of times, as if it found that unlikely. He was right, the three of us looked more like space pirates than intellectuals.

"I shall connect you," it said after a while and the IGU logo appeared once again. One day I'd find out what animal they'd adopted as their mascot. There had to be a reason for it.

A tired-looking Professor Katila flashed into view. Her third eye was closed as if part of her was sleeping. Curious. I'd never had the chance to study Karangi physiology in detail, but I was sure it was fascinating.

"How can I help you?" she asked, clearly suppressing a yawn. None of us had checked what time it was on the IGU station, so we may well have woken her from her sleep. Not exactly the best way to make a good impression on the person who'd grade us at the end of our course.

"Professor, we're about to land on the planet we've chosen and we could do with some advice," Xil said politely.

"Which planet?"

"Peritus. Earth."

Her third eye flew open. "Earth. Now that's an unusual choice. May I ask why you decided on that planet?"

"Boobs," Matar whispered. I cringed, hoping the microphone hadn't picked up his comment. Our Professor was female and I didn't want to offend her. I'd always been ambitious and I wanted to do well in this assignment.

"The females there are compatible with our species and fulfilled all other criteria we'd come up with," Xil said smoothly. "Their lifespan is a little shorter but the advantages of a match with a human outweigh the differences."

Her third eye blinked while the others stayed open. "None of my students have attempted to abduct a human in a while. They're a strange kind. No physical defences to speak of, but their minds are sharp. They're willing to sacrifice a lot to get what they want."

That matched our research. Humans were weak and yet not.

"Humans exist in various colours, just like you Kardarians, but just like with you, they're all the same on the inside. I'd recommend choosing a female that's not too small unless you don't plan to use her for...physical purposes."

Her third eye twitched with amusement.

"Thank you for the advice," Xil said and bowed his head. "Anything else we should know?"

"It sometimes helps to keep them in only one room in the beginning until they acclimatise to their new life. They can be both irrational and curious, and you really don't want them running amok around your ship."

I exchanged a look with the others and cringed. Yes, we'd already experienced that with the last female we'd tried to abduct. We'd learned from that. This time, all our escape pods had been biolocked to the three of us. Same with the ship controls and the board computer. The female wouldn't be able to get off this ship unless we let her - which, of course, we wouldn't. She was ours to keep.

"Is there a particular continent we should choose?" Matar asked.

"I'm not an expert on Peritus geography, but as far as I know, it doesn't matter. In the past hundred years or so, their governments have worked hard to make sure everyone on the planet has equal opportunities and resources. However, I assume you have read O'ltg'si's research on socioeconomic influences on abductions?"

I nodded enthusiastically, while the other two pretended to know what she was talking about. I smirked. I'd enjoyed that particular research and thought it might come in handy.

"It can be beneficial to abduct someone from a poor background," Professor Katila summarised the study. "That plus no or very few family ties will make them quicker to adjust to their new life."

"A poor orphan," Xil muttered. "Makes sense."

"How do we identify one, though?" Matar asked the Professor. "I assume they don't run around with 'I am an orphan' signs on Peritus?"

Katila chuckled. "No, they don't. But you could hack into their government databases and find the information that way. Or you simply go to one of the poorer districts in whatever settlement you land and search for an abductee manually. Either way, I wish you the best of luck with your assignment. Document everything as best as you possibly can so that I can give you a good grade."

She smiled and ended the transmission.

I glanced at the guys. "Are we going to do the database thing? I'm sure Matar can hack whatever security measures they use."

Xil shook his head. "I feel like going hunting will be more fun. Plus, it'll give us more material for our assignment reports." He rolled his eyes. "Remember, this isn't just an abduction, it's also a practical exercise for the IGU."

It wasn't hard to forget that, not after having spent the past week reading copious amounts of research papers and listening to virtual lectures. I felt as prepared as I could be. The last few times we'd tried to abduct a female, we hadn't known what we were doing. This time, we were ready.

"Let's randomly choose a place," Matar suggested. "I can let the computer run through all the names of towns and cities on Peritus and have it stop at a random time."

I nodded. "Sounds as good a method as any."

Xil inclined his head in agreement. "Start it. I'll be the one to say stop."

Matar moved his hands in a strange dance; inputting data into his implanted comms device. It always looked strange to us because we couldn't see the interface he saw in front of him. I was glad I hadn't decided to get the same implant. I liked my vision without the influence of others.

"Starting now," he said after a moment.

Xil and I waited, locking eyes. My breathing was growing faster as I realised the significance of this moment. We were finally choosing where to go. Where to find our perfect female. In a few hours, we'd hold her in our arms. She might be riding my cock by the end of the day.

I resisted the urge to touch myself. She'd do that for me, soon.

PRACTICAL ASSIGNMENT

ABDUCTING A HUMAN

The heat outside was suffocating. The air inside was even worse. The shack I currently called my home didn't have air conditioning. It didn't even have electricity.

I wiped the sweat off my face, very aware that it would be back within minutes. My body was wet all over. An entire lake was pooling beneath my boobs and I didn't even want to think about my armpits. No deodorant was strong enough for this kind of heat-induced sweating.

It had to be the hottest day of the year. The hottest day in years. I didn't have a thermometer but I didn't need one to know that staying outside for too long would be lethal. Yet I had errands to run and staying home would mean another evening without food to keep the hunger at bay. I had to leave my shack, there was no way around it.

I covered my purple hair beneath a large sun hat and made sure my sunscreen film still covered my skin. I'd stolen it, but it had been worth the guilt. My skin had always been prone to sunburn and this high-tech film prevented it almost entirely. I'd have to recharge it soon, but for that, I needed to find somewhere with an open electricity port. In this town, those were rare. The world may have recovered from the wars and natural catastrophes in most places, but not here. This was a dirt hole that I'd tried to escape ever since my parents had abandoned me. Problem was, leaving was hard if you had no money. So I'd spent the past few years trying to make not only a living but also to put away some savings. And failed. I didn't even have enough money to pay for my dinner today.

Hopefully, Chadra would have some work for me. I adjusted my hat one last time, making sure its wide brim would throw some shade over my eyes - both to protect from the sun as well as unwanted attention - before leaving my shack. I didn't bother locking the door. If someone wanted to break in, they'd be able to do so without much effort. Besides, I had no valuables to steal and I doubted anyone would take the few things I had. They wouldn't bring them any money at the market. Most of it had been found or stolen. I'd become good at repairing broken things so that I could use them nonetheless.

I hurried along the dusty road leading into town. My shack was at the very outskirts, in the slums, although of course, nobody called them that. Slums had existed two centuries ago, but not any longer. No, we weren't supposed to exist. The people in power ignored us and we ignored them in turn. This was a lawless, dangerous place, but it wasn't like I could afford to live anywhere else. I paid exactly zero rent because, well, I lived in a tiny wooden hut with a leaky roof. Not exactly luxury.

The shiny dome of the spaceport at the edge of the desert glinted in the sun. I blinked and looked away before I could start having fantasies yet again, dreams of leaving not just this town, but the entire planet. Those were childish. They were vacancies to work on spaceships, yes, but I had no skills and qualifications that would ever get me there. No, I was destined to stay here, starving, always hoping for a miracle.

Chadra's shop was empty and refreshingly cool. It was a ramshackle store that was filled with all sorts of unnecessary crap, but the owner was kind and often had work for me. I gave two marble statues a questioning look. Not exactly something people in this part of town would buy.

"Those are new." Chadra appeared from behind a curtain, barely managing to squeeze through the doorway. She was big, no, massive. Three of me could have filled her clothes and there would still have been space. Her white hair was braided around her head like a crown, giving her a somewhat pompous appearance, especially when paired with her slightly upturned nose that always made her look arrogant and aloof.

"What are they for?"

She shrugged. "Coat stands? Oversized garden gnomes? I'm sure I'll find a seller eventually. But I doubt that's why you're here."

"Got any jobs for me? I could do with some work."

Chadra rolled her eyes. "You always do. Why don't you try to find a full-time job somewhere? You're a clever girl."

"Woman," I corrected. I barely reached the five-foot mark and people often thought me younger than I was. It was annoying but it also had its advantages. I'd been let off by the police more than once because I got them to believe I was simply a teenager, not yet of age, and therefore not worth the trouble.

"And nobody wants to employ someone like me. I never even finished school."

"Qualifications have nothing to do with intelligence. You're a quick learner. If I could, I'd employ you as my assistant, but I wouldn't be able to afford you. Still, you'll be pleased to hear I've got a job for you. A courier run to the spaceport."

I groaned. That meant I'd have to spend all afternoon in the burning heat.

"Want to say something?" Chandra asked with a smirk.

"No. It's fine. Great. Wonderful. What do you need me to deliver?"

She pulled a small parcel from a drawer, not much bigger than my hand. Jewellery, maybe? It had to be something small yet valuable. Chandra wouldn't have something delivered if it wasn't worth it.

"Don't ask questions, don't look at the customer for too long. Just get to the spaceport as fast as you can and ask for a Mrs Lester."

"Can I get a scooter?" I asked hopefully and to my surprise, Chandra nodded.

"You'd never get there fast enough by foot. But if it gets even the tiniest scratch, I'm going to have to take it off your wages. And because I don't pay you much, it's going to take years for you to repay, so you better don't have an accident."

I gulped, but it wasn't like I had a choice. I needed the money.

Chadra pulled a bundle of keys from her pockets and threw one of them at me. I caught it easily and grabbed it tightly, unable to suppress a grin. I'd not ridden on a scooter in years. This was going to be fun.

Half an hour later, I was on the side of the road, my knees bleeding, the scooter wrecked. And my head hurt like hell. I hadn't worn a helmet because there hadn't been one. Something wet tickled my cheek. Tears? I rubbed my face before looking at my hands. My skin was stained with red. A head wound. Just what I needed.

I let myself fall back onto the hot sand. I didn't have the energy to get up and inspect the damage. This was it, the moment the last dream turned into dust. I'd have to spend years paying for what just happened, like Chandra warned me. Years of starvation. Instead of improving my life, I was making it worse.

I closed my eyes, unwilling to look at the damaged scooter any longer. I wasn't quite sure what had happened. It had suddenly stopped and I'd been flung through the air, over the handles and onto the hard ground. Everything ached. For some reason, the scooter had then started to drive again, on its own, right into a brick wall that had once been part of a house. Not anymore. The homes that had stood here had all been abandoned when the spaceport had been built five decades ago. Now, they were nothing but ruins.

My head was starting to pound as if someone was banging against it from the inside. I must have got hurt more than I first thought. I couldn't afford to go to a doctor or even call an ambulance, so I just had to wait until it got better.

The sun was quickly drying the blood on my face, turning it into something that felt like a mud mask. A wave of vertigo overcame me even though I was lying in the sand. The ground swayed beneath me and bile rose in my throat. Don't puke. Please don't puke.

The headache was getting worse. Was this the end? Was I going to die in a ditch, alone with no witness but the scorching sun? It would turn my body into a burned crisp before anyone removed my remains.

Even though this was the road to the spaceport, nobody had driven past since my crash. People would start passing by once their shifts ended later today, but now everything was quiet and deserted.

I let my mind drift, unable to stay focused. The pain pulled me away, wrapping me in its arms and telling me not to worry. I welcomed it. There was no point in resisting. Darkness lingered around the edges of my mind, waiting for me. Soon. For now, the pain wasn't ready to let me go quite yet. It explored my body, showing me all the places I'd been hurt in. My legs, my back, my head. I wished for the darkness to swallow me. I didn't want to have to wait. Any delay meant suffering. I'd fought all my life and now I was done fighting. It was time to simply give in to the temptation of everlasting sleep.

A shadow fell over my face, instantly cooling my skin now that it was no longer being grilled by the sun. Someone was talking from high above, several someones. Men. I couldn't make out their words, but I was grateful for the shade they gave me.

I waited for them to leave so that I could die in peace, but they didn't move. Something - no, one of them - touched me by the shoulders. I groaned. I was too tired to move, even opening my eyes seemed like too much of a task.

Cool fingers touched my cheek. Inside, I smiled. Such a nice feeling. It was lovely of them to stay with me while I died. I wouldn't have a funeral but this was even better. I was still alive and knew they were here. Funerals were kind of pointless for the dead person.

More fingers on my face. What were they doing? One of them touched my eyes, gently, ever so softly.

I wanted to see them, I was so curious, but when they pulled up my lids and let me see them, I regretted that.

The sight of a bright blue man with glistening fangs was the sight that finally drove me over the edge and into the waiting embrace of darkness.

LESSON 5

BASIC TECHNIQUES IN DEALING WITH AN ANGRY FEMALE

XIL

Thil had been our easiest abduction to date. Ironic, since we'd put the most work and resources into it.

We'd found the perfect female without having to spend any time at all on her hot, humid planet. Our randomly chosen location sadly hadn't brought us to lush forests or sparkling oceans. No, it had been a dirty hovel in the middle of nowhere.

"She's healing well," Havel reported. "I'm keeping her sedated though until all her injuries have been dealt with."

I nodded, pleased with how things were turning out. We'd carried her right into our med bay where Havel was now working on her.

She was gorgeous now that Havel had removed the layers of dirt caking her face. Her skin had a reddish sheen in some places but not in others. Maybe they were like my spots, designed for camouflage. In that hot and sandy place, orange and reds would be great to hide in plain sight. She was special, I knew that already. The way her eyes had widened in surprise when she'd seen us made my heart beat faster. She'd seen us as the saviours we were. We'd come to take her away from that place and she was grateful for it, I was sure of it.

"How long until she wakes?" I asked our healer.

"Two hours, maybe three. I want to make sure she's definitely not in pain."

I nodded. "Good. That gives us the chance to check in with the IGU and see if there's a new lecture to watch."

Matar groaned. "Seriously? Now? Can't we just stay here with her? I don't want to leave her, not now that we finally have been successful."

With a sigh, I had a screen descend from the ceiling. "We can watch it here."

I checked the IGU's student dashboard. A large questionnaire waited to be filled in about our abduction, but I clicked on the lecture instead.

Module 5: How to deal with an angry abductee.

I exchanged a look with the others, then let my eyes drift over our sleeping human. I doubted we'd need that lecture. She was going to be grateful that we rescued and healed her. She had no reason to be angry. If everything went well, she'd find ways to show her gratitude. My cock twitched, growing hard. It had been semi-aroused ever since we'd brought her onto our ship. I was aching to plunge into our human's depths to find out what she felt like. There'd be enough time for that though. This was only the beginning.

Professor Katila appeared on the screen. Her third eye was closed and she had a strangely serene expression as if she'd just emerged from a trance.

"Welcome, students. If you're watching this lecture, I assume that you have successfully abducted a being from another planet. You may think that the hard work is done, but you'd be wrong. The act of abduction is easy. The hard part is yet to come."

I gulped. That didn't sound promising in the slightest.

"Your abductee will be scared, no, terrified. You've ripped them from their home and from everything they've ever known. Depending on what planet you chose, they may have never seen an alien before. You need to be aware of that and proceed slowly."

My cock didn't agree with that statement. Down, boy. You'll get your chance.

"You will have to draw on all the cultural research you've undertaken. If you don't speak their language, fit them with a translator."

"Already done," Havel whispered, clearly pleased with himself.

"Communication is key. Sit them down and patiently explain that you have abducted them. Tell them that there is no way they're going to return to their home planet. It's important to be open with them from the start. They will get over the shock more quickly that way. Introduce yourselves and make sure to answer any questions they may have about your species. If you have any physical features that may be unfamiliar to your abductee, show them at this point. Be open about your differences and highlight the similarities. Once this step is done, tell them what your plan is, whether that's research, companionship or something else entirely."

Her third eye blinked open lazily and she used her slender fingers to wipe the sleep from it.

"If you require help with how to do what I call *the talk*, you can find several pointer sheets in your files. They'll give you helpful conversation starters. As always, you can contact me with questions. Our next lecture will be all about probing, an essential skill for every capable abductor, even if you don't plan to conduct research on your subject. I'll see you then."

The screen turned black. That was a quick lecture. Not that I was complaining. Sometimes Professor Katila droned on and on, giving us more information than I could ever process. Not today.

I looked at our sleeping human. *Ours.* Havel had removed her clothes to access all her wounds, but he'd immediately covered her with a sheet. We'd barely got a look at her body and seeing her full, round breasts push against the fabric from beneath wasn't enough.

"Uncover her," I ordered. "I need to see what we abducted."

"Who," Havel corrected drily but he did as I'd asked.

She was small, much smaller than a Kardarian female would ever be, and didn't have enough flesh on her bones. Was she supposed to be this way or was she emaciated? We'd have to find out once she woke. Her hips were wide and strong, perfect for birthing our offspring. She only had five fingers and toes each, but I'd read that this was the norm for humans. I curled my six fingers into a fist. Maybe Havel could give her those extra digits to make her look a little more normal.

"I love her breasts," Matar sighed in contentment. "Look how they'd fit into my hands."

He got up, but Havel stepped in his way. "No touching until she's awake."

Matar growled, his tail slapping against the floor. "You don't tell me what to do."

"But the Captain does." Havel shot me a stern look.

I wanted to touch her too, but our healer was right, this wasn't the time to explore her body. "Later," I said. "Sit down. It will be more fun when she's awake and can tell us how good it feels."

"Can't you wake her now?" Matar complained. "She looks healthy to me."

Havel rolled his eyes but checked his medical instruments. "In theory, I could. But are we all feeling ready to have *the talk* with her?"

I nodded. "I'll take the lead. Havel, try to keep your fangs hidden for now. Matar, no sudden tail movements. We don't want to scare her."

Both of them inclined their heads in agreement, before Havel started adjusting the machines that were keeping our human unconscious.

"It'll take a few minutes for her to fully wake. Be patient. Let her wake up naturally and take in her surroundings. Maybe we should all move back a little."

The three of us retreated to the back of the room. I didn't want to be that far away from her, but Havel's advice made sense. We had to go slowly or we'd end up in the same situation as last time when our abductee had run around the ship like crazy, threatened us with our own weapons before jumping onto an escape pod. I shook my head to dispel the memory. The embarrassment of that still hurt.

The human moaned softly, but her eyes stayed closed.

"This could take a while," Havel whispered. "I've tried to find out as much about their physiology as possible, but a lot of it is still guesswork."

I shushed him with a glare. She didn't need to hear us talk about her like a lab experiment when she first woke up.

We waited in silence, the tension rising with every minute that passed. Finally, her eyelids twitched and she let out another moan. That sound woke something in me, a feral instinct to protect this female. I clenched my fists to prevent me from storming to her side to hug her to my chest. She was *mine*.

She opened her eyes but didn't sit up yet. All she could see was the ceiling, which was probably the blandest ceiling in the entire ship. Our vessel was old but we made sure to keep it clean and homely. We spent most of the year on the ship and it therefore had to feel like a place we wanted to spend time in. Matar had decorated most of the walls with colourful, abstract paintings. He growled at anyone who commented on them, but I knew he was secretly proud of his art, even though it didn't fit into the image of the macho, growly, aggressive male he tried to be.

The med bay, however, hadn't been painted and was boring shades of grey and white. With a white sheet covering most of her body, her dark hair stood out even more. Kardarian females didn't have manes like that. They had short, wiry tendrils sprouting from their scalp, but nothing as soft and lush as this. I couldn't wait to have tiny Kardarians with long, soft manes on my arm, looking up at their papa with adoration.

"Hello?" she asked, her voice hoarse as if she'd screamed a lot. Maybe it was dehydration.

"Did you give her that oxygen-hydrogen fluid humans like?" I whispered to Havel.

His eyes widened. "I forgot. I made some but I only gave her standard fluids to rehydrate her, not what they call water."

I was tempted to rip off his head, but we needed our healer.

"Get her some right now."

"Shouldn't we wait-"

"What the fuck?" the female suddenly exclaimed and we turned back to her. She'd sat up and was staring at us. Time to follow Professor Katila's instructions and start *the talk*.

"Hello, female," I began, "you have been abducted and are now on the Jade, my ship. You will not return to Earth. You will become our mate and breeder and you will be happy with us. Do you have any questions?"

She blinked several times, then rubbed her eyes. Was there something wrong with her? I shot a panicked look at Havel, but he didn't seem too worried.

I realised I'd forgotten part of my speech and quickly continued. "I am Xil, Captain of this ship. This is Havel, our healer, and Matar, our engineer. We are Kardarians, one of the most powerful species in the galaxy. We are compatible with you, although you may need some practice to accept our cocks because you're so small. We don't know yet if we're compatible for breeding, but we will find out. Oh, and-"

I ripped open my uniform to expose my mottled chest. "I have large spots and scales. Havel has fangs. Matar has a tail. Besides that, we aren't all that different from you. Except that you're missing fingers."

"Very well done," Matar whispered. Havel looked pleased with my speech as well.

The female, however, didn't react as I'd planned. Not at all. She started laughing. She threw her head back and laughed, her entire body shaking from the giggles breaking from her chest.

"Is she reacting to the drugs you gave her?" I asked Havel.

"I doubt it. Maybe it's her way of communicating her happiness at the situation?"

I shrugged. Humans were strange, so this may as well be her showing us how pleased she was with us.

"Do you have any questions, female?" I asked, hoping she'd take the hint and stop laughing.

She gasped for breath in between giggles, causing concern to rise in my chest which turned my scales a darker shade of yellow.

"This is a joke, right?" she asked breathlessly. "Is this my punishment for breaking the scooter? Did Chadra put you up to this?"

Again, the three of us exchanged a look. Chadra? Punishment?

"If you'd like to be punished, we'd be happy to comply," Matar said smoothly. "I've heard some aliens expect punishment when they're abducted. I'd be happy to spank you if you wish."

The female immediately stopped laughing and stared at Matar. "Spank me?"

He held up a hand. "Slap you on your bum."

"I know what spanking is. What the hell? Why are you doing this?"

"It's part of our culture," I explained. "We've wanted to abduct a female for so long and you're just what we were looking for." I didn't tell her that we'd failed many times before. She didn't have to know that. I wanted her to see us as strong, capable males who'd given her the perfect abduction experience.

"Abduction experience," she echoed. "I think the joke is over now. Can I just get my scooter back and leave?"

"You cannot leave," I said as gently as I could. "I already told you that. We're in space and on route to Kardar. You will never return to Earth. We are your mates and this ship is your home."

To my surprise, she snorted. "Yeah, sure. You're great actors, I give you that, although you should work on your script. No aliens would ever talk like that."

"But we are aliens," Havel interrupted. "Here's proof of what the Captain has been saying."

The blinds to our right shot up, revealing a large window. Outside, space was endless and beautiful. I'd always loved looking at the stars, wondering which ones I'd visit in my lifetime. I smiled at the sight, then turned to the female to see her reaction.

Her mouth had fallen open, revealing her very flat teeth. Not a single fang in sight. Havel was the only one of us with pronounced fangs, but even Matar and I had sharp teeth that could rip a piece of flesh off a bone. Yet more proof that humans were incapable of defending themselves.

"That's...it can't be real," the female muttered. She slipped off the bed and walked to the window with slow, unsteady steps. Havel moved to help her, but I held him back. I wanted to see what she'd do next.

She lay her hands against the window as if trying to touch the stars outside. I smiled. She was already starting to understand the beauty of our surroundings.

"This is a simulation," she said, her voice becoming steadier. "I don't know how you're paying for it, but this has gone on long enough. Don't you dare charge me for it. I'm going to have to work years to pay off Chadra's scooter already."

"I don't know what you're talking about, female, but this isn't a simulation," I assured her. "We can have a true simulation at some point so we can show you our planet, but now isn't the time. What is your name?"

I knew I should have asked that earlier, but luckily Professor Katila wasn't here to grade us on our performance. We'd simply tell her that everything went smoothly.

"That's none of your business," the human snapped. "And I'm leaving."

To her detriment, the three of us were standing right in front of the only door leading out of the med bay. And there was no way we'd let her go. Not after the escape pod drama.

"Sit down and ask us questions," I told her and pointed at the bed. "You're supposed to ask about your new life and us."

She raised her eyebrows and I realised they were brown rather than pink. Curious. "I'm *supposed* to?"

Matar nodded enthusiastically. "It's what it says in the manual. You're full of questions and we'll do our best to answer them. It will calm you down and prepare you for the next step."

"What's the next step?" she asked, her voice wavering a little.

Havel grinned, happy to have reached his favourite subject. "Probing."

LESSON 6

PROBING FOR BEGINNERS

She stared at me as if I was the alien. Something to inspect and examine and then put into a display case. I didn't think she'd fully comprehended that this was real. It wasn't a joke and it didn't have anything to do with her scooter. Not that I understood what all that was about. We'd found her next to a crashed vehicle, but I didn't know why anyone would dress up as aliens as a result of that happening. Humans were strange.

"Probing?" she asked in a high-pitched voice.

I nodded, smiling in anticipation of something I'd looked forward to ever since I'd seen the module in the IGU course description.

"It's an important part of any alien abduction," I explained. "Abductees expect to be probed. If you look at human reports of abductions, most of them report probing, so we wouldn't want to disappoint you."

"Disappoint me?" she screeched. I didn't know female voices could go that high. It actually hurt my sensitive ears.

"Exactly. We know you want to be probed and I'll do my best to make it all you've ever imagined."

Her eyes grew even wider. It had to be a human way to show excitement.

"What kind of probing would you prefer?" I asked pleasantly. "In our lectures, they've taught us various methods but since it's the first time for both of us, I thought you should choose."

"What kinds are there?"

I grinned, satisfied that she was interested. "It all starts with the basic exam. Taking blood, measuring your body weight and size, counting your teeth, cutting off some of your mane for analysis, and so on. I have to admit that I've already completed most of that while I tended to your injuries. It was essential to be able to give you the best treatment possible, but I apologise. We can redo those things if you'd like."

Her lips parted but she didn't reply, so I continued. "The basic examination is usually followed by the actual probing. I can insert probes into your various orifices to look at your insides. I've read humans quite like anal probing, but as I said, it's your choice. I've prepared several different instruments to make it as pleasant for you as possible. What do you think about anal probing?"

The female coughed. I frowned, immediately worried that I'd overlooked an injury, but a quick look at my med scanner showed me that her lungs were intact. Maybe it was because we still hadn't given her that magical water humans required.

I rushed to the fabricator. I'd already programmed the chemical formula for water, so it took only seconds for a glass of liquid to appear in front of me. I offered it to the female and she grabbed it, downing it in one go.

"That wasn't poison, was it?" she asked as soon as she'd set down the glass. "Although, I guess that would be better than probing."

"No poisons, but I'm sure I could find some hallucinogens for you," I offered. "Or maybe some sedatives to make the probing even more comfortable."

"You mentioned lectures," she muttered. "What do you mean?"

"We're taking a course in alien abduction," Xil explained before I could. "We wanted to make sure that this abduction goes as smoothly as possible for everyone involved."

He didn't mention our previous failures.

"This is real? I'm really in an alien spaceship?"

Finally. I nodded. "Yes, you are. Should we repeat our introductory talk?"

"No, it's fine." She gulped visibly and I couldn't resist checking the med scanners once again to make sure her throat was alright. Maybe she'd had too much of that oxygen-hydrogen liquid. I'd have to do some more research into how much of it was safe for humans.

"Now that we've established this is real, could we progress to the probing?" Matar asked impatiently. "I've been looking forward to this too."

The female shook her head. "No probing."

"But it's part of the process," Xil argued. "There's no way around it. We may fail our assignment if we don't do it."

She made a strange noise that was somewhere between a cough and a laugh. "You're getting graded on this?"

"We are," I confirmed. "But don't worry, we've had excellent grades in the modules leading up to this. We're top of the class."

"Thank goodness for that."

Her voice had a strange vibration to it, but I hadn't read about this happening so I didn't know what that might mean. Excitement? Relief? There was so much learning to do. I was starting to think that humans were far more multi-faceted than I'd realised.

"Probing," Matar reminded us. "Now."

I walked over to my probing trolley that had all the instruments I'd require. I'd crafted most of them myself after studying human physiology. Most of the tools I'd have used for Kardarians were too big for our dainty little female. She was even smaller than I'd anticipated.

I chose one of the smallest tools and held it up so our female could see how unthreatening it looked. "Shall we start with the anal probing? Please roll around so I have better access. You can hand that sheet to Matar; I think subjects generally prefer being naked during probing."

She looked down at herself and grabbed the edge of the sheet covering her. "I'm naked," she stated.

"Yes, you are. I had to undress you when I looked after your injuries. Is that a problem? Did you want to experience the undressing while you're conscious?"

TRISH

This was one weird dream. I was starting to think that I was still lying by the side of the road, unconscious, having some strange concussion-induced visions. That was the only explanation. Even if I really had been abducted by aliens, I very much doubted that they'd ask my opinions about probing. Aliens didn't do that. They just did what they wanted before dropping you off back on Earth with your memory wiped. Or they sold you as slaves. Or...well, anything except this.

The blue alien seemed intent on stuffing that metal rod into my arse. I'd always loved anal sex - when I say always, I mean the two times my ex tried that with me before we split up - but this was something else entirely. What would happen if I said no? Would they still continue? They didn't seem intent on harming me, but they'd been brainwashed into thinking that this was part of the abduction process.

I laughed hysterically, causing them to look at me with confusion. Abduction process. Their words, not mine. Definitely a crazy dream.

"I'm glad you're happy about this," the blue alien - Havel, I believed - said with a grin. His fangs glistened in the bright light of the room, making a shudder run down my back. Maybe it was a good idea to do what they said. Those fangs looked lethal. I bet they were poisonous.

All three aliens were massive, hulking males full of hard muscles and tempting abs. They were drop-dead gorgeous, even with their scales, fangs, and tails. One tail. I couldn't help but look at it again. The green alien had rolled up his sleeves, exposing dark markings along his arms. Tattoos or birthmarks? Who knew. His tail was wrapped around his left leg like a snake, but I'd seen him pound the floor with it earlier. I wanted him to turn around so I could see if he had a hole in his (very tight) trousers where the tail sprouted from...his tail bone? Was it part of his bum? Or higher? I didn't dare ask him. He gave me the most dangerous vibes of the three of them. The yellow alien was the captain of the ship, but he had a good-natured smile on his face while he waited for the probing to begin. He'd shown me his mottled, scaled skin earlier. His shirt was still open, exposing pecs that were to die for.

My mouth watered at the sight. I shouldn't ogle them like that. They'd abducted me and were planning to stuff instruments into my - what had he called it? - orifices. My arse was just the beginning, I was sure of it. Another shiver ran down my back, but I wasn't sure if it was fear or excitement. It had been a while since I'd had anyone look at me with such fascination, even adoration.

Don't give in to the aliens, Trish. They've probably given you some drugs to make you fancy them. Maybe they played with my vision, too. What were the chances of all three of them looking this hot? Perhaps they were ugly monsters with tentacles and warts, and I only saw what I wanted to see.

"Are you speaking English?" I asked, suddenly realising how effortless our communication had been.

The yellow alien laughed. "No, we don't speak your primitive language. Havel fitted you with a translator as soon as we got you onto our ship. It's a brain slug, embedded in your right ear."

I must have misheard. Brain slug. He meant brain plug or something like that. Not slug. Not a slimy animal.

"They feed off soundwaves and then transmit the information right into your brain. You're speaking your language, but our slugs transform it into Kardarian. They've been fitted with microchips that can add whatever language we want. Because we weren't sure where on Earth we'd find you, we added all eight thousand languages spoken on Peritus."

I ignored every single thing he'd said and deleted it from my memory. I was good at that. I'd experienced too much crap to want to remember it all.

Instead, I clung to the last word, one I hadn't heard before. "Peritus?"

"The intergalactic name for your planet. I'm not sure why you call it Earth. You've got so many oceans yet you didn't call it Sea or Ocean."

I cocked my head, surprised. I'd never thought of it like that.

"I have no idea why," I admitted. "Maybe it's because we all live on land. We're not made to live in the sea."

"Yes, you don't have any gills," the blue alien said with an almost disappointed look in his large, expressive eyes.

"Let's start the probing. Anal first?"

I couldn't believe this was happening. I was surrounded by aliens who wanted to look into my arse. With metal probes. And yet...my nipples were getting hard and warmth gathered between my legs. The thought turned me on. I was one crazy lady. I hadn't been with anyone in way too long; it was no surprise I was reacting like that. I was having sex withdrawal symptoms, that had to be it. That's why my mind was conjuring these things. Unless they were real.

That possibility was becoming more and more likely. I doubt even my mind could come up with brain slugs, especially not slugs embedded with microchips. That was one step too far.

"Turn around," the green alien ordered impatiently. "I'm starting to get hungry." His tail thumped on the floor as if to underline his words.

Time to make a decision...

"Is it going to hurt?" I asked, barely able to believe that I was actually considering it.

"Of course not," Havel replied with a frown as if that thought insulted him. "Unless you want it to. Is that what humans imagine alien probing to be like?"

I quickly shook my head. I didn't want to give him any ideas.

He seemed relieved at me not wanting it to hurt. And that relief was what made me turn onto my stomach. The white sheet slipped away, exposing my naked back. And my bum.

Had I shaved before I'd been abducted? It had been a couple of days, at least. Without a boyfriend, I often couldn't be bothered.

I snickered to myself. I was worried that the aliens might dislike a few hairs rather than fearing their probing.

"I've coated in the instrument in a cooling gel," Havel explained. "It will prevent pain and will help the probe glide in more easily."

Alien lube. How lovely. They'd really thought of everything. I wondered if that was part of their course. Had he practised this? Maybe on the other guys? The thought made me wet. Those three aliens, naked, probing each other...

Something cool touched my arse and all other thoughts fled my mind. Warm, soft hands spread my cheeks and the cold instrument was gently pressed against my rosebud.

I tensed, but then hands gently ran over my back and my shoulders and I instantly relaxed. I barely noticed the probe gliding into my arse, I was too occupied with one of the aliens massaging my shoulders. I didn't know if learning how to do this had been part of their strange abduction class, but if it had, I wanted to hug their teacher. It was heavenly.

"What now?" Havel whispered after he'd fully inserted the probe.

"What do you mean?" the captain asked. "Continue probing her."

"But this is it. I've inserted the probe. It's done. But it doesn't feel like it's enough."

"Wasn't there supposed to be a camera attached? To see her insides?"

The medic sucked in a breath. "I forgot! Klat, I'm an awful prober!"

He sounded genuinely upset, so much so that I turned my head to look at him.

"You're doing great. It feels lovely."

It really did. I was dripping wet even though none of them had touched me anywhere besides my back and my arse. The probe was slowly becoming warm while it filled me with a pleasant pressure. I ached to touch my clit, but that would have been entirely inappropriate. The aliens didn't seem to see this as something sexual. It was only me who was craving more.

"It does?" he asked, still unsure. "Shall I try another probe, a larger one?"

I straightened my neck again so they couldn't see my expression and grinned. "Yes, I think you should."

He pulled out the instrument, making me feel very empty indeed. I needed something bigger. An alien cock would have been perfect, but I'd settle for a larger probe.

I was crazy. I was being probed by aliens and I was *enjoying* it.

"Spread her open," Havel ordered, his voice hoarse. Maybe it wasn't just academic for him either.

Hands grabbed my cheeks and pulled them open. Cool air hit my opening just before cold metal was pressed against it once more. I tried to relax, but this one was a lot bigger than the one before. Havel pushed it in slowly, but with steady pressure, helping overcome my body's resistance. I moaned when it was fully inserted, stretching me. My clit was throbbing, aching to be touched.

"What a curious sound," the green alien muttered. I kept forgetting his name, but this wasn't the time to ask.

They kept stroking my back, my bum, even my legs. My body was putty under their skilled hands as they massaged me into blissful oblivion. The probe in my arse seemed to get smaller, or maybe I was just getting used to the sensation of being filled to the brink. By now, I wouldn't have said no to an alien cock to complete the probing.

"Probe me," I moaned before realising I'd even done it.

Havel chuckled. "She seems to enjoy this. I think we'll get top grades on this."

"All credit goes to you, my friend," the captain replied before running his fingers through my hair. Now that he'd spoken, I could identify who of the guys were standing where and doing what to my body.

"Where shall we probe her next?" Matar asked.

"Female, do you want to continue?" Havel addressed me. "You still haven't told us your name."

"Trish," I groaned. "Don't stop."

The medic moved the probe in my arse and I almost came. Fuck. I was being probed by aliens and I was about to orgasm because of it. What was I turning into? Some sex hungry hussy ready to serve her alien masters? No way.

"We won't stop until you want us to, don't worry. Trish." He rolled the R in my name. I loved it. "Trish."

"Trish," the other two aliens echoed.

"I like that," Xil said, a smile audible in his voice. "We won't have to give you a new name."

I shouldn't be surprised that they were considering that as an option. These guys were crazy. And amazing at giving me pleasure.

"I'm going to remove the anal probe," Havel announced. "Then you're going to turn around so we can probe your other orifices."

That word took away some of my arousal. There had to be a better, sexier term for my holes.

"Don't," I moaned. "Keep it in. Do both at the same time."

Silence met my words. They hadn't expected that. I chuckled. It probably wasn't in their abduction course. Did that make it an extracurricular activity?

"Alright," the medic said after a while. "But turn to your side, we don't want you to get hurt. It'll be more comfortable that way."

The way he cared about my wellbeing while probing me was almost endearing. I was starting to think that these aliens had their hearts in the right place, despite their abduction fetish. They could have gone about it in a more violent manner, yet here they were, asking me how I wanted my probing to be done. Maybe that was why I wasn't reacting like a normal abduction victim should.

Instead of running, screaming, attacking them, I was dripping wet and begging for a probe in my pussy.

I rolled onto my left and spread my legs. Matar grabbed my right leg and held it in position, saving me from having to expend any energy on it. I was now on full display, yet I didn't care.

"She's leaking," the captain said, sounding worried. "Female...Trish, is that normal? Are you unwell?"

"Normal," I managed to say before breaking into laughter. "Totally normal. Don't your females get wet when they're aroused?"

All three guys sucked in a breath, clearly shocked.

"No, they don't," Havel said after a moment's silence. "Is this water? Can I test it?"

For a moment, I thought he'd asked to taste it before I realised that he was a medic and probably interested in me from a scientific point of view.

"Go ahead," I offered, still laughing. "If your females don't have natural lubricants, doesn't it hurt them when you...you know. Wait, do you even have cocks? Like humans?"

This time, it was their turn to laugh.

"We do, sweet female," Matar chuckled. "Some of us even have more than just one."

I sat up a little to look at them. "What? More than one? How?"

Matar turned to the captain with an evil grin. "I think you'll have to show her, Xil."

"I don't think this is part of the probing," the yellow alien protested, his cheeks turning a dark ochre. "We're probing her, not she us."

"How many do you have?" I asked when he didn't start pulling down his trousers.

"Two," he replied without looking at me. "Some of us Kardarians are born with up to three. These two are lucky to only have one."

I frowned. "Why lucky? Most human men would happily have two dicks."

"It can get difficult. Even painful."

He didn't expand on that, leaving me burning with questions.

"If he gets an erection, he needs to get relief for both cocks," Havel explained, playing the helpful medic. "Most females don't like being penetrated by both at once and aren't always willing to be fucked twice, so he'll have to do it manually."

There were worse things. But also, what woman would say no to two alien cocks? I hadn't seen them yet, but the exoticness of it alone made me even wetter.

"To answer your other question," Havel continued, "we secrete a gel which gives us smoother access."

A gel. How neat. I wanted to see, feel, taste that.

"Let's proceed with the probing," Matar growled impatiently. "Black Oboto help me, it's getting uncomfortable watching her like that."

I shot him a look. His tail was no longer wrapped around his lower leg but had moved up instead, now protectively curled in front of his crotch, as if he didn't want me to see his erection. I wondered what that tail could do...

Something cool touched my nether lips and I gasped. I hadn't realised Havel had approached me with the second probe.

"Let me know if this is uncomfortable," he said softly and began to push in the probe. It felt like a smooth, metal dildo that was just the right size to stretch me without becoming painful. I moaned as my pussy sucked it in. Havel pushed in as far as he could before gently turning the probe, pushing it against my inner walls. I moaned loudly when the two probes touched, only separated by a thin layer of skin.

"Fuck," I groaned, barely clinging on to control.

"Does she want intercourse?" Xil asked.

All I could do was moan. Havel kept moving both probes, twisting and turning, making me quiver on the bed.

"I'm not sure," Havel replied. "I don't think it's part of the usual probing procedure. Maybe it's a human thing?"

"I need to go," the captain bit out and ran out of the room.

"He'll have his hands busy for a while," Matar teased, but I didn't care. I was teetering at the edge, ready to take the jump if only someone touched my clit. It looked like I'd have to do it myself.

I reached down and rubbed my bud. It only took a single flick and I exploded, coming hard and fast. I moaned, whimpered, groaned, tossed from side to side, making the probes inside of me move and prolong the orgasm I was riding.

I didn't know what the two aliens were thinking or doing. All I cared about was the heat rushing through my body, the trembling originating in my core, the waves I didn't want to miss.

It took me forever to come back from my high. When I finally opened my eyes - I hadn't even realised I'd closed them - I was alone with Havel. He was still holding both probes, but his hands were shaking slightly.

"Can I pull them out now?" he asked cautiously as if he expected me to grind down on them again.

I nodded, not quite able to form words yet. My insides were still shaking. This had to have been one of my best orgasms ever - and it had been in front of three aliens who'd just abducted me. Not exactly what I'd imagined when I visualised having the most amazing orgasm.

Havel carefully removed the vaginal probe - with a squelching sound that made me blush - before slowly pulling out the anal probe. I felt empty and strangely alone as if I'd been abandoned.

Abandoned by alien probes. Now there was a blockbuster title.

LESSON 7

SEDUCTION FOR INEXPERIENCED MALES

Xil found me in the engine room where I'd hidden after putting on a new uniform. I'd not had an accident like that since my metamorphosis when I'd first discovered the pleasures that previously boring body part could bring me.

"She's quite something," the captain stated.

I didn't turn around from the pipe I was hammering into submission. This blunt, physical work was just what I needed right now.

"Havel is cleaning her up, then he'll ask her about her probing experience so that we can submit her statement along with our assignment. I think she enjoyed it, so I'm expecting top marks for us."

I didn't care about grades. What I did care about was that my cock was already getting hard at the thought of Havel cleaning her between her legs. For our medic, this may have been strictly academic, but not for me. Nor for Xil.

"What have we done," I sighed. "I'm never going to be able to concentrate on my work again, not when I know she's on this ship. Did you see how she quivered? How hard her nipples were? How soft her skin felt?"

"Stop it or I'll have to take another cold shower," the captain growled. "But it's good to know we made the right choice when abducting her. She's perfect, more than perfect. She's a dream come true."

I nodded. "She really is. What's the next step now that she's been probed?"

"Seduction," he said, suddenly sounding a little worried. "We've never tried that before in our previous abduction attempts. Maybe that's why we always failed."

"It can't be that difficult, right? She was aroused by some simple probing, so we'll just offer to probe her again and she'll be happy. If we do it often enough, she'll get used to our touch and she might be willing to fuck without probes involved."

Xil laughed. "I don't think you understood the concept of seduction. It's not all about sex."

"It isn't?"

"No. I read this one paper on human courtship and it mentioned giving her plants. Not sure why, maybe because females like to eat healthy stuff?"

"We don't have any plants," I pointed out. "The fabricator can make vegetables, but I doubt it can make anything that's still alive and growing."

"Then we'll have to buy her one at the next space station we stop at. We should watch the next lecture as soon as possible so we know how to proceed. So far, everything Professor Katila has taught us has been effective."

He was right. I'd been worried this course might be a waste of time, but it had turned out to be the best thing we could have done. Thanks to the IGU, we now had our own female on board.

Our comms beeped simultaneously. Havel was paging us. I opened the call and his hologram appeared above my wrist, grinning at us.

"She's fallen asleep. I'm monitoring her vitals and will be alerted as soon as she wakes up, so how about we use the time to listen to the next lecture?"

Xil and I exchanged a look and grinned.

"We were just talking about that," I replied. "Meet you on the bridge?"

I gave the broken engine part one last longing look, then adjusted my uniform and followed Xil to the other end of the ship. I was never going to get any work done with our female around. She was sleeping and still I wasn't able to fix what needed fixing. This was going to be harder than I'd anticipated.

Havel was already on the bridge and had opened the lecture on the main viewscreen. I took my seat, crossed my arms in front of my chest - I didn't want to appear too eager - and waited for the Professor to speak.

"Hello, students. This lecture is split into two parts, depending on the purpose of your abduction. If you want your abductee for companionship and mating, continue watching. If you abducted her for other reasons like research or servitude, please skip to the second part now."

We waited in silence until she finally continued.

"This lecture may be called 'seduction for inexperienced males', but please be assured that this will be interesting for all genders and levels of experience. I like to say that learning is never over, no matter how good you think you are at a subject. I myself still like to expand my knowledge, even though I've conducted hundreds of successful abductions.

"Seduction isn't just about getting your abductee into your bed, nest, roost or whatever sleeping arrangement your species prefers. It's about forming a lasting bond that combines friendship with something deeper. Your end goal is to make your abductee love you with all her heart or hearts - or whatever anatomy her kind associate with love. You do not necessarily have to have the same feelings for your abductee, but it helps if you want to keep her as a long-term mate.

"Every species has different courtship rituals and it's your responsibility to research how your abductee likes to be wooed. You can combine that with the traditions of your own species, but make sure that at least half of your actions correspond to what your new female is used to. You don't want to confuse her unnecessarily.

"I know you will be eager to proceed as fast as possible, but be aware that seduction can take time. Start slowly, take note of how your female responds to your advances, then adjust your strategy accordingly. Give her your full attention. Make her feel adored and cherished. Protect her from all outside threats, even if you don't perceive them as important. Always remember that your abductee may never have left her planet before and everything is new and strange to her. A simple wormhole jump could traumatise her if you've not prepared her well.

"As your first assignment in this module, I'd like you to make a list of all the seduction strategies you've read about during the research phase. Then sort them by intensity. If you have the choice between giving her a sweet treat versus marking her with your saliva, choose the former to start with. If you find a strategy that works well for your abductee, repeat it again and again, even if it becomes boring to you. Your abductee will let you know when she's ready to proceed to the next step."

She smiled, her third eye glazed over as if she was reminiscing over a past abduction. I was impressed that she'd abducted hundreds of beings. I hadn't thought it possible for a Karangi, known for their benevolence and kindness, to do this kind of work professionally, but maybe Professor Katila was an exception to her species' customs.

"Before we end this lecture, please be reminded to submit your practical assignment reports as soon as possible. Seduction is not part of the abduction assignment so you don't need to wait to complete this module before submitting your reports. However, if your probing went exceptionally well, you may include a short summary of it in your assignment."

Havel grinned happily at that. I was sure he expected us to get bonus points for our successful probing.

Xil switched off the screen, also smiling. This crew had never been happier. Even my own lips curved into a smile. I wasn't used to that movement. I was known for being grumpy and I did my best to live up to that expectation.

"Havel, finish your report," Xil commanded. "I'll read over it when you're done, but I think you're best placed to write it. Definitely mention the probing and if our female agrees, include a quote from her. Maybe have her rate the probing on a scale from one to ten."

"I'll be disappointed if she says anything lower than nine," Havel muttered. "Although, I did forget the cameras so..."

"Matar and I will make a list of seduction strategies," the captain interrupted. "Hopefully, we'll be done with that before she wakes up so that we can get started right away. I want her to be ready for mating as soon as possible."

His eyes flicked down to his crotch and I couldn't help but follow his gaze. He was hard, just like me. Havel was already walking out of the room so I couldn't see if he had an erection too, but I wouldn't have been surprised if he had. This female was messing with our bodies already and she hadn't even touched us.

With a sigh, I created a piece of virtual paper and began jotting down what I'd read during the Learn phase of the 4 Ls. I felt Xil watching me, but I didn't pay him any attention. I was intent on doing well with this seduction thing and hopefully be the first our female decided to mate with.

1. Opening doors for her (*note to self: programme doors not to open automatically*)
2. Give her a plant (*note to self: research what colours she likes*)
3. Sing to her while she's a floor above from you (*does it work if she's in the same room?*)
4. Write love letters (*are comms acceptable or do we have to procure real paper?*)
5. Sit next to her while someone else plays a string instrument (*may be difficult to find a musician;*

     *research if recorded music or a live stream of a
     musician is acceptable)*

6. Have food together and have a fire burning instead of normal lights
7. Give her lots of boxes full of tiny food pieces
8. Wear lacy undergarments
9. Write poetry (*note to self: find a poetry generator*)
10. Send yourself (*not sure what is meant by this, more research needed*)
11. Watch recordings of other couples
12. Smile a lot and swirl your moustache (*should we get fake facial hair?*)
13. Hold her hand as often as possible

Xil looked over my shoulder.

"That's a great list," he muttered. "You really did your research."

It made me feel surprisingly good to hear that from him. It wasn't that I didn't feel appreciated on this ship, but this was something unfamiliar and I had never expected to be good at it.

"I don't quite get the bit about lacy undergarments," Xil said thoughtfully. "What does lacy mean?"

"Fabric full of holes," I supplied, glad I'd looked that up a few days ago. "It should be easy to replicate."

"I don't wear undergarments. Do you think it's essential?"

"It came up again and again," I sighed. "I'm not happy about it either, but humans seem to see this as an essential seduction strategy. They call it lingerie, I believe. We could even cut up some of our uniform trousers. I don't think it matters as long as there are lots of holes."

"Enough holes for our dicks to be seen?"

"Exactly. I think it's supposed to be a teasing thing, where she can see our assets but would still have to undress us."

Xil licked his lips. "That does sound tempting, now that you say it like that. But that's probably for later, we should start with something where we're fully clothed. I wouldn't want to overwhelm her." He tapped on his comms, then looked at me triumphantly. "I've locked her door, so now she can't exit her room without one of us opening the door for her. That should be a great start to our seduction."

I nodded. "Great thinking. Let's put the door opening in first place. I suppose she might be hungry when she wakes up, so we can give her tiny food pieces next. For some reason, humans eat them out of a box rather than from a plate, but the fabricator should be able to replicate that. What next?"

"We'll have to wait until we arrive at the space station before we can get her a flower or a string instrument. I won't allow open fire on this ship so we can't do that until we're back on Kardar. We could write her letters though, maybe even now while she's asleep, and then she can read them when she wakes. I bet Havel could even come up with some poetry."

Xil raised his eyebrows. "Havel? Poetry? You're kidding."

"If not, we can probably find a way to generate some simple poetry. Or we'll look in a human book for something some human male has written in the past. I doubt she'll know every human book by heart, so she'll never notice. Especially if we use a really old book."

"Good idea. We can also do the singing from a floor below, but we have to plan that so that one of us is with her to see her reaction. Maybe two of us can sing so it's loud enough to penetrate the walls."

I rubbed my tail, a clear sign that I was getting nervous. "Why do you think we have to sing in another room? Do humans not like it when they see someone else sing? Does it destroy the attraction?"

"You were the one who put it on the list, I'd never heard of it," Xil admitted. "I could sing a drinking song, or maybe a lullaby my mother-"

"Drinking song," I interrupted. We didn't want her to go to sleep. We wanted to mate with her and it was essential that she was awake during that. I wanted to hear her make those sweet sounds again, where she sounded like she was in a happy sort of pain. Pleasant distress.

"Havel can join you," I said. "I'll be with her since it was my idea."

Xil didn't look happy about it but then inclined his head. "Then I shall deal with the tiny food pieces. She's small, so I suppose they have to be even tinier than they'd be for us. Size of my fingernails, maybe?"

I nodded. "That or smaller. She really is tiny."

"What kind of food should I get? Maybe something from Kardar to introduce her to our cuisine?"

"Make a mixture of Kardarian and Peritan food," I suggested. "That way we'll see what she likes best."

I quickly sorted the list anew and added some notes for Havel, since he hadn't been here with us.

1. Opening doors for her (*Havel, we've locked her door*)
2. Give her lots of boxes full of tiny food pieces (*Xil will do this*)
3. Write love letters and poetry
4. Xil and Havel will sing drinking songs while Matar is with her a floor above
5. Wear lacy undergarments
6. Watch recordings of other couples
7. Hold hands whenever possible

In future:

1. Give her a plant (*note to self: research what colours she likes*)
2. Sit next to her while someone else plays a string instrument (*may be difficult to find a musician; research if recorded music or a live stream of a musician is acceptable*)
3. Have food together and have a fire burning instead of normal lights

I deleted the bit about facial hair and sending ourselves since I didn't know how that would contribute to seducing Trish. Maybe if all our other strategies didn't work, we could return to that.

"We can get Havel to find recordings of human couples," I suggested when I was done with the list. "I'm sure he came across some when he was researching human psychology and physiology."

"Yes, he showed me some," Xil said with a wide grin. "Humans can be very flexible when they want to be."

TRISH

As soon as I woke, the memories of what happened made me sit up straight. I wasn't confused at all. I knew exactly what happened. It made me both queasy and breathless. A sexy kind of breathless, that is. I'd been probed by aliens. For real. And I'd enjoyed it. It was so amazing that I passed out in the end after the best orgasm of my life. I dimly remembered one of them carrying me into a sort of shower and washing me, but I had no recollection of him bringing me into this bedroom.

It was tiny, reminding me of a ship's cabin. I guessed that's what it was, now that I thought about it. The bed was attached to the wall and looked like it could be pulled up, creating more space. Metal shelves and cupboards graced the walls to create as much storage as possible. Instead of a window, a large screen hung opposite the door. It was blank though. No alien soaps for me to watch.

They'd dressed me in a simple dress that resembled a pale blue sack with holes for my head and arms. Not exactly the height of fashion, but I supposed I should be grateful I wasn't still naked. They'd even provided a pair of slippers made from something that reminded me of felt, yet it was softer beneath my feet.

My stomach growled, reminding me that it had been a while since my last meal. How long had I been on this ship? I knew neither how long I'd been unconscious when they'd abducted me nor how long I'd just slept. For all I knew, I could have been here for days. A shiver ran down my back at the thought. Would anyone miss me? Chadra would probably be the only one, mostly because I destroyed her scooter and couldn't pay for the damage. She might also miss having me for small jobs that she didn't want to do herself.

I got up. It was time to explore this spaceship, hopefully without stumbling upon one of the aliens. I needed some time to process what had happened.

Problem was, the door didn't have a knob or handle. I stepped close to it, hoping it might have a sensor that would open it automatically, but nothing happened. I pressed my hands against it and pushed, without success.

They'd locked me in like a prisoner. I supposed it was to be expected. They'd abducted and probed me. For some reason, they were intent on following every alien abduction stereotype imaginable, which I guessed included being locked into a room. At least this wasn't a cell. And I had clothes. I should be grateful for small mercies like that.

I banged my fists against the door and started shouting for them to open it. Just like I was supposed to behave, right? I couldn't help but laugh at the absurdity of the situation. I hadn't just been abducted by aliens. I was part of some kind of academic assignment they were conducting and therefore had to be the perfect abduction victim. This was ridiculous.

"Let me out!" I yelled as loud as I could.

I looked around the room again, almost hoping to spot a camera that I could wave to. Or destroy. Both options sounded tempting.

"Aliens, come and unlock this door!"

Footsteps sounded in the distance. Someone was running towards me. Had they heard my calls or was this just a coincidence? Maybe their cameras were too hidden for me to see. It didn't make sense for there not to be any. I had been abducted; of course, they'd want to keep an eye on me and see if the probing had any aftereffects. I bet the blue medic, Havel, would be keen to document everything I did. It was almost endearing if I hadn't been kidnapped.

The door slid open, revealing a grinning Matar. The green, tailed alien seemed pleased at himself for some reason, even though I scowled at him.

"Why did you lock me up?" I snapped. It was probably a bad idea to snap at my captors, but I was hungry and to be honest, after the probing I didn't take them too seriously. I didn't think they were dangerous, but there was a high chance I was wrong. Perhaps this was my mind trying to protect me from the truth.

"So I could open the door for you," he replied as if that made any sense at all. "Are you pleased?"

"No. I'm not."

His face fell, disappointment distorting his alien features. It was strange how his expressions were so human, in a way, or at least similar enough for me to recognise his emotions.

"Do you not like doors being opened for you?" he asked, sounding a little unsure.

"I don't like locked doors," I shot back at him. "Am I your prisoner?"

He raised his eyebrows and I noticed how perfectly shaped they were. Just like everything about him. He was gorgeous from top to bottom, even his tail. Alright, maybe his tail wasn't gorgeous, but it was exotic and strangely attractive. It made me want to reach out and see if it would curl around my hand.

"You're not. You're going to be our mate."

He - or one of the others - had said that before. A joke, surely? I wasn't mate material. I wasn't their species, nor was I particularly beautiful. Only pretty girls got abducted, that was universally acknowledged. Or maybe clever ones, to work for them and tell them all of Earth's secret. I was neither.

"I'm not. I want you to return me to my home." I stood as straight as I could and looked him right in the eyes. It took all my willpower to do that. His gaze was intense, sucking me in. His eyes were as green as the rest of him, but small silver specks shimmered within his pupils, making them sparkle. They had to be the most beautiful eyes I'd ever seen.

I forced myself to look away. I didn't want to swoon over my abductor. This wasn't the time to develop Stockholm syndrome.

"That isn't possible," he said surprisingly gently. "We'd fail our assignment. But don't worry, we'll look after you. We've already made a list-"

He broke off and bit his lower lip as if he'd said more than he'd intended.

"A list?"

"Of things to make you happy," he admitted. "Opening doors is on there, but it seems you don't like that. I shall erase it immediately."

A white rectangle appeared in front of him, covered in small, neat writing. I tried to read it, but it was written in *alien*. Whatever language they spoke. The translator - I didn't call it the disgusting thing it really was - only worked for spoken words, it seemed. And I was fine with that. I didn't want a worm in my eyes, thank you very much.

Matar ran his fingers over the projection and the top line disappeared. On one hand, I was curious about what else lay in store, while on the other hand, I dreaded to find out. Being locked inside my room just so he could open a door for me wasn't a good start. What would be next, starving me so they could sate my hunger?

My stomach growled again. Matar jumped back, his tail erect, his eyes wild as he searched the corridor for a threat.

I rolled my eyes. "It's just my stomach. I'm hungry."

He frowned. "Your stomach speaks? Is that normal for humans?"

"It doesn't speak. It makes growly noises."

Matar shook his head. "No, it spoke. Loud and clear. It said 'electricity'. Or maybe 'power', those words are very similar in my language."

This time, it was me who stared at him in confusion. "I assure you, my stomach doesn't talk. It has no mind of its own. It was just a grumble."

The green male didn't look as if he believed me, but he let it drop. "Xil is preparing food for you right now. Come, I'll take you to our canteen. I shall show you the ship afterwards, especially the floor above."

"What's there?" I asked curiously as I started following him.

"You'll see," he hedged.

We ignored several locked doors along the brightly lit corridor, heading straight to a large, open-plan room that seemed to act as both kitchen and living area. Most tables and chairs were covered with...things. Empty plates. Random gadgets. Electronics I didn't recognise. Something that looked like a yellow bath duck but definitely wasn't one. These guys didn't like to tidy up, that much was clear. I'd give them a minus point for that. When you invited someone into your home, you cleaned it first or at least made it look less like a mancave.

Matar seemed to realise the issue and simply wiped off all the contents from the closest table, beckoning me to sit on the only empty chair. I shrugged and took my seat, waiting for him to join me. He kept standing though, his tail knocking on the floor as if he was nervous. He pressed some buttons on the computer thingy he had on his wrist.

"She's here, klatting get to the canteen now," he snapped at whoever he was talking to.

"On my way."

That was the captain's voice if I wasn't mistaken.

"He's prepared food for you. I hope it'll be what you imagined."

I frowned at him. "I didn't imagine anything. It's not like I planned to be abducted. I guess I should be happy you're feeding me at all."

"Of course we're feeding you," he replied, clearly offended at the thought of letting me starve. "It's what good abductors do. We're going to look after you from now on. Whatever you want, just tell us and we'll make sure you get it."

"Really? Whatever I want?"

He grimaced. "Within reason. If you want a lavva fruit or a tribitt, that's doable. If you want a bigger spaceship or a weapon of mass destruction, it would be less likely that we can fulfil your wish."

"What's a tribitt? My translator didn't get that one."

"A furry, long-eared animal that many Kardarians keep as pets, especially females. They're fluffy and quite intelligent but also very mischievous. I'm not sure what our Captain would say about having a pet on the Jade though."

I grinned. "I want one."

Matar looked as if he regretted this conversation. "You need to ask Xil-"

"Ask me what?"

The captain had entered the canteen without me noticing. I whirled around and took in his broad, muscular form. During the probing, I'd been kind of out of it, but now I took the chance to look at him properly. His head was bald, just like that of the other two, but strange ochre patches made it look less bare. The same mottled jaguar pattern he had all over his body - I remembered when he'd torn open his shirt to show me. The skin on his face and scalp was smooth, like that of a human, no scales like on his chest. Of the three men, he was the most human-looking, if you ignored his bright yellow skin colour, his scales and his dark orange eyes that didn't have lashes.

His dark blue uniform had silver stripes along his arms and legs, only highlighting how his bulk stretched the fabric. Why did they have a uniform when this ship wasn't military? And they were only three guys living on the Jade, so it didn't make sense to me. Maybe some weird alien tradition, just like their desire to probe humans.

"She wants a tribitt," Matar sighed.

To my surprise, Xil shrugged. "Then we shall get one. We should reach Kepler Two in about a week, so until then, we can make a list of everything Trish needs." He gave me a warm smile and held out a metal box. "For you."

Was he giving me a present? These aliens were so weird. Half of the time I didn't know if they were serious or if this was just some kind of twisted game. Maybe they were toying with me, waiting until I felt safe only to pull the floor from under my feet and show me their true, monstrous natures. I mean, what kind of alien gave the woman he'd abducted a gift?

I sat it down on the table and carefully opened the lid, half expecting poisonous scorpions or other lethal critters ready to sting me. But no. Inside was a grid made of something that looked like shimmering plastic, separating the box into thirty-two compartments, each of them filled with some kind of food. At least I thought it was food.

The portions were tiny, the size of half of my thumb. Xil had taken finger food to a new level. Some of them didn't even constitute one bite. How small did he think my mouth was?

One compartment contained a single blue leaf. Was that even edible? Next to it was something that looked like a bright pink mealworm. No thanks. Some of the *things* were clearly meat, while others could have been meat, plant, or something in between. Nothing looked familiar at all. I supposed they hadn't used their stop on Earth to restock.

"Do you like it?" Xil asked. He was watching me intently, clearly eager to get a reaction out of me. It was almost adorable, having this big, dangerous alien begging for my approval.

"Is that how you eat?"

His enthusiasm turned into confusion. "No. We eat proper portions. Isn't this what human males give their females when they want to seduce them?"

Why would I want-

"Chocolates." I started laughing. "This is what a box of chocolates looks like. Now I get it."

"What's chocolates?" Matar asked. He looked just as downtrodden and disappointed as Xil. I felt sorry for them and tried to contain my laughter. It was hard though. This was hilarious.

"Chocolate is a sweet deliciousness made from cocoa beans. You can get it in all shapes and forms, but if you go on a date, the guy might give the woman a box of chocolates. Small, expensive ones with different fillings." I looked down at the box. They'd kind of got the concept...except that they'd used normal food instead of chocolate. I couldn't help but smile at Xil. "You did well, it's almost the same. Thank you."

A grin lit up his face and his cheeks turned a darker yellow. An alien blush, how very sweet. I was starting to realise that there was something sweet and cuddly inside those big, burly men.

"Try them," Matar encouraged me. "That red piece is grilled oro steak, a delicacy from our home planet."

It didn't look like it had been grilled or cooked in any way. It was bloody. Or maybe that was a sauce. I told myself it was red gravy and gingerly took the piece of meat. I gave it a cautious sniff, but it actually smelled quite nice, like peri-peri chicken.

I wasn't a picky person. If you were poor, you ate whatever you found, even if it was out of date, dirty or come from shady sources. This was alien food, however. There may be harmful substances in there. Germs my body wasn't used to.

"Havel has made sure it's all safe for you to eat," Matar reassured as if he could read my mind. Maybe he could. I didn't know anything about their species.

"Where is he?" I asked to stall for time. As appetising as the meat smelled, as disgusting did it look as it oozed with red fluid.

"Practicing," Xil replied, then pursed his lips. "Ignore I said that. It's a surprise."

That sounded ominous. A drop of liquid fell from the piece of meat, landing on a white disk that looked like a tiny pancake. It immediately turned a disgusting shade of orange.

"That's strange," Matar muttered. "Must be some kind of chemical reaction." He took the mini pancake and gave it a sniff. "Do you mind if I taste this, female?"

"My name is Trish. And go ahead."

He bit off a tiny piece, leaving teeth marks on the disk. His teeth were triangular. Weird. But not the weirdest thing I'd seen since waking up on this spaceship.

"Still tastes good. Those are some of my favourites."

He put the half-finished pancake back in its place in the box. Eating something someone else had bitten into didn't seem to be against their etiquette. A pancake with blood and alien spittle. Just what I'd always dreamed off. Still, it looked more appetising than the meat I was still holding.

I squeezed my eyes shut and almost threw the piece of meat into my mouth. It was chewy as if it had been cooked for too long, but it didn't taste bad. The spices were different from anything I'd ever eaten before, but definitely edible. This wouldn't become my favourite food though. The aftertaste was strangely sour, making me wish for something sweet. Maybe that pancake?

I took it, not hesitating this time.

I gagged as soon as its flavour registered. It tasted like puke. I spit it out, catching it in my hand. At least I hadn't thrown up all over the box. That should count for something.

"Not to your taste?" Xil chuckled, not seeming to be offended. "Try some of the plants. Havel said humans must eat a lot of plants. Something about mini vitas."

"Vitamins." I grinned. "What would you recommend?"

He pointed at a ball of cooked leaves that reminded me of spinach. It was even green. That seemed safe.

Still, it took some force of will to nibble on it. The nibble turned into happy chewing as flavours of cinnamon and caramel caressed my tongue. Now this was what I'd expect a suitor to give me. If all their vegetables tasted this good, I was going to become a vegetarian.

"Do you have more of that?" I asked as soon as I'd reluctantly swallowed that amazingness.

Xil nodded. "I can make you an entire bowl. But first, you need to go with Matar. Havel is ready." He pointed at his wrist computer as if that meant anything to me.

What were they going to do next? More probing? Likely, if Havel was involved. He was deeply passionate about it. He'd even asked me questions about how I'd found the probing while he'd cleaned me, but I couldn't quite remember what I'd answered. It was all a bit of a blur.

I left the weird food box on the table and followed Matar to a circular column at the other end of the room.

He pressed his hand against what looked like smooth bronze metal and it rotated until an opening appeared. The inside of the column was lit up with fluorescent blue lights.

Matar stepped inside and again put his hand on the wall before realising that I hadn't followed him.

"It's the elevator," he explained with a smirk. "It'll take us upstairs."

"It's very small."

His tail waggled. Like a happy dog's. "Yes. It is. We'll have to stand very close."

"Can't we go one after the other?"

"No, it's not programmed to your biosignature yet. The captain can do that later, but we don't have time. Come on. I won't hurt you."

Strangely enough, that hadn't been my worry. That scared me a little. I should have been afraid of him, of all three aliens, but I wasn't. I just didn't want to be pressed against him, feeling all those muscles...

Or maybe I did want to. But I shouldn't. It was a bad idea.

With a sigh, I stepped into the elevator, pointedly turning my back to Matar. I left a few inches between us, but sighed again when I realised the column doors couldn't close like that. I shuffled back, careful to avoid touching him, but he wrapped his arms around my waist and pulled me against his chest.

The doors slid close and with them, any chance of getting out of his embrace. His hands were tight on my hips, holding me in place. His chest was hard against me while something even harder pressed into my lower back. Heat shot into my core, making me just as aroused as he was. Fuck. This wasn't happening. I couldn't be horny.

I wriggled against him, but he didn't let go of me. No, he groaned, clearly pleased I'd rubbed his cock. Unintentionally. Totally unintentionally.

Luckily, the door opened again, revealing an unfamiliar corridor. I hadn't even felt the elevator moving, but to be honest, I had been a little distracted by Matar's erection. Did he have one or two cocks? I knew Xil had two but I couldn't remember if Matar had mentioned how many he had. I snorted. What a strange world in which a girl would have to find out how many dicks her partner had.

Matar reluctantly let me go and I jumped forward, putting several feet of space between us. It was safer that way.

"Come, this way." He pushed past me, not trying to touch me. I was both relieved and disappointed. I hurried after him until we got to two massive double doors, looking much thicker than any I'd seen before. Matar typed something into his wrist communicator and the doors slid open. A blast of warm, smelly air hit me at the same time as my ears were assaulted by the noise of a rocket launch. Well, not quite as loud, but it almost made me want to cover my ears.

"One moment, I thought he'd switched them off," Matar muttered and continued pressing buttons. I took the time to peek into the room. Lots of pipes, wires, lights, and cables surrounded six large columns similar to the one the elevator had been housed in. In the centre of the circular room was a glass ball filled with a flickering green flame. I had no idea what any of it was, but it didn't need a genius to figure out this was the engine room.

With a hiss, the noise stopped, leaving only blissful silence.

"Ten minutes," he announced. "Then I have to turn them on again."

I had no idea why he'd even turned them off. I hadn't asked him to show me the engines. I wasn't good with electronics even on Earth and I bet these machines were a lot more advanced than anything I'd find back home, even on the spaceport. I'd never been inside a human-made spaceship, but I doubted it was anything like this one.

Matar put a hand on the small of my back, gently pushing me into the room. I let him, revelling at how good his touch felt. I became aware of the heat between my legs once more. What was this alien doing to me?

When we got to the green flame, the metal floor gave way to a grate, revealing the room beneath us. And down there stood Havel and Xil, looking up with grins on their faces.

"What's going on?" I asked Matar, but he didn't reply. His hand was still on my back. I should've stepped back from him, but my legs didn't move.

Something nudged my leg. I looked down only to find his tail possessively curling around my knee.

"Your tail is touching me," I whispered.

"So it is."

"Why is it doing that?"

"Sometimes it's hard to control it. Many, many generations ago, all Kardarians had tails. They were like an extra limb and we could use them as such. Now, only some of us are still born with tails and those who do have lost the ability to fully control their tails. With some practice, it's possible to get rudimentary control, but when I don't concentrate on it, it sometimes takes on a life of its own."

A sentient tail? I had a hard time believing that. Maybe he simply wanted an excuse to touch me.

I didn't get a chance to interrogate him further. Beneath us, Xil and Havel opened their mouths and began to howl in unison. It sounded like they were in agony. Were they being attacked? Their howls turned louder and louder, tearing at my heartstrings.

"Help them!" I shouted at Matar, panic freezing my mind and body.

"You want me to join them?"

He didn't sound worried at all. Just confused.

"Do something!" I cried, unable to take their pained yowling much longer.

In an instant, his hands were on my hips again and he spun me around. Before I knew what was happening, his lips were on mine.

LESSON 8

THE MATING HABITS OF HUMANS

"It's working!" I shouted jubilantly, breaking the song.

Xil stopped too, looking up with a surprised expression. He hadn't expected our singing to be this effective either.

Above us, Matar and Trish were kissing. She was wrapped in his arms, her lips on his. My cock twitched with jealousy. It should have been me up there. I was the one who'd successfully probed her. It was me who'd introduced her to our abduction skills. I remembered how it had felt to slide the probe inside her, imagining that it was my cock...

"I can't believe that worked," Xil muttered. "I would have bet against it. Why did our singing make her kiss him? Shouldn't she come running to kiss us?"

We watched as their kiss turned more and more passionate. Xil's jealousy was almost palpable, or maybe I was projecting my own onto him.

"Let's go," I growled after a few minutes. "At least this might mean that she'll be ready for the next stage."

Xil's frown lessened. "Mating."

"Kissing is a good step towards that. I was worried humans might not be into kissing, but it looks like they love it as much as Kardarians. Let's hope they love to fuck even more."

The probing had shown that she was compatible with us. She would need some time to adjust, but she'd be able to take us. Maybe even Xil's two cocks at once. Luckily, they were one above the other and not next to each other like with some other alien species. That would have made finding a position awkward, but like this, he could rut her from behind in true Kardarian fashion.

"Have you prepared a room?" I asked as we left Matar and Trish alone.

"Yes, I did that after I made her food. She didn't like most of it, by the way. We'll need to experiment some more."

"That was to be expected. Her palate will be used to some vastly different things. It's a pity we couldn't find more human recipes for our replicator."

He shrugged. "She'll just have to get used to it. But yes, the room is ready. I had the bots build a bed large enough for all of us. I also prepared some underclothes with holes in. Now you just have to select some videos of human couples to watch. I don't know if Kardarian couples work, so let's not risk it."

I nodded. "I've got some videos I found during the early research phase when we started to consider humans. I'm sure one of them will work."

I didn't mention that I'd watched them many, many times, and not for strictly academic reasons. Watching humans fuck was hot. I understood why human couples might watch that together, although I didn't understand why they ate plant seeds while doing so. I wanted to kiss her and then maybe replicate some of the positions, not eat. Well, maybe eat her... I'd tried some of the juices that had leaked out of her. The taste had almost made me come by itself. I ached to taste her once again.

No plant seeds for her. Definitely not. There were going to be no distractions that could stand in the way of our mating.

I followed Xil into the room he'd prepared. It was one of the storage rooms, but he'd managed to turn it into a cosy space by adding soft lights and fabrics. I'd never taken him for an interior designer, but I had to admit he'd done a stellar job, especially in the short time he'd had.

My comms beeped and as soon as I saw who the message was from, I activated the holo screen so that Xil could see it too.

"Professor Katila's marked our assignment already," I told him, my voice shaking a tiny bit. I wanted to do well, but had we done enough to pass?

"It's not the probing grade," I said after opening the attachment. "It's for the abduction itself."

"I don't want to look," Xil admitted. "Just tell me if we passed or not."

"Choosing on physiology alone lacked insight... needed assistance from teacher... good choice of abductee... initial speech overwhelming..."

"Tell me," Xil growled. "Now."

I quickly scrolled to the end and my hearts skipped a beat. "We passed. Just about. I can't believe she detracted points for calling her for help. She keeps telling us to ask questions so she shouldn't penalise us for it. And we didn't choose her just because of her boobs..."

Xil put a hand on my mouth, silencing me. "We passed. That's all that counts."

He looked happier than I'd ever seen him. "Does that mean we've passed the entire course?"

"Mmmmmrmmppfhh."

He removed his hand, allowing me to speak with an apologetic wink.

"No. All our grades will be added up and then an average will be calculated. This practical assignment is weighed pretty high though, so unless we did really badly in other parts of the course, we should pass."

Another bing interrupted me. Our probing grades had arrived.

My fangs extended as nerves threatened to take the better of me. I was desperate for a top grade in this. I'd thrown my hearts and soul into preparing for our female's probing and I thought it had gone exceptionally well. Professor Katila had counted the speech into the abduction assignment, so I didn't have to worry about that. It was only the probing and that had gone splendidly, right? We'd made our little abductee come. That alone should give us the highest grade possible.

"Do you want me to?" Xil offered when I didn't open the message.

I nodded, suddenly feeling weak in my knees. This was

just a grade, just a test. But no, it was so much more. My honour as a medic was at stake. I had to do well. Had to.

"She praises your preparation and dedication... she likes that you created your own probes... but you shouldn't have offered our abductee a choice..."

"But that would have been impolite!" I protested. "I wanted her to feel safe and by giving her control over what was happening, she felt more confident."

Xil shrugged. "Just saying what Professor Katila wrote. Let me continue."

I sighed and sat down on the bed. I was starting to think we might not get a good a grade on this as I'd hoped.

"Us touching her was unprofessional," the captain grunted. "We should have restrained her instead. And she says your probing was useless. It held no scientific value because your probes didn't actually film her insides or measure things like her temperature."

I stared at him, unbelieving. "But..."

"We failed," Xil interrupted. "We klatting failed."

"It can't be. It went so well. She even said that she enjoyed the probing. I-"

I covered my face in my hands. The day had started so well yet now, I just wanted to punch something. Or someone, namely Professor Katila.

"She says the abductee should not have been consulted on whether she liked the probing or not, at least not during the procedure," Xil said, still reading our results. "And while the Professor appreciates that we didn't want to harm her, the probing turned sexual rather than academic, especially with all of us touching her."

He grimaced. "I don't regret touching her boobs."

I didn't regret probing her either. It had been a special experience and I wouldn't let the Professor taint the memory of it. Of course, we hadn't wanted to hurt our female. She was going to be ours for the rest of our lives and starting that relationship with pain was a bad idea. Surely our teacher understood that?

Klat.

"We failed one and passed one," Xil summarised. "What's next?"

"They'll take a look at all the reports we've submitted since we started the course. If our average grade means we've failed, there'll be a final interview with both us and the abductee...Trish. That could save us."

The captain looked grave. "Let's assume that we failed the reports too. That means that Trish's opinion could mean life or death for us. In a figure of speech, anyway. I guess the course doesn't matter as much, not now that the abduction was successful."

"True, but I still want to pass."

"Me too," he admitted. "It would feel like a failure if we don't. We can't do much about our own interviews, but we can make sure Trish only has the best to say about us. We need to make the mating a success. We've prepared well, but will it be enough?"

"We've got a large bed, lacy underclothes and recordings of human couples. We can also hold hands while lying on the bed to tick off another seduction strategy. Plus Matar is kissing her just now, that should count for a lot."

I wished it was me in Matar's position. I couldn't wait to feel her lips against my fangs, my venom dripping onto her tongue. Our ancestors' venom could be lethal, but what we were left now only had a slightly intoxicating effect, increasing positive emotions and sensations. Fanged Kardarians were highly prized prostitutes for that reason.

"Let's get changed," Xil said and produced a stack of black clothes. Those had to be the ones he'd made. I wasn't keen on wearing something when in bed with Trish, but if it was their tradition to wear damaged clothes, then so be it. Maybe she'd take pleasure in making the holes even bigger so she could access my cock.

I changed in record time, eager to be ready in case Matar and Trish joined us. I ended up wearing a black shirt than only covered the top half of my chest - and that only in pieces since holes and loose threads were too copious to count - and tight black leggings with one leg longer than the other. Again, Xil had made sure to add as many holes as possible without tearing the fabric into pieces.

His own outfit was similar, except that he wore shorts that didn't leave a lot to the imagination. One of his balls was clearly visible, while his two cocks strained against the fabric. Maybe we should provide Trish with some scissors to make it easier to unwrap us.

Xil left Matar's clothes by the door. He'd just have to get changed as quickly as possible once he got here.

While the captain went to get some drinks, including the water liquid Trish needed for survival, I chose one of my favourite human copulation videos. It had two males and one female in it. Hopefully, that wasn't too removed from tradition. I could have chosen a couple, but I thought this would make it more obvious to our female that all three of us wanted to get involved with her. We'd abducted her together and we'd mate her together. Maybe not all at the same time since she lacked the orifices for that.

***

XIL

When I returned to the bedroom, I met Matar and Trish in the corridor just outside. Her lips were red and swollen. Had Matar hurt her? If so, I'd punch him until his green skin turned blue.

She stared at me as if she hadn't seen me before. Had he taken her mind while kissing? Anger roared through me and I barely managed to hold onto the tray topped with four drinks.

"What are you wearing?" she asked in a strange voice. Her eyes wandered up and down my body, lingering on my crotch for a long time. I checked to make sure neither of my cocks was showing, but they were mostly hidden, with only some of my skin peeking beneath the black fabric.

"Clothes, with holes," I said proudly. "Do you like it?"

"Holes..." she muttered, clearly impressed. Her face did weird things, contorting and quivering.

"Is everything alright?" I asked, starting to get concerned at her behaviour. Matar had to have damaged her.

When she didn't reply, I turned to him, growling. "What did you do to her?"

He flinched. "Nothing. We kissed. A lot." He smiled sheepishly. "And my tail may have slipped under her clothes."

I gaped at them. He'd started the mating process without us? Had he penetrated her with his tail? This was completely out of order.

"Get inside, change," I snapped, pleased he immediately followed my command, almost running into the bedroom. Even though the three of us were all in this together, I was still the captain. I was in charge and I'd make sure the mating would be perfect for our female.

I smiled at her even though I was still confused by her expression. "Did he do something to you?"

"No. At least, nothing I didn't want him to. But...explain to me why you're wearing this? Is this some sort of tradition?"

I stared at Trish. Had I misread her completely? "It's your tradition, is it not? We read about humans wearing special clothes when trying to seduce each other. Garments with lots of holes to tease. I think Matar called it lacy."

"Lace. Oh my goodness, did you try to make lingerie?" she

squealed and covered her mouth with her hands. "That's so adorable!"

Adorable hadn't been what I'd tried to go for - sexy, masculine, seductive had been my intention - but I'd take it.

"Is it what you'd wear on Peritus?"

"Peritus? Ah, you mean Earth, I keep forgetting you have a different name for it. And no, not quite. Usually, it's the woman who wears the lingerie, not the guys."

I looked down at myself in disappointment. I'd thought I'd got this right, but it seemed we'd failed yet again. Chances of passing the IGU course got slimmer with every moment.

"Hey, but you look great," she said and reached out to me, only to pull her hand back just before she touched my chest. "Thank you for trying to make this like what I'm used to. Not that I've ever owned any lingerie-"

"You haven't?" I asked dumbfounded. "But how do you - or have you never-"

"It wasn't a necessity and I didn't have money for anything that wasn't essential," she explained without answering what I'd tried to ask. I supposed it didn't matter if she'd mated before. She was ours now and she'd never return to whatever human male she'd shared her body with.

"We'll make you as much lacy clothes as you want," I promised. "You can show me how they're supposed to look like. But now, would you like to join us in watching a recording of a human couple?"

Her gorgeous eyes widened in surprise. Her pupils were much larger than ours, only leaving a small ring of colour around them, but I thought that only made her more attractive.

"Are we going to watch a movie? A romantic one? That's so sweet. Will there be popcorn?"

"What's that? My translator didn't get that."

"Snacks. Something to eat while watching."

"Why would you want to eat?" I asked. "I was planning to hold hands with you."

And copy some of the things happening on the screen, but it didn't feel right to say that yet. I wanted to surprise her.

"That's very sweet."

I wasn't sure why she kept describing everything as sweet. Did she think we were like confectionary? Humans were strange. Although maybe she expected my seed to be sweet. I had no idea if it was. I'd never asked a female to taste it. Was that something humans did?

The thought of it made my cocks swell further. I was about ready to burst. The anticipation had made me hard and ready for her. I hoped the recording Havel had chosen wasn't too long. I had no patience to sit and watch other people fuck without being inside Trish.

I pressed a button on my comms to open the bedroom door for her, incredibly pleased that I'd remembered that part of seduction etiquette. She gasped as soon as she entered, then began laughing so loud it almost hurt my ears.

"What on Earth have you done to your clothes?" she exclaimed. "Get out of them, that's about the unsexiest thing I've ever seen. You look like you're vagrants."

I didn't know what a vagrant was, but I liked that she wanted us to undress. I got out of my lacy outfit quicker than I thought possible. I followed her into the room, proud of how high my erect cocks were reaching. Maybe she'd let me rut her right away, without the delay of watching that recording.

She turned to look at me, did a strange gurgling sound and swirled around again. "I meant put on something else, not get naked," she squeaked. "I didn't need to see that." She realised the other two had undressed too and squealed again. "Nor that."

I exchanged a look with the other guys. What was the point of getting dressed again if we'd discard our clothes soon after? It seemed like a waste of time.

"Does my physique disappoint you?" I asked.

She slowly turned to me, her eyes fixed on mine, although the concentration on her face made it obvious that she was having to force herself not to look at the rest of my body. "Not exactly. But this isn't right. You abducted me. You shouldn't be naked. You shouldn't be this...big."

She covered her mouth again. I wondered why she kept doing that. I added it to my mental list of questions that I'd eventually ask her. Now wasn't the time.

"I'm slightly above average size," I said proudly. "But if you consider I have two cocks, I am very much above average."

Her face turned redder and redder. "Thanks for letting me know."

"You're welcome. Havel assured me after the probing that you'll be able to take all of us."

"All of you?" she repeated in a high-pitched voice. "At the same time?"

"If you want us to," Havel said smoothly. "We'd love nothing more."

Trish staggered back and sat down on the bed. "This is too much. I should be running, I should be freaked out. Why am I not freaking out?"

"Because we chose you as our female," Matar said, his tail curling around her ankle. She didn't seem to notice or if she did, she didn't mind. "We chose you because we knew you'd be able to cope with this. You're strong, you're beautiful, you're perfect. We've travelled across the galaxy to find you and you were worth every single lightyear."

I nodded, impressed at how eloquent our engineer had suddenly become. Maybe he should try and write some poetry for her after all.

"Every lightyear," I echoed. "Worth it."

"So that means I shouldn't feel bad about...wanting you?" she asked.

My hearts beat so hard it almost hurt. She *wanted* us.

"We want you too," Havel said. "You are all we ever wanted. You don't have to be afraid of your feelings. Everything is new to both you and us. There are no rules. We make our own rules, our own traditions. If we want to wear clothes with holes, that's fine. If we want to walk around naked, that's also fine."

"As long as the Captain agrees," I grumbled, just to make sure she understood that I was still in charge, no matter Havel's pretty words.

"Let's get comfortable," the medic suggested. "The bed is big enough for us all. Do you want to watch that *movie?*"

Trish nodded. "But can you at least slip under the blanket? Seeing you all naked is...well, I'll need time to get used to that."

Nudity was nothing special or embarrassing for Kardarians, but I was aware not all species felt that way. Maybe we could persuade her to stay naked eventually. Drops of golden precum rose to heads of my cocks as I thought of how convenient it would be to have her always available, no need to undress. I could find her whenever I felt the need and plunge into her depths.

Yes, abducting her was the best thing we could have done. And no matter what Professor Katila thought about our probing, it had shown to me that Trish was perfect for us. And that she was willing. She may need a little persuasion, but deep inside she wanted us just as much as we wanted her. It was only her mind telling her to take it slow, while her body betrayed her. Even now, I could smell her arousal.

All three of us joined her in bed and dutifully pulled a blanket over the bottom halves of our bodies. She didn't ask us to fully cover up all the way to our necks, so hopefully, that was a good sign.

She was squeezed in between me and Havel, with Matar on the medic's right. He'd already had his kiss with her and should, therefore, wait his turn. We hadn't talked about it, but it was proof of how well this crew knew each other. Soon, Trish would be part of us. She'd be our family, gluing us all together. Our mate.

Havel's eyes glazed over as he used his comms to select the recording. The large screen at the other end of the bed flickered on, revealing three humans in a dark room. The lights had been strategically positioned to highlight only parts of their bodies, adding to the mystery and suspense. The two males caressed the female between them, stroking her hair, her body, then one of them kissed her on the lips.

"Ehm, that's not a romance movie," Trish laughed. "Are you watching porn?"

"Yes, this is a pornographic recording," Havel confirmed. "I found it in your planetary database. Is it not to your liking? I have others with just a couple or several females or-"

"You don't usually watch porn on your first date," she explained. "We watch films about two people falling in love. Usually, there's something that stops them coming together but when they finally do, it's even sweeter." She smiled. "Romance isn't all about sex, you know?"

I nodded, proud that I knew that. "Yes, you're right. It's also about other things. Like seduction and wooing and kissing."

For some reason, she rolled her eyes, but she didn't say anything. I reached out to hold her hand. Her fingers were so much thinner than mine and I was worried I might crush her delicate hand. She didn't pull back, not even when Matar took her other hand and lifted it to his mouth. He kissed her thumb, then the other fingers one by one. With each kiss, Trish became redder. Was there a limit to how red her skin could become? I didn't want her to be permanently red like a luovi fruit. I hated those. They were too sweet.

One of the males in the recording went to his knees and pressed his face against the female's arse. His nose sunk in the valley between her cheeks. The camera didn't show what his tongue did but I bet he was tasting her. He wrapped his hands around her thighs and pulled them apart, giving him better access. I took in every detail, committing it to memory. I'd do that with Trish someday. In fact, what was stopping me from tasting her right now?

I let go of her hand and pulled up her dress until I was able to touch her sex. I was too impatient to do anything but plunge a finger into her. She was warm and tight and her inner muscles contracted around my finger as if they were hugging my cocks. Klat. I'd planned to pull out and lick off her liquids, but now that my finger was deep inside her, I couldn't stop. She moaned when I started moving, exploring her insides. This was much better than probing. The probe hadn't been able to tell us what it would feel like to touch the warm, wet skin that led to her womb. I would plant my seed into her. Right now.

I threw back the blanket, my cocks twitching when cold air hit them. Trish moaned, but she didn't protest. On the contrary, her eyes were closed and her lips parted as her breath turned faster and faster. She liked it. I grinned. This was only the beginning.

Something nudged my hand. Matar's tail. Its tip had swollen; something I'd never seen it do. I hadn't realised his tail could change shape. It almost looked like a cock, which instantly turned it into a competition. Still, I wanted to see what would happen, so I pushed my finger to the side, giving the tail space to enter her too.

It pushed against her entry, needing some force to fit. Maybe I should pull away my hand, but I didn't want to leave her. The tip of Matar's tail twisted and turned until it slid in, aided by the liquid leaking from Trish's sex. It shot into her, hard and deep, deeper than my finger could reach. That was unacceptable. I had to match it.

Trish groaned and threw her head from side to side. "More," she moaned. "More."

She didn't have to tell me twice. I finally pulled out and licked the finger now glistening with her wetness.

Her nipples were hard and pointed, inviting me to suck on them. Havel was faster. He licked them first, one after the other, then wrapped his lips around one and started sucking. The sound of it nearly drove me insane.

If he had her breasts, I'd take her pussy. It was time for Matar's tail to leave. I grabbed it and pulled it out gently for Trish's sake. I didn't want to hurt her in my frenzy to have her for myself. The tail's end turned and pointed at me as if it wanted to protest, but then Matar pulled it to himself and licked it, tasting her. I realised I hadn't done that yet, even though it was why I'd first penetrated her.

I sucked on my finger and her taste exploded on my tongue. I stopped breathing as an overwhelming need took over. I had to be inside her.

My cocks were already covered in the gel that would make it easier to fuck our little human without causing her discomfort. She was full of her own liquid, but I wasn't sure how effective that was. I grabbed her waist and pulled her around until my cocks were pointing at her sex. Havel growled in protest as her breasts were ripped from him, but Trish only moaned, looking at me from half-closed eyes.

"Are you ready to be mated?" I asked her. It felt right to say those words.

"I am," she moaned, barely more than a whisper. "Fuck me."

That was all the encouragement I needed. I positioned my lower cock at her entrance, not wanting to overwhelm her with both at once. I pushed in just a little bit to make sure my gel was working, then when she didn't show any signs of pain, I rammed my cock into her in one hard, confident stroke.

She screamed, her hands gripping the bedsheet, her hips jerking upwards to let me plunge in even deeper. I grabbed her even tighter and fucked her, letting go of all inhibition. I was wild, a predator taking his prey. My upper cock rubbed against her folds, enough to get me close to coming. I usually needed to fist it, touching it from all sides, but this human was far better than my own hands could ever be.

I groaned as I set a fast rhythm, sweat pearling on my back. Havel's mouth was back on her nipples while Matar's tail nudged her lips open until she took him in, sucking him like a cock. I was going to have words with Matar about that tail of his. The engineer was watching without touching himself, but he was hard and there was no doubt he was waiting his turn. We'd all take her today. This first mating was for all of us.

"I'm so close," she gasped. "Just keep- aaaaaaaarrh!"

She threw her head back and let out a scream as her body began to shake, her inner walls fisting my cock. That was my undoing. With a scream that equalled hers, I came, one cock filling her with my seed and the other shooting it all over her belly, creating a beautiful golden pattern. As I watched, it seeped into her skin, staining it like a tattoo. Our mating mark. Now it was time for Havel and Matar to do the same so that every male in the galaxy knew that she was ours.

It was hard to leave her welcoming depths, but as the captain, I had a responsibility to my crew. They were in need of relief and it was their turn.

I pulled out as slowly as I could. This wasn't goodbye; this was just the beginning. I'd get to know every part of her body, inside and out. Maybe again later today. We'd have to discover how often she could be mated with before she needed a break.

I retreated to the end of the bed and leaned against the cool metal wall. I needed a shower, but there was no way I'd miss watching Havel and Matar mark her.

Havel had already taken my place, his single cock ready to enter her.

"Do you want this?" he asked while caressing her breasts. He seemed obsessed with them. Not a surprise, they were stunning.

"Fuck me already, you stupid alien!"

He laughed and did as she'd asked. Trish grabbed Matar's arm and pulled him closer until his cock was close enough for her to touch. Instead of stroking him like I'd expected, she directed him to her mouth. Oh A'Ta, she was going to swallow him like his tail. More seed spouted from my cocks. This was reaching a new level of mating frenzy. I started rubbing myself, impatient for them to be done with her so I could have another go.

Matar was careful with her, clearly afraid to hurt her, but she grabbed the base of his cock and pulled him into her mouth. He should be glad that she didn't have fangs like Havel. That would have been dangerous. She sucked him, taking him in deep, making choking noises that were almost my undoing. I closed my eyes, touching my cocks, imagining it was her. She was addictive, more so than any drug I'd tried during my wild metamorphosis years.

I only looked up again when Havel roared his release, his blue seed spurting all over her abdomen. Before it could sink into her skin, the liquid turned into single drops forming a circle around the strange indentation on her belly. Only when they were in position did they turn into permanent marks the colour of Havel's skin.

Matar never made it to her pussy. He came moments after Havel, just about managing to pull out of her mouth before shooting his seed on her breasts with a guttural groan. It first accumulated around her nipples, then ran down her mounds leaving beautiful blue stripes like the rays of a burning star.

Spent, he lay down on his back by her side, entwining his fingers with her. Matar's tail lazily curled up on her stomach, right above the bright blue marks. I was about to join them when my comms beeped. Not now. I checked the caller, ready to reject the call, but it was Professor Katila. If she contacted us, it had to be important.

I made sure the video function was switched off before greeting her. My voice was husky still, but hopefully, she wouldn't notice.

"I hope I'm not disturbing?"

I exchanged a look with the guys who grinned at me. "Not at all. What can I do for you?"

"I have looked at your grades and I'm afraid it doesn't look good for you. You've shown promise in some areas of the course, but you've failed several important parts of the abduction process. Even if you perform well in an oral examination, it won't be enough. There is however a way for you to pass the course and gain your certification."

"How?" I asked sharply while Matar gasped. I realised he'd not seen our results yet. Poor guy. Havel started whispering to him and Trish, explaining what had happened.

"First, I will have to talk to your abductee and ask her some questions. If what she says is satisfactory, I will let you know the next step."

I didn't like that she didn't divulge all the information immediately, but she was the teacher and we the students. The authority lay with her.

"Alright. She's with me just now, would you like to talk to her right away?"

Trish blinked tiredly, taken aback. She shook her head, but it was too late.

"Yes, that would be fabulous. You can stay on the line but please don't interrupt."

I felt a little like a child again, being chastised by my elders. I hated that feeling. I was the captain of this klatting ship; I deserved respect.

Matar helped Trish up and let her lean against his chest while Havel offered her a drink. She emptied the entire tumbler in one go, then licked her lips that were stained green from sucking Matar's cock. That colour should fade though; I'd never heard of a mating mark becoming permanent on a female's face. Not that it would make her any less beautiful, but she may not want to walk around with blue stains on her lips and chin for the rest of her life.

"Abductee, please report your state of health," Professor Katila commanded, suddenly sounding reserved and clinical.

"Ehm, I'm well," Trish muttered, shooting me a questioning look. "I was injured back on Earth but when the guys abducted me, they healed all my injuries. Actually, I don't think I've ever felt better."

She grinned at the three of us, clearly referring to the aftereffects of the mating. Our human - no, our mate - seemed to be glowing with joy. Pride filled my heart. I was proud of how she was handling her abduction, proud of having her as my mate.

"Did the abductors explain to you why they abducted you?"

"Yes, they did. I thought I'd already said that when Havel interviewed me for his assignment."

"They explained to you that they wanted you as their mate and breeder?" the Professor asked.

Trish blushed a little. "They did."

"And you weren't scared when you heard that?"

"Of course I was scared. Although, I first thought it was a joke. Then I was scared. Then I realised it may not be as bad as it sounded. Now I think this is the best thing that could have happened to me. I had no one on Earth. Now I have three guys desperate to make me happy."

"Now? Does that mean you've mated?"

Trish looked at me as if looking for reassurance. I nodded encouragingly and she rewarded me with a smile.

"Yes. We have."

"Was the experience satisfactory?"

Our female snorted with amusement. "You could say that."

"Good. I assume that means you're content to continue the abduction experience without resistance or escape attempts?"

Again, Trish laughed. "Yes, I don't plan to run away from this."

She looked at Havel, then Matar, then me, appraising our naked bodies. I looked down at my cocks, thanking them for being able to pleasure Trish so thoroughly. I wasn't sure if our personalities were enough to keep her with us. We'd failed with the lacy clothes and the recording of the couple. I glanced at the screen where the female was impaled on both men's cocks, unmoving. Havel must have stopped the video at some point. It would make a nice wall decoration, inspiring us for the next mating.

"Excellent. I need you to be fully compliant for the next stage. We are setting up a new course for advanced learners. Only those who've completed the first abduction certifications can take part."

"Does that mean we passed?" Matar interrupted eagerly.

"We will need case studies for the course," the Professor continued, ignoring the engineer's question. "If you agree, we will follow you three as you progress with your abductee. As part of the course, other students will analyse your behaviour to learn from it. This means you will be recorded on camera most days during the experiment. I will give you pointers in what to do and how best to proceed, but in the end, the decisions on what to do with your abductee is up to you. At the end of the course, I will decide whether you get the certification or not."

"Certification for this course or both?" Havel asked.

"I will mark you as passed for this course as soon as you agree to be our case study. I will even raise your grades a little to give you a 'good' rather than a 'passable'. I really think you're the perfect group of individuals to learn from. What do you say?"

I looked first at Matar and Havel, then at Trish. Matar looked angry but gave me a curt nod. Havel was more enthusiastic, clearly ecstatic that we might pass the course after all. Trish showed me her thumbs. I didn't know what that meant, but her smile said enough.

"We say yes," I told the Professor. "We're going to do it."

I reached out and took Trish's hands in mine.

Our abduction adventure wasn't over yet.

ALIEN ABDUCTION FOR PROFESSIONALS

THE INTERGALACTIC GUIDE TO HUMANS #2

LESSON 1

TAKING YOUR ABDUCTEE TO A PUBLIC PLACE

I patted the wall, stroking it like a pet. "You're a good little ship, Jade," I muttered. "Please don't fail."

The hull groaned in response and the floor beneath me shuddered.

"This can't be normal," I exclaimed, glaring at the guys who'd been telling me that everything was okay.

"No, it's not," Xil sighed. "We should have taken the long way round rather than flying through the nebula. It's too late now. You better put on your seatbelt, it might get even bumpier."

He himself was already strapped into his chair, looking very much like the starship captain he was.

"By A'Ta, what the klat are you doing?" Matar's voice came through the intercom. He was down in the engine room, fixing something – his favourite pastime. To be fair, the Jade constantly needed repairing. She was an old lady who'd seen better days, but she'd been well looked after. The colourful corridors were proof of that, painted by Matar himself. It was the only time I'd ever seen him embarrassed, when I'd told him how much I liked his art. He'd muttered something about randomly throwing paint at the walls and that it was nothing, but I knew how pleased he'd been by my compliments.

"Our captain decided to show off," Havel explained mildly. "Which is why we're now flying through a radioactive nebula instead of taking the scenic route around it."

"I wasn't-" Xil protested but was interrupted by a bang against the hull to my right. I jumped and realised I'd not put my seatbelt on yet. I quickly did so, just in case. I trusted Xil's flying abilities, but this was the first time I'd encountered a nebula and wasn't quite sure what that entailed. Until now, flying through space had mainly consisted of endless darkness with the occasional bright stars glittering in the distance. Not much different from looking up at the night sky on Earth, except that they were much brighter and everything felt more *real*. It was hard to describe the feeling of frightful wonder that overcame me whenever I looked out into the depths of space. Today though, we were going to visit a space station - a treat for me before we were turned into guinea pigs for Professor Katila.

"Get out of there!" Matar shouted. "The engines are overheating, and the radioactive energy is affecting the shields. The Jade is too old for this, you should know that."

"She can do it," Xil insisted. "We're almost through. Don't you want to spend extra time on Kitt-Y-6? This short cut will get us there before lunchtime."

"There might be some pawan steaks left. Trish, you need to try those. They'll fill you up and... never mind."

"What?" I asked.

"Make you horny," Xil chuckled. "Not sure if it's the same for females, but if I eat an entire pawan steak, my cocks will be hard for hours."

"How is that even possible?"

The Jade shook and groaned even worse than before, stopping the guys from answering. I was intrigued, but really, none of us needed aphrodisiacs. I'd lost count of how many times the guys had been inside me, how often I'd sucked them off, how often I'd had them between my legs. I should be sore, but Havel had given me a dose of medical nanites that were helping with any damage both space radiation and too much sex could do to my body.

Space was dangerous, they'd told me that from the start. There wasn't much research on how humans fared if they spent more than a couple of months in space. I supposed that would be an extra bonus for Professor Katila. I was a guinea pig for both her research and her teachings. At least the guys were only used as examples for Katila's lessons.

Again, the ship made noises reminding me of a cry for help. The Jade was suffering. Xil looked conflicted, but he didn't change our course.

"Not much longer," he said soothingly. I wasn't sure if that was meant for the ship or me or him. "Almost through."

I clung to my chair as we swerved and rattled through the nebula. I was starting to feel like I was about to be sick. As much as I appreciated a shortcut to get to the space station a little quicker, I didn't think it was fair on the Jade nor on my stomach.

Kitt-Y-6 was the closest space station to Earth - or Peritus, as the entire galaxy except humans called it - and my guys had promised me a treat once we got there. I was excited, but also a little trepidatious. I was about to meet a whole lot of aliens. I'd only just got used to my own three aliens and the three-eyed professor who kept checking on us via video link. According to Havel, at least two thousand different species were strewn across the universe. And since not all of the universe had been explored, it was likely that there were many more. The majority of them weren't spacefaring civilisations, so I'd only get to meet around a hundred different kinds of aliens. I snorted. That was still a hell of a lot. Havel, Matar and Xil were all Kardarians, yet they had very different features. Havel was blue and had fangs, Xil sported yellow scales and two cocks (my favourite attribute!) and Matar's green skin was speckled with silver spots that sparkled in bright light. I wasn't sure what wonders would await me at the space station with so much diversity within one species.

"Are there some kind of rules on Kitt-Y-6?" I asked to distract myself from the ominous rumbling the Jade was producing. "To stop people from eating each other?"

Xil laughed. "Yes. All space stations are neutral zones. No eating, no fighting, no blood-sucking, no mating."

"No mating?"

"There have been intergalactic wars brought on by lovesick aliens," Matar explained. "If the wrong species come together to mate, it might even have catastrophic health impacts."

"Not just for the couple," Xil added. "Badengas emit a toxic gas when they climax. It's supposed to protect them from predators during mating, but there was once a case where an entire space station had to be evacuated due to a Badenga having a little too much fun."

I snorted with laughter. "I can see why that would be a problem. I guess we can wait with the mating until we're back on the Jade."

Xil gave me a heated look. "We could always start now..."

The ship lurched to the right and it took all my willpower to prevent my stomach from emptying its contents. No, can't say I was in the mood for sex. As hot as my three males were, puking on them wasn't high on my agenda.

"How much longer?" I winced.

"A half of your Peritus hours," Havel replied. "Which is about twenty IG clicks."

He's explained the intergalactic time system to me before, but I found it very confusing. Since no species wanted to agree on which planet's rotation to use as a day, they averaged the amount of waking and sleeping hours most sentient species need. One IG day was about 27 Earth hours, while ten IG days made up an IG week. I kept getting mixed up with all the numbers, but luckily the guys had done their research and knew how to convert times and dates to what I was used to.

"Aaaaaand we're out of the nebula," Xil announced. Everyone breathed a sigh of relief, me loudest of all. The danger of puking was over.

"You better get changed," Matar told me. "You showing this much skin might be dangerous, even on a station like Kitt-Y-6."

Yes, it probably was a bad idea to go shopping while wearing nothing but my panties and a flimsy bra.

I met the guys at the airlock. Xil had parked us in the station's spaceport and bought us an electronic parking ticket valid for something like six Earth hours. Enough time to explore. The guys had been making plans for days about what they wanted to show me.

"Ready?" Matar asked me and took my hand.

I nodded. "Let's go shopping."

He slapped his tail on the ground, a gesture that I'd learned is close to him rolling his eyes. All three males didn't seem to think much of shopping, but I'd assured them that it was an essential pastime for Peritan women. I may have accidentally let them believe that it was necessary for us to survive...oops.

"Remember the lesson," Xil told the guys. "We show Trish the best shops and will buy her whatever she looks at for at least thirty Peritan seconds. Some things we can buy in front of her, others we will have to do in secret to surprise her later."

"You know I can hear you, right?"

Xil ignored me. "We do have a budget, so let's avoid the more expensive places. No trip to the exotics market for you, Havel. We can't afford that."

It was kind of sweet how they'd planned this entire trip with the same academic fervour they'd shown during the abduction, probing and mating. I knew they loved me, just like I loved them, and it wasn't all just because we were part of Professor Katila's course.

"Matar, Havel, remember that this excursion won't be filmed for the IGU," Xil reminded them as if he'd read my mind. "We will have to write a detailed report later on, so maybe make some notes. We don't want to disappoint the professor."

His last sentence was dripping with sarcasm. None of us was thrilled with the arrangement, but it had been the only way them pass their Alien Abduction for Beginners course. In return for a 'good' grade, we agreed to act as a case study for Professor Katila's Alien Abduction for Professionals class. The guys were given lessons every week that we then had to put into practice. This, taking me into a public place, was the very first one since we'd signed the contract.

To be fair, the lesson wasn't technically about going shopping. That was just a bonus. No, they were supposed to expose me to other aliens without becoming jealous. They were also told to make sure I felt safe and didn't panic, but I didn't see much chance of that happening. I was buzzing with excitement, and there was no space for fear or worry.

DEPRESSURISING COMPLETE, the computer announced, and the airlock doors slid open, revealing a massive hangar full of spaceships.

It was big enough for at least four football pitches, maybe more. The ceiling was so high that I couldn't see how far it reached. All around us, the noise of engines, machines and aliens talking in dozens of languages pushed against my ears, making me stumble back. I hadn't expected it to be quite this intense. Even though I was sure those ships ran on a fuel not found on Earth, the air smelled of oil and petrol.

Xil put his hand on the small of my back and gently pushed me forward, out of the Jade and into the chaos of Kitt-Y-6.

Circling around strange-looking space ships, we hurried out of the hangar to a sleek elevator.

"Hop in," Matar said with a grin. He seemed just as excited as me about being on the space station.

As soon as all four of us were inside the spacious cabin, the doors closed and a holographic...thing appeared in the centre. It was clearly alien, but I wasn't sure what gender, age, or even what materials it was made from. It resembled a block of yellow gelatine with several slits all around it that could have been eyes, mouths or something altogether different. It bobbed gently up and down and grew in size every few seconds before constricting again. Breathing? Without that movement, I would have assumed it to be some kind of artificial intelligence, but I instinctively knew it to be sentient. The being looked the same from all sides, so I wasn't sure if I was looking at its front or back. I supposed it didn't matter.

"Shopping platform three," Xil requested, clearly used to this alien's strange appearance.

"Have you completed your immigration forms?" the being replied in English. Well, it probably didn't, but I heard English, so that was all that mattered.

"We have," Xil confirmed and lifted his hand, pressing a button on his wrist communicator.

The gelatine blob vibrated, then turned from yellow into red.

"Invalid forms. You will be taken to a secure location."

I stared at the guys. This sounded bad.

"There's been a mistake," Xil argued, his voice calm and collected. "Check them again. Everything is as it should be."

The blob's expression didn't change - because it didn't have an expression in the first place - but its red faded into a dark orange.

"Full biosignature required. Please press against the walls and stay still until I tell you to move."

This was becoming stranger and stranger. Not how I'd imagined a shopping trip to the space station. It didn't bode well for the rest of our time here.

"Stand against the wall," Xil told me. "It's painless, just a quick scan to confirm that we're the species we say we are."

"How could we pretend to be another species?" I asked and stepped back until my bum hit the cold elevator wall.

"There are ways. Not that I'm familiar with any of them, of course." Xil gave me a wink.

The elevator began to shake slightly, and I was glad I was pressed against the wall for support. My skin tingled, and a shiver ran down my back.

"Scan complete. Three Kardarians, one human. Interspecies sexual contact confirmed."

"Why do they need to know that?" I whispered, a blush heating my cheeks.

"What is your relationship with these males?" the cube asked me, flashing an alarming red. "Mate, slave, partner, adopted sibling, teacher, student, breeder, nurse, pet-"

"Mate," I interrupted it before it could go any further. "I'm their mate."

It felt good to say that.

The alien stopped flashing and returned to a calming yellow. "Truth verified. Please note that slavery is forbidden on Kitt-Y-6. Should your relationship status change, please notify one of the attendants. Transporting you to shopping platform three. Have a pleasant time."

LESSON 2

SHOPPING FOR RICH(ISH) MALES

I slammed my tail against the elevator when we exited. That klatting thing had spoiled the beginning of our excursion. Trish seemed a little downcast, but her expression brightened as soon as she took in our surroundings. It had been a good choice to start with platform three. This was the place where merchants from all across the galaxy came to show off their bestselling wares. The other shopping platforms were more specific, while this was a treasure finder's paradise. There was everything from food to clothing to technology.

"This is amazing," Trish gasped. I had to smile at seeing her so stunned. I remembered my first visit to Kitt-Y-6. It was unlike any other space station. Others were more strict with what could be sold, while here the only rule was no slaves and no weapons. Of course, some merchants would sell you guns and ammunitions if you had the right passwords, but as long as no violence erupted on the station, the officials turned a blind eye.

"What smells so delicious?" our human asked and wrinkled her adorable nose.

"About a hundred different dishes," Havel laughed. "You'll have to be more specific."

"Let's have a wander," I suggested. "When you see or smell something interesting, we'll stop to take a closer look. The only thing we really need is some more clothes for you, but I assume we'll end up with bags full of other stuff."

Xil, Havel and I had listened to a lesson by Professor Katila on shopping with females. It had been an eye-opener. I had no idea females were this obsessed with acquiring new possessions. Katila had given us some pointers on how to resist, but I knew I couldn't resist whenever Trish fluttered her eyelashes and looked at me with a pleading expression that promised I'd be rewarded for giving in. We'd need to stock up on some of her favourite foods and treats, or I wouldn't get to see that lash-fluttering as often. She had a strange taste and liked dishes I wouldn't have touched even if someone paid me to eat them, but after all, she was a different species.

"What's that?" Trish asked and hurried towards a garishly purple stall. "Are those earrings?"

"Translators," the shop owner replied with a charming smile that made me want to punch him. "Not all people want theirs implanted or some kind of ugly device. This is the most fashionable way to show that you're open to other cultures and willing to talk to them."

"That makes no sense," Xil grumbled. "You could easily lose them and then you're stuck without a translator. No, implants are the way to go."

"Look, over there," I said quickly and pointed at another stall. "I think they have piki cakes."

"Pikis!" Havel roared and ran there as if he was starving.

Just like I'd hoped, Trish forgot all about the weird translator jewellery and followed Havel to the food stall. The owner, a massive Intaran female with enough body fat to last her through several famines, wasn't as charming as the other seller. She simply looked at us as if she knew she had no need of charm and sales pitches. Everyone loved piki cakes. I didn't know how it was possible, but almost every species in the galaxy enjoyed these small, moist cakes. The recipe was closely guarded, and I'd never met a piki seller who'd even say if there was meat, plants or something else entirely in them. Not that it mattered.

"Fifty cakes, please," Havel ordered.

The Intaran's expression changed to something more pleasant, while Xil scowled at Havel. Fifty cakes were excessive and would swallow a large part of our budget. Professor Katila had warned us that we'd have to adjust our budget when shopping with a female, but this wasn't Trish ordering an extortionate amount of cakes.

"Where shall I deliver them to?" she asked. "It'll take me a while to wrap them all."

Havel pressed his communicator against the receiver on her table to transmit our parking spot data. "Give us four to go, the rest can be delivered. No need to hurry, we'll be here for a while."

"I assume they're some kind of delicacy?" Trish asked when we walked away from the stall. "You seem to be very keen on them."

Havel laughed. "Wait until you've tried one. You'll never want to eat anything else."

"Which is impossible because we couldn't afford it," Xil muttered, but humour glinted in his eyes. He loved piki cakes just as much as the rest of us.

The medic handed Trish one and she unwrapped it eagerly, revealing the dark red cake. It was stamped with the traditional Intaran symbol that marked it as an original. Many people had tried to replicate them, but none had succeeded.

Trish took a first bite and her eyes widened. "This is amazing. What's it made of?"

"Nobody knows," I explained, "but don't let that stop you. It's not harmful."

She stopped eating. "You don't know? How can you eat something without knowing what it is?"

Havel chuckled. "Do you really care after tasting it?"

Trish took another bite, then shrugged. "Point taken. I'm glad you ordered that many."

We continued walking while enjoying our piki cakes, ignoring the other food stalls for now. We might return to them later, but the cakes would sate us for a while. Despite their small size, they were as filling as a full meal.

"Let's have a look over there," Xil said and led us towards a tech stall. "I could do with some upgrades to my communicator."

I suspected that wasn't what Trish was interested in, so I took her hand and pulled her the other direction. "You do that while Trish and I will continue to explore. Get me some upgrades too. My holo screen has been flickering recently."

Before the others could protest, we disappeared into the crowd. I was glad to be alone with Trish. Living in such close quarters on the ship, it was hard to spend some time with just her.

"Where are we going?" she asked.

I shrugged. "Wherever you like. Shall we look at clothes?"

Professor Katila had emphasised how important clothing was to females. Especially shoes.

"Yes - wait, what are those?"

She hurried towards a pet stall. Oh no. Xil had told me to avoid those. Larger animals were sold on one of the other shopping platforms, but pets and smaller service animals could also be found on this platform. Klat. Xil would kill me if I allowed her to get a pet. But looking at her expression as she took in the animals whining, barking, chirping and meowing from their cages, I knew that it was too late.

"Welcome, welcome," the owner called from behind a massive aaven who was getting its scales polished. Those six-legged beasts were prized as guard animals, but they were also great with children and would often be the first mount of juveniles living in rural areas. No, we were not getting an aaven.

"What are you in the mood for, my dear? We've just had a delivery of loovins. They're aquatic, but each comes with a floating liquid-filled bubble so you can take them with you wherever you go. They're long-lived, very loyal and don't make any noise."

He pointed at a stack of glass balls, each housing a strange-looking creature with fins twice as large as their bodies. I had no idea why anyone would want those as a pet. The word pet implied that you could touch and stroke the animal, but I doubted you could do that with loovins.

To my relief, Trish ignored both the aaven and the loovins. Instead, she stared at the tribitts housed in a large cage beneath the stall. I remembered how we'd once mentioned them in conversation. I dimly recalled that Xil even told her she could have one.

The little long-eared creatures were a sorry sight. While the other pets were all in pristine condition, the tribitts looked like they'd not been brushed in days. They were well-nourished but clearly hadn't been given the same attention as the other animals.

"Those are tribitts," the owner said dismissively. "Very old-fashioned. Nobody wants them nowadays. I only keep them because nostalgic tribitt enthusiasts need new breeding females for their herds."

"Ooooooh," Trish exclaimed. "You told me about them, Matar. You didn't say that they look like rabbits!"

"That's because I have no idea what a rabbit is," I chuckled. "But if you say so..."

"What's a rabbit?" the stall owner asked curiously. "Are they cute?"

"Very," Trish replied with a dreamy expression. "I used to have one as a child. They have ears just like these tribitts, but they're a bit smaller and less colourful. Mine was white with beige spots, but you'll also find black and brown ones."

"That sounds dull," I remarked. "It would make them hard to spot."

She laughed. "That's the point. In the wild, they're prey and need to camouflage."

"They're not bred to be pets?" the seller asked with a strange expression. "You take them from the wild?"

He looked horrified at the idea.

"No, but their ancestors were wild. Wait, does that mean tribitts don't exist in nature?"

The stall owner shook his head. "All these pets were created to be just that. Pretty, cute, easy to look after, house or space ship trained. Most of them listen to simple commands, while others are more intelligent. Tribitts can be too clever for some owners, especially when it comes to food. They're known to learn how to open drawers. I've even heard of some that can manipulate a fabricator. That could be just a myth, but I wouldn't put it past them. Devious little beasts. I don't know why they were even created. Now, my dear, how about one of these gorgeous Sliviean poro'la? They like to ride on their owner's shoulder and are excellent at removing body hair."

One look at Trish told me that we'd leave Kitt-Y-6 with a tribitt. And when she looked at me and began to flutter her lush eyelashes, I knew I had no choice.

"Which one do you like best?" I asked, repressing a sigh.

Most of the tribitts in the cage were a shade of dark purple with bright pink ears. Two were golden with dark stripes, and-

"The green one," Trish said determinedly. "It's the same shade as you. So pretty."

My heart did a little jump at that. She chose that tribitt because it reminded her of me. I would have bought her a dozen tribitts just to hear her say that again.

"Are you sure?" the owner asked, clearly not happy about it. I guessed the other pets were more expensive than the tribitts. After he'd told us that they were out of fashion, he couldn't charge a lot for them, not without losing face. That suited me just fine. We'd have more left in our budget to buy Trish other things. I wanted to treat her to a necklace I'd seen the last time we'd been on Kitt-Y-6. It was unlikely it was still available, but it would suit her perfectly.

"Yes," Trish replied without hesitation. "That is if you're okay with that?"

She turned to me.

"Of course," I said quickly. "Anything for you."

Trish smiled. "I'll give you a proper thank you later."

My cock hardened. I knew exactly what she had in mind.

I squeezed her hand, a promise of other squeezing I was planning on doing later. Her breasts were made for me, perfectly fitting into my hands. I loved massaging them, using just the right amount of pressure to make her moan and gasp.

"Do you need a basic tribitt accessories set with that?" the stall owner asked, clearly hoping to increase his profits. "It includes a harness, leash, food bowls, litter tray, some toys and a first-aid kit."

"First-aid?" Trish asked with wide eyes. "Do they get injured easily?"

The male grinned. "No, that's for the owners. Tribitts can be moody."

I rolled my eyes. "Don't listen to him. If you treat a tribitt right, he'll never scratch or bite you. But we'll take the set. I assume they're vaccinated and microchipped?"

"Yes, they also have sensors implanted, so you always know where your tribitt is and how it's feeling. There's an app for your communicator."

An app to monitor your tribitt. How silly.

He opened the cage and grabbed the green tribitt by its ears. It let out an angry bellow, but the seller didn't seem to care. I was starting to regret buying from him, but it was too late. The way Trish looked at the tribitt meant she'd already fallen in love with it. Not that I could blame her. The little animal was adorable. While most of it was green, it had small pink spots beneath its eyes. Its paws were a lighter green, the same as the insides of its long ears. Trish had been right. It was almost the exact colour I was.

"Do you want a cage for it?" the seller asked. "Or I can put the harness on it and you can carry it around with you. I should warn you, though, they go crazy for piki cakes so don't let them anywhere near that stall."

I sighed. That was going to be a problem.

LESSON 3

THE INTRICACIES OF MATING TOYS

I tried to be as quick as possible with getting my essential purchases done. I'd give Matar a good talking-to later for stealing away Trish. That klatting male was going to spend tonight alone in his bedroom, without our human.

While we squeezed through the crowd, Havel played around with the gadget he'd just bought. It was a ring that changed colour depending on Havel's mood. I didn't know why he needed it. Our healer was one of the easiest to read males I'd ever met. Maybe he'd got it for Trish, but since Kardarians and humans were so similar in looks and behaviours, it was really unnecessary. Oh well, it was his money. The IGU paid us for being their case study subjects in addition to giving us the chance of another certification, so we had some money to spare.

"I want to get her a present," Havel suddenly said. "Any ideas?"

I'd had the same idea, and it irked me that he'd said it first. Now he would think that I was copying him.

"Maybe we should ask one of the assistants," I suggested, unwilling to tell him what I'd planned to get Trish. "They might be able to recommend something."

Havel nodded and flagged down one of the AI globes swirling above our heads. Years ago, they used to have real people do this, but they switched to AIs for a 'better service'. To save costs, more like.

"How can I be of assistance?" the AI asked in a seductive female voice. Did they all talk like that or had the AI determined that we'd react best to this voice?

"We want to get our human female a present," I told the flashing globe. "Do you have any suggestions?"

"Data on humans is lacking," the AI replied, managing to sound almost regretful. "Switching to generic female profiles. Does the female like cooking?"

"No," both Havel and I said as one.

"Does she like fashion?"

"We want a present that's something special," I said before it could ask any more stupid questions. "Something that isn't a commodity. Something pretty and valuable. Something that shows her that we love her."

I regretted saying that last bit. Admitting my love for Trish to an AI felt weird.

"Maybe a present that her and I could use together," Havel suggested.

Again, I hated him for coming up with that.

"I know just the thing," the AI chirped. "Follow me."

It led us through the crowd, occasionally hovering above a stall as if it was deciding whether to stop there or not, before continuing. We were halfway through the shopping platform before it finally landed on the roof of a busy stall. Males of all species, sizes and colours were standing around it, staring at the wares on offer. I exchanged a look with Havel. This was a good sign.

Those males were likely buying presents for their females, too.

Instead of waiting, I squeezed through the shoppers until I was pressed against the table. A strange selection of objects was spread out in front of me. I had no idea what any of them were, although some of the long objects' shapes reminded me of something. No, that couldn't be... could it?

"Welcome," a shop assistant in barely any clothes greeted us. She was showing more skin than I liked. In the past, before we abducted Trish, I may have found the female attractive, but now I just found it irritating.

"Are you looking for a toy to use with a male, female or other?"

"Toy?" Havel asked.

"Mating toys," the Ferven said, rolling her eyes.

Havel and I looked at each other again. Neither of us knew what this was about.

"Sometimes, you might want to add some more spice to your mating," the female explained with an exasperated sigh. "In the beginning, it's all exciting and new, but at some point, you'll run out of techniques and experiences to try. That's when our famous mating toys come into play. We've got toys for all species and preferences. Kardarians are one-cock-species, correct? Maybe your female would like to experience what it would feel like to be with a two or even three-cock-male? We've got some beautiful replicas, either standalone or as a strap-on."

I wanted to rub my eyes in astonishment. Fake cocks? What was the galaxy coming to? Next, they'd come up with fake pussies and fake boobs.

"Some of us do have two cocks, actually," I told her and flicked my gaze downwards for a second to make it very sure that I was one of those males.

"Apologies," she muttered, but I ignored her and let my gaze wander over the stall's offerings. And instantly corrected my view of the universe when I realised both fake boobs and pussies were available. Including the rubbery replica of a four-boobed Ankanis female. How peculiar. Why would anyone prefer to play with this instead of the real thing? I supposed there were lonely males out there with no chance of ever abducting their own female. Havel, Matar and I were lucky to have found Trish, the most perfect female in the entire galaxy.

"Our female has four Kardarian cocks to choose from," Havel said drily. "What else do you have?"

"Take a look at these magic balls," the Ferven said and held up a chain of three fist-sized balls made of some kind of rubbery material. "They vibrate, and the deluxe version can even emit mating hormones, depending on the species. Or maybe you'd like your female to experience the pleasures of knotting?" She pointed at a strange ring. "Just push this over your cock and at the end of your mating, it will activate, locking you inside your female. You can set the time yourself or you can have it choose a random time. It can be most satisfying to be inside your female for hours, without neither of you able to break the link."

My cock hardened at the thought of being bound to Trish in that way.

"I'll take one," I said before Havel had the chance.

"Would you like small, medium or large?" she asked and held up three different sizes. As much as it pained me to admit, the large one was about three times the girth of my cock. I had no idea what species that was made for, but it had to be some kind of giant.

"Medium," I admitted grudgingly.

She grabbed a box from under the table and handed it to me. I pressed my communicator against the receiver, and it automatically took the credits from my bank account. I'd not even checked how much this knotting ring cost. That was so unlike me. Being with Trish was changing me in all sorts of ways.

"What can I get for you?" the Ferven asked Havel. "How about this little remote-controlled vibe?"

"What's a vibe?"

"Really, don't Kardarians know anything?" she huffed, before putting on a fake smile again. "It's a vibrator. She'll insert it and it will vibrate when you want it to, stimulating her from within. Of course, you can also give her control over it, but most males prefer to be the ones to do the honours. Again, vibes come in all shapes and sizes. What species is your female?"

Havel didn't reply and turned to me instead. "I might just get her some more piki cakes. This is so strange. Who says she even likes these toys? She might be offended if we give them to her."

I gulped. I hadn't thought of that. Hopefully, she didn't mind. Trish loved mating, so she'd also love this, right?

Without another word, Havel walked away from the stall. I grabbed my box and followed him, now very much doubting my purchase. I was going to have to talk to Professor Katila. Her advice about shopping for our female had been completely useless so far.

TRISH

The little tribitt purred in my arms, looking up at me with his beautiful black eyes. There was a certain intelligence to his gaze. I couldn't wait to be back on the ship to play with him. Matar had promised to download a guide to tribitt husbandry to the reading device the guys had borrowed me. The animal looked a bit like a rabbit if you ignored the tiny antennae sprouting between its ears and the colour of its fur, so maybe he had a similar temperament and needs. The seller had reassured Matar that the tribitt was litter trained and wouldn't soil the ship. We'd see if that was true. After seeing how that guy had kept the poor little tribitts, ignoring them in favour of fancy pets that were in fashion, I didn't trust his words.

One of his ears stroked my chin and I laughed. "Aren't you the cutest little bunny," I cooed.

"Tribitt," Matar corrected. "Have you thought of a name yet?"

"No, but I think I'll discuss that with all of you later. If this is going to be our family pet, we should all have a say.'

"Family pet?" he repeated slowly. "I like the sound of that. Family."

I would have hugged him if I didn't have a snuggle tribitt in my arms. I didn't want to squeeze him to death between Matar and me, but I made a mental note to give him that hug later. Maybe paired with a kiss.

"What now?" I asked.

"Are you hungry?"

"Nope, not in the slightest. That cake has made me so full that I don't think I need any food for the next week or so."

He laughed. "And I bet you'll want another piki cake then?"

"You know me so well." I grinned at him. "Is there anything you'd like to buy?"

"Giving you that tribitt has been enough. I don't need anything for myself."

"It's not about needing something. Shopping is all about treating yourself to something you want rather than need."

"Yes, I think I remember Professor Katila saying that. But what if all I want is to spoil my little human mate?"

Warmth spread through my chest and it had nothing to do with the furry animal pressed against me.

"Then maybe I should spoil you... if I had any money." I sighed. "Not having a job and my own money sucks. I hate relying on you for everything. I don't get why the IGU won't pay me like it does you. I'm part of the case study, aren't I? I should be reimbursed for my troubles, too."

"You're right. As much as I love to care for everything you may desire, I understand the desire to be independent. Maybe we should all give you a share of our pay. That way, it's like a salary from the IGU, even if they don't pay you themselves."

I frowned. "I suppose that would be a good solution. And next time we speak to Professor Katila, I might demand that she pay me if she wants me to co-operate."

"I wouldn't suggest that," Matar said with a sigh. "I've heard stories of her being quite nasty to people who didn't follow her rules. Everyone thinks she's kind and benign because she's a Karangi, but there's something cold behind those three pretty eyes."

"Well, if you're going to pay me my salary, that means I can buy you something now." I smiled. "And I know just the thing."

"Trish!" a familiar voice called from behind me.

I swirled around to see Xil and Havel make their way through the busy crowd. A group of very tall aliens that reminded me of humanoid giraffes stood in their way, but when Xil glared at them, they hastily stepped aside.

They didn't see the little tribitt until they finally reached us, which explained the shocked looks on their faces.

"A pet?" Havel asked before his surprised expression turned into one of adoration. "It's soooo cute! Can I hold it?"

"It's a male," I grinned and handed the green bunny to Havel.

"You've adopted another male?" Xil growled. "Aren't three enough for you?"

I stared at him, but then his scowl cracked and a wide smile appeared on his face.

"Just messing with you. He's adorable. I wondered if you'd buy one after we'd talked about it a while back. I wasn't sure if you'd remember."

"I couldn't resist." I watched as Havel petted the tribitt, rubbing it between its ears. The furry creature purred and sighed in contentment. Awwww. So cute. I was dying of cuteness.

"Does he have a name?" Havel asked, repeating Matar's earlier question.

"No, let's do that later. What did you guys buy?"

Xil didn't meet my eyes. "I'll show you back on the Jade. Let's not do it in public."

"Yeah, let's not," Havel chuckled. "But I can show you mine."

He handed the tribitt to Xil, who immediately grinned goofily and started muttering to the animal. The tribitt seemed to be enchanting everyone. I had no idea why they'd gone out of fashion. I couldn't imagine a cuter pet.

"Hold out your hand," Havel asked and rummaged in his pockets.

Curiously, I did as he'd asked. Had he bought some kind of bracelet for me? Or a ring? Was he going to-

He pulled out a wrist communicator, similar to the ones he and the other guys wore, but smaller and on a leather armband rather than metal. Small pearls had been woven into the material, turning it into jewellery. He slid it over my wrist and fastened it.

"We can set it up on the ship, but I thought it was time for you to have one. You'll be able to control everything on the Jade, communicate with us and whoever else you want, watch those Periton videos you like, use it to-"

I hugged him tightly, pressing a kiss on his cheek. "It's perfect. Thank you."

He wrapped his arms around me and pressed me tight against his chest. I breathed in his scent and wished we were on the Jade already. I needed to thank him and Matar for their gifts, plus I was curious about what Xil had got for me. It had to be something naughty if he couldn't show it in public.

"Maybe I give you mine now so I can get a hug, too," Xil grumbled from behind me.

I laughed and took the tribitt from him. "Later. I promise. What else is on our shopping list?"

My new little pet yawned and wiggled its head into my armpit. Its ears were flat against its head and its eyes slowly fluttered close. Despite the noise around us, it had fallen asleep. No idea how it did that, but I guessed he was used to being surrounded by noise and people. He might even get scared on the Jade where it was a lot quieter, with only the hum of the engines and our voices. Sometimes music, too, but I didn't care much for the Kardarian rock the guys loved so much, and I hadn't been able to convince them of listening to Earth music, either.

"Clothes for you," Xil said. "And we should get some parts for the ship. Matar, that's your job. Didn't you say you needed some kind of special bolts?"

"I did," Matar replied grudgingly, clearly not happy about it. "But can't we get them together after we've been clothes shopping?"

"You've already had alone time with Trish," Havel snarled. I looked at him in surprise. Why was he so angry?

Xil put a large hand on my shoulder and steered me away from Matar and Havel. "Let's get you some clothes. I saw this Ferven female earlier with a very fabric-less outfit. It reminded me of that lingerie you told us about."

I laughed when I remembered how they'd tried to make their own lingerie once. In a misguided attempt to seduce me, they'd cut holes in their clothing. I still didn't know how they could have been that stupid, but I believed it was due to the ridiculous lessons the Intergalactic University had taught them. A lot of what they knew about humans was wrong. Very wrong. Hell, they didn't even get the name of our planet right. They called it Peritus, although apparently it had been given that name long before the first life had developed on Earth. Still, it felt weird to call good old Earth by another name.

"Shall we get you some?" Xil asked eagerly.

I shook my head but stopped immediately when the tribitt started mewing in his sleep.

"I think I could do with some proper clothes. You know, jeans, shirts, jumpers, maybe even some bras. But nothing too fancy." It's not like we were meeting a lot of other people. I grinned at the thought of other spaceships docking with the Jade in space so we could have a cup of tea with random aliens.

While the guys had some friends outside of their trio, most of them were back on their planet, just like their family. One day, we were going to travel to Kardar so I could meet their parents, but not yet. Kardar was far from Earth - Peritus - and we had better things to do. That's what Xil said, anyway. He hated his father, but I didn't know why. He'd only mentioned his mother once or twice, and I hadn't wanted to pry. He'd tell me at some point, I knew that. We had no secrets from each other, but some things didn't have to be discussed.

The guys led me to a row of clothes stalls. I gaped at the garments. Of course, I should have known that I wouldn't find any Earth clothes here, but it was still a shock to see how different everything was. A shirt to my left had four armholes and it shimmered in all colours of the rainbows even though I could swear that it was white. Something that looked like a hoodie for a two-headed species had an inbuilt screen, showing text in an alien language on its front. Advertising, a political message, quotes from a song? I couldn't read it.

Xil flagged down a little AI globe - I'd seen other aliens use them - and asked it to lead us to a shop catering to humans. The ball whizzed away and we hurried to follow it through the narrowing walkways until we got to a rather sorry looking area. Barely any shoppers, dusty stalls, depressed sellers. Not exactly what I'd hoped for.

"Maybe we should go back," Havel suggested. "This looks seedy."

"Stall 429Y has the best clothes for humanoids," the AI chirped, sounding almost offended. "Please take a look."

It stopped above a lacklustre shop that had clearly seen better days. While other stalls used flashing lights, signs, garish colours and sexy shop assistants to lure in the crowds, this one had nothing but a tired looking alien with one large eye and no nose. The rest of him looked somewhat human in the sense that he only had two arms and two legs, without tentacles, tails or talons. After seeing dozens of different alien species today, I'd gained a new perspective on what was possible.

Xil pointed at a dark green blouse. "This would suit you. Plus, it matches the tribitt."

"And me," Matar grinned. "I love seeing you in my colour."

"You should also get something in yellow and blue then," Havel insisted immediately. "No favouritism."

"We don't stock yellow," the shop owner said in a monotonous, tired voice. "But we do have various blue shades. How about this skirt?"

He rummaged in a stack of barely folded clothing and pulled out a monstrosity of a skirt. It looked like a dishevelled chicken and a blueberry had a baby. And then added lots of frills. It was so ugly that it could probably count as fashion somewhere in the galaxy.

"No, thanks," I muttered. "Do you have any jeans?"

"Jeans?" he asked, clearly not recognising the word. Maybe my translator didn't know that.

I sighed. "Trousers, thick cloth, hard to destroy. Usually blue. Do you have anything like that?"

"Wouldn't you prefer something more flattering?" the alien insisted and held up a see-through blouse that would have barely covered my boobs.

"It would suit you," Havel whispered from behind me. I elbowed him in the stomach, and he groaned. "Alright, go with something else instead. But it would still look great on you."

I sighed. "Is there somewhere I could try on some of these?"

The cyclops nodded towards his right. "There's a changing pod over there."

I handed the tribitt to Matar and randomly grabbed a couple of items, not convinced I'd like any of them. Still, I didn't want to disappoint the guys by being too choosy. After all, we'd walked for ages to get to this stall and I didn't want to stay in this seedy area any longer than I had to.

The changing pod looked a bit like a port-a-loo, just more space-y. A silver door slid open when I approached, revealing a small room with mirrored walls. As soon as I stepped inside, the door closed. A light above me flickered into life, but even so, I felt a little claustrophobic without a window. Yup, just like a port-a-loo.

I quickly undressed and tried on the first shirt. It wasn't too bad, although it wasn't flattering in the slightest. I'd take it anyway, just to have something to show for. This shopping trip wouldn't be for nothing. The two pairs of trousers both didn't fit, although I might be able to wear the looser ones with a belt. I should check the stall if they had any. The puke-coloured jumper I'd grabbed was surprisingly comfortable. It looked horrendous, but it was warm and soft. The Jade was usually warm enough to walk around in t-shirts, but who knew when we might visit a colder planet. Better to be prepared.

The final item was a tank top that I wouldn't have chosen if I'd had given it a proper look. It ended above my navel and together with its extremely low cleavage, it didn't leave much to the imagination. The fabric's feel reminded me of neoprene except that it was thinner. My nipples poked through the fabric. Definitely not something I'd wear in public, and if the guys saw me wearing it, I wouldn't keep it on for long. They'd rip it off my body before ravishing me where I stood. Yes, I was speaking from experience.

Suddenly, the pod shook, and I stumbled back against the wall. The cabin swayed, leaning to one side as if someone was trying to push it over from outside.

"Hey, I'm in here!" I shouted as loud as I could. "Stop that!"

Nobody replied, but the movement continued. I dropped to my knees, feeling safer close to the floor. A lurch made me gasp. The pod was being pulled into the air. Fuck. What the bloody hell was happening here?

"Stop!" I cried. "Help!"

It was useless. The pod swayed as if it was swinging in the air. Were they transporting it somewhere else? This couldn't be happening. How did a shopping trip turn into this? All I could hope for was that this was an honest mistake and not an abduction. I doubted I'd ever come across abductors as friendly and cute as mine again.

Fuck. I continued shouting, but nobody heard me. Or if they did, they didn't care.

With nothing else to do, I put on my own clothes again, then wrapped my arms around my knees and hoped that my guys would find me soon.

LESSON 4
INTRODUCTION TO RESCUING YOUR FEMALE

"**S**houldn't she be back by now?" I asked, checking the time. "It's been ages."

"Females can take a while when trying on clothes," the Brontes said, looking unconcerned.

We declined. If his *refreshments* were the same quality as his stall, we'd likely end up with food poisoning.

"Maybe ping her communicator," Xil suggested. "Just to check if she needs help deciding."

My present for her was already coming in handy. I'd made the right choice, even though it had taken me forever to decide.

I dialled her communicator's ID and waited for her to respond. I hadn't shown her how to use it yet, but all she had to do to pick up a call was press one very obvious button or use voice control. I'd made sure the device had human English installed as a language.

"The changing rooms are data-insulated," the Brontes told me. Was that a smirk on his thick lips? "We don't want customers to be disturbed while trying on clothes. It's an intimate process, after all."

That didn't make sense to me, but I didn't know much about fashion. I bought my clothes in bulk and put on whatever was on top of the stack in my wardrobe. Now that we were part of Professor Katila's case study, we had to wear slightly more formal clothes, but Trish had assured me that my black garments would be fine.

We waited for a little while longer until I couldn't stand it any longer.

"I'm going to check on her," I announced and headed off to where we'd last seen Trish. She'd disappeared behind the stall, but when I scanned the dirty, rubbish-strewn area at the back of the shops, there was no changing pod. Strange. A few doors led away from the main shopping area into the belly of the space station, but those were out of bounds and likely locked. She wouldn't have gone into one of them. So where was Trish?

I called out to the others, but they were already close behind me.

"Where is she?" Matar asked and sniffed the air. 'I can smell her scent, she's been here, but where did she disappear to?"

"Let's ask that Brontes," Xil growled. "He can lead us to that mysterious changing pod."

A strangely muffled cry made me look up just in time to see a silver pod disappear through a hatch in the ceiling.

Someone had taken Trish.

I exchanged a look with the guys and without another word, we broke into a run.

It took us way too long to reach the nearest elevator. It took even longer for the warden to understand why we wanted to go to the platform above even though none of the shops there were currently open. By the time we finally burst out of the lift, my heart was racing. My fangs were fully extended, ready to rip into whoever had taken our Trish.

I checked my communicator. "Five life signs further ahead. One of them human."

We ran as fast as we could, Xil in the lead, Matar and I flanking him. Matar's tail was wrapped around his waist so as not to get in the way, but I knew he'd use it to fight our enemies as soon as we got close. The three of us had trained together. Yes, we'd been traders before we'd started our Alien Abduction for Beginners course, but that didn't mean we didn't know how to fight. On Kardar, every youngling learned how to defend themselves. Hatcheries taught combat skills in addition to academic subjects. With three sentient species living on the same planet, there had been many wars in the past. Right now, an unsteady peace kept everyone in check, but I was sure that one day, Kardarians would have to fight again.

The platform lay deserted, only a few lamps illuminating our path. Empty stalls, the tables covered in grey fabric, gave it a ghostly feel. Dust covered the ground. I didn't know why this platform was no longer used, but it was the perfect hideout for whoever had stolen Trish from us. It was lucky the elevator warden had agreed to take us here. Involving the station security would have taken way too long.

We sprinted in silence, faster than we'd ever run before. Finally, a silver pod glinted in the distance. My fangs poked my bottom lip as adrenaline pumped through me. Battle lust threatened to overwhelm me even though we hadn't even seen the abductors yet.

While running, I took a look at the communicator again. The life signs were moving away from us, but we were faster. It wouldn't be long before they came into sight.

Beside me, Matar was breathing hard, and I felt exhaustion creep up on me, too. None of us did much exercise. Now I regretted that. We'd done some weightlifting before we'd abducted Trish - the course had recommended for us to look our best so to attract our female - but that was a while ago now. I swore I would do regular cardio as soon as we were safely back on the Jade.

Finally, four figures came into view. Large, bulky, bipedal. It was too dark to see much more than that. I increased my speed even further. They weren't going to get away. One of them carried something on his shoulders. Trish?

"Ari, dial Trish," I commanded my communicator. I usually preferred manual input, but I wanted to keep my eyes on the abductors.

A traditional Kardarian folk dance started playing in front of us. Yes, they had Trish with them. I was glad I'd already set up her communicator.

"Stop!" Xil roared as soon as we got close enough for them to hear us.

They didn't even turn around, just kept running. Where were they even going? There was nothing up here. If they wanted to take them to their ship, they'd have to use one of the elevators, but they'd passed two of them already without stopping. Not that I wanted them to take a lift. I wasn't sure if the warden had alerted security. There was no time to check.

Once we got closer, I finally recognised the aliens. Tarpartians. Yuck. Since they hadn't actually developed spaceflight yet, there weren't many of them. They had the advantage of their planet having an extraordinarily strong gravitational pull, which had led many a spaceship to crash land on Tarpa. Scavenging parts and repairing ships, they'd somehow managed to reach nearby space stations. While they weren't very bright, they'd soon become known to be excellent bodyguards. They were loyal, tough, greedy and lacked morals. They'd do pretty much anything for the right incentive, like abducting a human. I doubted it was them who'd had the idea. They were just lackeys for whoever had really orchestrated the kidnapping. Had this been random or had they wanted Trish for some reason? In most places, humans weren't known at all since the only ones travelling the galaxy were those who'd been abducted. Peritus was making its first small steps towards the stars, but it would still take a while for them to be able to reach their closest planets, let alone a space station like Kitt-Y-6.

No, it had to have been random. That changing room had been a trap for the first person to step into it.

"Stop right now!" Xil bellowed once more.

The Tarpartians didn't care. Luckily, they were slower than us. They were about our height but had a lot more bulk. And I wasn't talking about just muscles. Their body fat index had to be through the roof.

Just when we got close enough to launch our attack, they turned around as one, guns drawn, pointing right at us. Trish was slung over the shoulder of the tallest Tarpartian, struggling against his grip.

"Don't worry, Trish," I called out to her, and she lifted her head. Her hair was dishevelled and her eyes were rimmed with red, but otherwise, she seemed unharmed.

"Thank A'Ta," Matar exclaimed under his breath.

Even though I didn't believe in the deity, I felt the same relief. Now we just had to deal with the guns. We carried no weapons, so we had a problem. Not one I couldn't solve though. They were basic beta-laser-guns, the cheapest on the market. Perfect. Without taking my gaze off them, I typed into my communicator. I'd practised this so often I could do it in my sleep.

"Leave," the Tarpartian carrying Trish burped. Yes, he burped. It was how Tarpartian language sounded to anyone who wasn't a native speaker. Our translators turned it into actual words, but while the translation was delivered right into my brain, I could still hear their burping. It was disgusting. Probably one of the reasons why nobody wanted Tarpartians anywhere near them if they could help it. Unless of course you needed a scrupulous bodyguard. I assumed most people hiring them told them not to speak if it could be avoided.

"Return our human," Xil snarled. "She's ours."

"Not anymore," the grey alien burped. His mouth was so large that it created an echo chamber for the sound.

"What do you want with her?" I asked, playing for time. I still needed a moment to work on my communicator.

"None of your business," the Tarpartian on the right burped. "Now run off before we shoot you."

I pressed the final button and coughed, signalling Xil and Matar. The deed was done.

"Then shoot us," Xil grinned. "What are you waiting for?"

"No!" Trish shouted and struggled even harder. I hope she didn't hurt herself trying to get away from her captor. She had no chance of escaping his grip, as much as it pained me to admit that. Maybe we should teach her some self-defence skills. It wouldn't help her much when confronted with a burly Tarpartian, but it might aid her in less dangerous circumstances. You never knew what deranged aliens who might encounter in space.

The Tarpartians looked at each other.

"She told us not to harm them," the male carrying Trish muttered, barely loud enough for my translator to pick up his words.

"We should have taken stun guns," the one on the left whispered, and I realised it was a female. She looked exactly like the males, only her voice was slightly softer and her mouth smaller. Her burps were just as disgusting, though.

"I'm sure she won't mind if we kill them. She's only interested in the female," the Tarpartian who'd threatened us said.

"Come on, shoot us," I shouted. "Stop wasting our time!"

"What are you doing?" Trish screamed. "Are you insane?"

I wished I could have told her what was going on, but there was no way to safely do so. In fact, her panic helped us. The Tarpartians didn't suspect a thing.

"Fire on my command," the largest one burped.

I turned to Xil and Matar and gave them a wink, just in case. Everything was going to be fine.

"This is your last chance-"

"Just klatting do it," I interrupted him. "This is getting dull."

I forced myself to take on a relaxed, almost bored posture.

The Tarpartian snarled and pointed his gun right at me.

"I warned you..." he burped and fired.

Except that nothing actually happened. He stared at his gun and pressed the trigger once more. Nothing.

Xil roared and launched himself at the closest Tarpartian. Matar and I followed suit, using their distraction to attack. Before he could react, I reached the one on the right and plunged my fangs into his fleshy neck. I didn't have any venom, not like other fanged species, but that didn't matter because I hit an artery and blood poured into my mouth. I pulled back and spat out the sour blood, before kneeing him in the groin. He went down, clutching his neck, looking at me in shock. I wasn't sure if this would be enough to make him bleed out - I'd never fought a Tarpartian before - but for now, he was down.

"Havel, take Trish!" Xil commanded, and I didn't hesitate.

The male who'd been carrying her had simply dropped her on the floor to defend himself. Idiot. I ran to her side and scooped her into my arms before running away from the battle.

"Are you alright?" I demanded more harshly than I'd intended. "Are you hurt?"

"I'm fine, thanks to you. They didn't hurt me. Said their employer didn't want me harmed."

I growled. As soon as she was safe, we'd go after that employer. One of the Tarpartians had said that it was a female. That made it even more mysterious. A male may have wanted Trish as his human sex slave, but it was unlikely that a female would desire the same. Of course, some females preferred their own sex, but why choose a human?

We reached the closest elevator and the doors slid open. As soon as we were inside, I pushed the button, locking us in. No warden waited for us; the spot in the centre where they usually hovered was empty. Maybe this elevator shaft wasn't used anymore. I didn't care. We were safe now.

I set Trish down to inspect her, just in case she was injured after all. They'd bound her hands with wire, but it didn't take me long to get it off her. As soon as her arms were free, she clung to me. I held her tight, breathing in her scent, feeling her press against my body. Only now did the shock of almost losing her sink in.

"Trish," I whispered, but then there was no more time for words. I captured her lips and kissed her like I was starving. She cupped my face and locked me in place, returning the kiss just as passionately. She tasted sweet and spicy at once, even better than piki cakes. Her tongue swiped against my fangs, and I realised they were still more extended than they should be. I concentrated and slowly retracted them until just the tips poked out between my normal teeth. I didn't want to hurt her.

I held her, vowing to never let her go again. I was going to get a leash and keep her by my side, not letting her out of my sight. She was too precious to endanger. We should never have left her alone. From now on, one of us would always be with her. Especially until we knew who'd wanted to abduct her.

My communicator beeped. It had to be the others. I realised they wouldn't know where we'd disappeared to. Without breaking the kiss, I pushed the button to take the call.

But it wasn't my friends who spoke.

"Congratulations, you've passed the test."

I was going to kill her.

LESSON 5

NEST BUILDING FOR DUMMIES I

I glared at the Professor, still not quite able to believe it had all been her doing. We were back on the Jade's bridge, all huddled together. I was on Xil's lap, but Havel had his hand on my thigh, and Matar leaned against me, his head on my shoulder. They'd not let go of me on the way here. Even while I'd showered and changed clothes, Xil had been with me. If Professor Katila hadn't been waiting for our call, I knew we'd be in bed now, all of us, claiming each other.

The shock still sat deep in my bones. Even now that I knew it hadn't been real, I was still on the verge of having a nervous breakdown. While I'd been carried off by that alien, I'd not allowed my fear to take hold of me. Now, it was close to overwhelming me. Only the guys' touch kept me from falling apart.

"You have done extremely well," Professor Katila said, giving us a smile. Bitch. "Top marks for all of you. Of course, you need to write a full report for our case study, but there's no doubt about your grade. You didn't hesitate once you found out your abductee had disappeared. You wasted no time in following her. I expected you to contact security or find some weapons, but I liked your method of disabling the Tarpartians' guns even more. Very effective. I also appreciate that you didn't kill them. I'd planned for that possibility, of course, but it does save me some paperwork."

"Why did you do that?" I accused her. "Do you have any idea how scary that was?"

She ignored me and looked at Xil instead. "You have proven excellent leadership. I might invite you to record a presentation on how you trained your team."

"I didn't train them," he said in a quiet, dangerous tone. "We grew up together. We had the same teachers. And if you were here right now, I'd show you some of the techniques they taught us."

Professor Katila didn't react to the threat. "As I said, I require a full report. That was your first practical assessment of this course, a second will follow soon. You'll have some time to prepare for that one."

"How generous," Matar huffed.

"Next, I'd like you to look after your female. She's been through quite a lot and needs to be reassured that she's safe with you. I've uploaded some presentations and readings on nest building for you."

I stared at her. "Nest building? Humans don't build nests."

Her third eye looked straight at me, making a shiver run down my spine. Her normal eyes were fixed on the guys, looking at each one of them in turn.

"You might want to get some building supplies from the space station while you're still there. Turn your bedroom into the ideal breeding environment. You'll want soft, warm colours, lights that can be dimmed, lots of pillows and soft furnishings. You already have a large enough bed, but maybe invest in a better mattress. You-"

"I don't need a nest and I don't breed," I hissed. I wanted to throw something at her, something sharp and dangerous.

"You may change your mind," she said, completely ignoring my protest. "Besides, Kardarians build nests, and we wouldn't want to deprive your males of that."

I looked at the guys. All three had murderous expressions painted across their faces. If Katila had been on the ship with us, she'd be dead by now.

Somehow, I doubted this arrangement would last much longer. How desperate were the guys to get their qualification? Now that they had me, they weren't' going to abduct anyone else. I was their one and only abductee. They were planning to go back to being traders again once they'd completed this course. Maybe I could convince them to do it sooner rather than later. Professor Katila gave me the creeps. I wouldn't have been surprised if she had more plans for my guys. And me.

"You have two days to complete this lesson," she continued. "Then we will have a debrief. I'll send you the time once I've squeezed you into my calendar."

She made it sound as if we should be grateful that she took the time for us. Urgh. What a bitch.

I breathed a sigh of relief when the screen went black. The only good thing about this conversation was that she'd distracted me from my fear.

Xil pressed a kiss on my shoulder. His lips were softer than ever. Yummy.

"We'll figure it out," he said soothingly. "I won't forget what she did to you. We'll make her pay for it."

The other two nodded.

"I don't care about that certificate," Matar growled. "She harmed our mate. There's no way I'm letting her get away with that."

"We," Havel corrected. "*We* will punish her."

Relief flooded me. I'd know they'd put me first, but it was good to hear how they were no longer motivated to complete their alien abduction course.

"Are you really going to build me a nest?" I asked them. "Humans don't have nests. Chickens, yes. Humans, no."

"Yes, we shall make you a nest, my little chicken," Xil laughed. "Whatever that may be."

I groaned. "A chicken is a bird, not a term of endearment."

"I think it sounds cute," Havel said, and I knew I'd made a mistake. From now on, I was going to be their chicken.

"Do Kardarians have nests?" I asked.

"We do. Males build them for their females as proof of their love and devotion," Matar explained. "They can take many shapes and forms. It's mostly a space for the couple - or multiple mates - to withdraw to. Somewhere to feel safe and at home. Unlike for egg-laying species, a nest isn't for incubating younglings. We use it to increase the bond between mates."

"And to breed," Xil added with another laugh. "That's why she suggested a better mattress."

I had to admit, I had no issue with more sex. After what we'd been through, I wanted them to hold me. To merge with me. To become one. It was the ultimate feeling of safety when I was in their arms. Nothing could harm us while we were together.

"I still find it weird," I admitted. "Nest sounds so... alien."

Matar snorted. "Glad you're only now noticing how you're an alien."

"You're the aliens," I shot back. "Humans are the centre of the universe."

"Of course they are," Havel said mildly. "Now you stay here with Xil or Matar while I start making that nest for you. We can order materials from the station without having to go outside again. They'll be delivered straight to the Jade."

"Can't I help?"

"No. Nest building is a task for us to do to honour our mate. But if you want, you can watch Katila's lesson about it and tell us the gist of it, just in case she asks us questions." I could hear him rolling his eyes without turning my head. "Every Kardarian male knows how to make a nest for their female. It's preposterous that she even sent us a presentation on it."

"I'll need snacks. Have the piki cakes arrived yet?"

The guys laughed. The sound dispelled all remaining anxiety, and I finally felt warm again. I was ready to forget about today's nightmare and move on to new, strange things. Like a nest.

In the end, all three of them disappeared, leaving me on the bridge with a piki cake and something resembling a smoothie. As much as I liked popcorn when watching films, this was even better. The cake dissolved in my mouth, letting flavours explode with every bite. I no longer cared what it was made of. All I cared about was knowing that we had lots of them stashed in the galley kitchen.

Instead of Professor Katila, another alien appeared on the screen when I started the pre-recorded lesson. I thought I'd seen some of his kind on the space station, but I didn't know the name of his species. He reminded me of a red frog with bulbous eyes, an enormous mouth and something like gills on his neck. His teeth were sharp, turning him from a harmless frog into a predator. He wore a toga-like robe, hiding most of his body. Only one arm was visible, making me curious how many limbs he was hiding beneath the toga.

"Welcome to this lesson," he said with a surprisingly soft voice. "Today we'll be discussing the traditional art of nest building. While all species have their own techniques, many share a common basic concept that we'll look at in detail. We will also examine why nests are the way to your female's heart or hearts and how you can use them to strengthen your bond. In the final part of the lesson, we will cover incubating eggs. If you belong to a species who doesn't lay eggs, you're allowed to skip that."

I was grateful for that. Although it might be fun to find out more about aliens who laid eggs. I couldn't imagine having an egg inside of me... but as the guys continuously pointed out, humans were just one of many species in the universe. The aliens I'd seen on the shopping platform had mostly been bipedal and breathed oxygen, but that's because we hadn't been on any of the other platforms. Xil had explained that there were various platforms depending on customers' needs, whether they needed water to swim in, nitrogen to breathe, lower gravity or other requirements. It would have been fun to take a look at some of those, but then, I wouldn't have been able to survive there without some sort of spacesuit.

I focused on the teacher again. I realised he'd never introduced himself. Maybe he'd done other lessons before and assumed students would know his name. For now, I decided to call him Professor Frog. Was that speciest?

"A nest is the ultimate expression of safety and comfort. It's the centre of your home, where you and your mates will be intimate. I don't just mean physical intimacy. In a nest, it is a common rule to be completely honest with each other. A space of truth and love." He smiled and I despite his teeth, he looked happy and benign.

"Materials used to build nests depend on what you can find on your home planet. Some species will weave branches and other organic materials. My own kind uses algae and our parents' dried excrements to form the perfect nest. As I can't cover every single species in this lesson, I challenge you to look up your own traditions in the handbook I've attached."

A bing sounded, and a holographic book hovered above my communicator. Havel must have linked it to the Jade already. I had no idea what to do, so I simply pretended it was a real book and opened it. Even though my fingers didn't touch the virtual pages, the communicator seemed to recognise my movement and flicked to the first page. Although I was sure that was just for me, the book was written in English. I bet it didn't take the shape of a book for everyone either. Was that the Jade's AI's doing or something within the communicator? I'd have to ask the guys.

A table of contents showed a long list of different species.

"Pause the lesson," I said, and Professor Frog froze on the screen. I was much more interested in what I'd find out in the book than what he had to say. I clicked on Kardarians and the book's pages magically flipped to the corresponding chapter. I felt a bit like a wizard. Harry Potter, watch out, there's a new mage in town!

I skimmed the chapter, skipping the bits I already knew about Kardarians. My mates had told me how they were one of three species on their planet, that they had a variety of bright skin tones, that they had various features like fangs, tails, pointy ears and even claws. It didn't mention two cocks, but maybe that was too specific. I'd never asked Xil if he was an anomaly or if it was common among Kardarians to have more than one dick.

Kardarians use the highest quality materials they can afford. Utilising local materials is frowned upon and items from other planets is preferred. The more exotic, the better. Often, the parents of the male/males will add something from their own nest, like a pillow or blanket. Sometimes, the female's father will cover the nest with his scent to warn the males that they'll have to answer to him should they mistreat their mate.

I cringed at that. Thank goodness that wasn't an issue for me. If my males mistreated me - not that they ever would -

I'd deal with them myself. No father needed and especially not his scent. Yuck. I wondered if the guys' parents would give me something for our nest once I met them.

I took one more bite of cake and continued reading.

Kardarian nests are comparatively small. They will fit the female and her mate or mates, but there's no space for furniture, offspring or other relatives.

Wait, relatives? Why on Earth would I want my relatives to be in a nest with me? That was weird. Were they supposed to watch while I slept with my guys? No way. I was surer than ever that I was lucky with my choice of mates.

While Kardarian males will take their female's opinion into account, they are very protective about their responsibility of building the perfect nest. They will continue to improve it until their female is completely satisfied. Once the nest is ready, they will mate in it repeatedly, often for several days, until the nest has taken on their scent. It's a way to stake their territory and show that they're a good match with their female.

Sex for days? Wow. Warmth pooled between my legs at the thought of being in my mates' arms, having them claim me again and again, only taking breaks to sleep and eat. It was kind of hot. Although I'd need some time to recover afterwards. The guys were *big,* and I could only take them so often until I got sore.

I pulled my mind out of the gutter and focused on the book.

Nests will be remade from scratch after each birth of a youngling. They increase by size each time, and it is assumed that the dwelling the family inhabits will also become larger.

Each time? How many children did Kardarians usually have? I wasn't planning on having kids any time soon, especially not several of them. I wanted to explore the galaxy together with my mates and children would only get in the way of that. One day, we'd settle down and start a family, yes, but not now.

I skimmed the rest of the text where it went into more detail of building techniques and strategies. The guys weren't letting me help with the nest anyway, so no need for me to study that. I closed the holo-book and continued watching the lesson. As interesting as some of it was, I had trouble concentrating. I wanted to know what the guys were doing.

If I'd had another piki cake, I might have been able to control my curiosity and stay on the bridge. Since I'd finished mine, however, I paused the recording. It was time to see what they were up to. And try out the nest.

LESSON 6

NEST BUILDING FOR DUMMIES II

Three males building one nest was a bad idea. Each of us had different ideas on how best to do it. And while they usually accepted that I was in charge, today neither wanted to back down. We all wanted to impress Trish, but we couldn't agree on what she'd want.

"This is impossible," I sighed after comparing our notes. After the first argument had almost turned into a fistfight, I'd decreed that we'd each write down our plans for the nest. Now we had three entirely different suggestions. Klat. Maybe we should have watched the IGU lesson after all. It may have explained how to solve disagreements between mates.

"Should we ask Trish to decide?" Havel asked, looking just as defeated as I felt. I didn't want to fight my friends, but there was also no way I'd back down from my plans. They were the best. Trish would love it. She'd fall into my arms and onto my cocks as soon as she'd see my nest.

"Or we could build three different nests," Matar suggested. "Then she can choose which one she wants to spend the most time in."

"We don't have space for three nests," I snapped. "Nor the time. Our parking meter is almost expired, and we haven't even ordered all the supplies we need. Staying for a second parking period will be expensive."

"Are you saying you don't like spending money on our mate?" Matar teased.

I growled at the engineer. "You know that's not true. But I want to be far away from here before Professor Katila comes up with yet another way to distract us."

"Trish is on her way here," Havel announced. "I put a tracker on her communicator after the incident earlier."

"Does she know?" I asked.

"Not yet. I didn't want to freak her out. We don't need it on the Jade, but from now on, I always want to know where she is. I don't think my heart will survive another kidnapping."

I had to agree with him. "Let's keep it quiet for now. What else have you installed?"

"All the usual. I added a Kardarian dictionary and software to help her learn our script. The translator will let her communicate with our families when we return home, but she won't be able to read any signs."

"Good thinking. Not that we'll go back to Kardar any time soon, but better to be prepared. I think she'll enjoy the challenge. Did you also add the Peritan books we downloaded during our research phase?"

Havel nodded. "Those and some of their films. For entertainment, if we're ever busy."

"I'll never be too busy for her," Matar said, but he shut up when I shot him a dark look. As our engineer, he was responsible for keeping the Jade in shape. With me flying the ship, it was Havel who'd be most likely to spend time with Trish during difficult periods. Not that I was planning to get into any space battles any time soon, but our bumpy ride to Kitt-Y-6 had shown how quickly a situation could escalate.

"I thought you'd have started by now," Trish said, stepping into the room.

"We've removed the furniture," I grumbled, aware that this wasn't going as planned. I didn't care about Professor Katila's grades anymore, but I didn't want to disappoint Trish. She deserved to be the happiest female in the galaxy.

"I can see that," she quipped. "Wasn't the bed supposed to stay?"

"We'll return that once we've decorated the floor and walls," Havel explained. "How was the lesson?"

Trish shrugged. "Quite enlightening. Is it true the father of the bride rubs his scent all over the nest?"

I exchanged a look with the guys. From the way she said that it was clear that she didn't approve.

"Sometimes," I hedged. "It's not necessary. Was the lesson about Kardarians in particular? Did they use us three as an example again?"

"No, but I was given a book that had a chapter on you. Well, your species. It said how important this ritual is for you, which is why I'm surprised that you're not finished yet. Or at least further than... this." She laughed. "Do you want me to build you a nest instead?"

"No," all three of us said, completely aghast. A female building her own nest? I'd never heard of such a travesty.

It would make her males the laughing stock of the entire planet. And Kardarians loved to laugh about each other. We'd never hear the end of it.

"Then what's the problem?" Trish asked.

I sighed and pointed at our three holo notes. "We can't agree on a plan. We all have different ideas, and none of us wants to back down."

"That's kind of adorable. How about I pick and choose bits from each of those plans? I'll try and make it so each of you has the same amount of input. I don't want you to fight over this."

"That would be great," Havel nodded before I could say anything else. "If you open the menu on your communicator, you can open a blank sheet of holo paper. Then just drag and drop the parts you want."

He fiddled with his own communicator and all our notes transformed into strange scribbles. That had to be her human way of writing. It looked ugly.

Trish sat on the floor - we should have left at least a chair in the room - and started reading through our plans. There was nothing for us to do but wait.

I wasn't a patient male. In fact, waiting was torture. I sat by her side to peek at her notes, but she turned her back to me.

"Don't look until I'm done. And don't you dare try and influence me."

She knew me too well.

"I'll get us some snacks," Matar volunteered. I hoped he meant Piki cakes by that. We'd given one to Trish earlier but hadn't taken any for ourselves. I'd make sure that she got most of them, but an occasional treat for us males was fine, too. Right? Or was I supposed to save them all for our female? Maybe I should. Before the kidnapping, I may have asked Professor Katila about that, but no klatting way was I going to contact her now.

My communicator pinged, signalling our time on Kitt-Y-6 was almost over. I suppressed a scowl and paid for a second parking period. We still hadn't ordered any supplies besides some basic pillows. Those wouldn't do for Trish's nest. Plus we needed to stock up on more food and fuel. In all the excitement earlier we'd lost track of those essentials. Shopping with Trish hadn't been the only reason we'd come to the space station.

I occupied myself by scrolling through the station's virtual catalogue, adding supplies to my basket. They'd be delivered to our ship before we left. At least now that I'd paid for a second parking period, we wouldn't have to pay a surcharge for fast delivery. And maybe... yes, we should take Trish to a restaurant. If she wasn't too scared to set foot outside the Jade again. I wouldn't think any less of her for that. It was a sign of her inner strength and resilience that she was sitting here with a smile on her face despite the ordeal she'd gone through just a few hours ago.

Just in case, I reserved us a table at the Outer Ring Restaurant. I'd never usually go there - it was way too expensive - but Trish deserved to be spoiled.

. . .

By the time Matar returned with Piki cakes and a tray of fresh fruit, I'd finished ordering supplies. Now, all we had to do was get the items we needed for our nest.

"I'm done," Trish announced and looked up from her note, smiling happily. "How do I translate this back into Kardarian?"

Havel reached out and touched her holo paper, flicking it to his own communicator. As soon as it landed there, it turned into our own alphabet. He sent copies to Matar and me, and we studied what Trish had compiled.

"Perfect," Matar exclaimed. "I think this is better than any of our plans."

Trish grinned. "Sometimes, it takes more than just the sum of the parts. Do I get some cake as a reward now?"

Faster than she could see, I grabbed her and pulled her against me, pressing my lips to hers. I kissed her passionately, hoping she'd understand how much I admired her. Loved her. She was the best mate I could have ever imagined.

"Xil, stop it," Havel said with a fake sigh. "You're the one who has to authorise the purchase. Go and order everything so we can get started on building the nest."

Instead of ending the kiss, Trish wrapped her arms around my back and clung to me. No way was I going to stop now. My cocks grew hard as her body moulded against me, a perfect fit. Our tongues danced, and it felt like our very first kiss once again. Every kiss with her was a new experience. It got better every single time, even though that was impossible. Our first kiss had been amazing, so how could it get even better?

Finally, I pulled away, breathless. Her eyes were wide, her lips swollen. I loved that look on her.

"Just send the klatting order," Matar said and pulled Trish to her feet, away from me. I immediately grew cold where she'd touched me. Being without her was like a brooding emptiness took over my heart, reminding me of how it had felt to almost lose her. It had been the worst moment of my life when I'd realised she'd been taken. I never wanted to feel anything like that ever again.

I quickly submitted the order, then snatched a piece of cake. If I couldn't have Trish, then I'd eat the second-best thing. As soon as we had our nest, I'd taste her, too. She loved it when I was between her legs, letting my tongue explore her most secret places. I enjoyed making her gasp with pleasure, have her grasp my head to prevent me from moving away.

"It won't be long before we get everything delivered," I told the others. "But I still want to build the nest without you watching, Trish. I know you've seen the plans, but I need it to be a surprise. It's tradition for the female to only see the nest once it's completed."

"I understand. I'll go and play with the tribitt," she said. "Hopefully he's done napping by now."

When we'd pursued her kidnappers, Matar had thrust the little animal at the stall owner. Luckily, it had still been there when we returned. I wasn't sure if the Brontes had been involved in Professor Katila's plot, but I hadn't trusted him one bit.

I watched as she left the room, a little sad that I couldn't go with her. But we had to build a nest. I looked back at the plans. We were going to have to hurry up or we'd never finish this today.

TRISH

The tribitt - I still hadn't decided on a name - was exhausted by the time the guys called me. We'd played for hours, and I'd started to get a good idea of the little space bunny's abilities. He was intelligent, and it shouldn't be too hard to teach him some tricks. The tribitt used his ears to communicate his mood. Hanging down was sad or tired, up straight seemed to be excited and him flicking them in my face was his way of telling me that he wanted food. Plus, a growl coming from his belly.

He also squeaked occasionally, and when I scratched him between his ears, he did something resembling a purr. It was the cutest sound ever.

Using my new communicator, I'd read up on tribitts and now knew that they ate almost anything. Very handy. I'd grabbed some stuff from the kitchen, and he'd scoffed down everything I gave him with no apparent preference for this or that. It would make feeding him easy. We could give him leftovers from meals without having to buy tribitt food. If that even existed.

The guide also mentioned that tribitts could get aggressive towards strangers, so I would make sure he'd cuddled with all the guys at least once. Although it would be fun to see the little green animal attack one of my mates. Would they fight back or simply let it happen?

I sat him into his bed, which was basically a large pillow I'd found in the cargo bay, and kissed him on his forehead. The tribitt yawned without opening his eyes. I smiled. Despite everything that had happened on the station, our shopping trip had been worth it.

I left him to sleep in peace and headed to the main bedroom. I had to admit I was a little nervous. The guys could be... intense when it came to their traditions. I sniggered when I remembered the first probing. They'd been so eager and at the same time terrified to make a mistake. By now, they'd accepted that we were all learning together, that it didn't have to be perfect the first time round - and that they weren't ever going to probe me again. One time had been enough, especially when knowing that they'd done a report about it for Professor Katila. She knew everything about our love life, and I hated that. Once we were done with the whole nest thing, I'd have to talk to the guys about perhaps dropping the IGU course. They'd be most willing to do so while the memory of my abduction was still fresh in their minds. And mine.

I shuddered and pushed that thought away.

Havel waited outside the bedroom, brimming with excitement.

"You're not allowed to enter until they give me the blue light."

"Blue? On Earth... Peritus it would be a green light."

"I'm blue, so it's a blue light," he said simply, as if that explained everything. "Did you have fun with the tribitt?"

Before I could answer, the door slid open. Xil and Matar stepped into the corridor.

"We're ready," Xil announced in a strangely sombre tone. Tradition bids us to let you enter the nest first and arrange it to your liking. If there's anything that you don't like, remove it. Then... ehm..."

"Strip naked," Matar interrupted with a wide grin. "We'll join you as soon as we get changed into our ceremonial outfits."

I was starting to realise that this was an even bigger deal for them than I'd thought, even after reading the lesson and reading the chapter on Kardarians. I guessed I wasn't used to them being so flustered and solemn.

With a nod, I squeezed past them into the room. The previously bright lamps embedded in the ceiling had been covered with red fabric, dimming the light but also reminding me of a brothel. Probably not what they were going for. The walls were hidden behind more fabric, black and more dark red. It made the room seem smaller, more intimate. But yes, definitely a brothel.

The guys had removed all furniture, even the bed frame. Instead, ten large mattresses, twice as wide as our original one, throned on top of each other in the centre of the room surrounded by hundreds of pillows. Not kidding. I wasn't going to count them, but there had to be at least a hundred pillows of various sizes. They ranged from cushions like you'd have on your sofa to fluffy monstrosities almost as long as me. Wow. They were mostly black, with some red and purple to make it look less like a funeral pyre. That's what it was. A pillow pyre.

I stifled a laugh just in case they were outside, listening to my reaction. They'd clearly put a lot of work and effort into this.

The mattress was covered in shimmering black fabric, similar to silk but with more sparkle. I ran my hand over it. Cool, yet soft. I bet it would feel amazing to have it against my naked skin. Of course, I'd find out soon enough.

I slipped out of my clothes in record time and threw them into a corner. It felt a bit weird to be naked without the guys in the same room. Hopefully, they'd join me soon. I made my way through the pillow mountains. Something hot hit my foot, and I suppressed a shout of surprise. Didn't want the guys to come in guns blazing. Rummaging around the cushions, I searched for whatever I'd stepped on. It was a stone, smooth and grey and very warm. A strange scent hit my nostrils and I gave it an experimental sniff. Yes, the stone was giving off a calming scent that I couldn't quite identify. Not flowery, more like smoke and spices. It made me think of a cold winter's night, sitting in front of a fireplace, wrapped in blankets, surrounded by my mates. I closed my eyes and breathed in the scent. It made me feel at home.

Of all the things in this nest, this was the best part so far. Maybe I judged a little too quickly. Were there any other surprises hidden beneath the pillows?

I put the stone on the bed, then went on my hands and knees to search. My fingers clasped around something hard and coarse. It felt like a branch or stick, but I couldn't dislodge it. I threw some of the pillows hiding it aside until I saw the strange item. It was twice as long as my arm and looked like a dried snake, with a thin body and round ends. Not kidding. *Please, don't let this be some kind of aphrodisiac food that I'll have to eat.* It didn't feel organic, though, more like pottery or stone. I'd break my teeth trying to eat it. One end of the almost-snake was screwed to the floor, which is why I hadn't been able to lift it. Curious. I'd have to ask the guys about it. Unless it was an oversized sex toy, I couldn't imagine it's purpose.

I covered it under pillows again - just in case it was a sex toy that they wanted me to fuck - and searched the other side of the room for more surprises. I found a pile of yellow leaves that smelled like vanilla and two more of the hot stones. They were smaller than the one I'd stepped on but had the same beautiful scent. I added them to their sibling on the bed. I wanted to have them close, not buried beneath cushions.

A knock on the door made me whirl around.

"Are you ready for us to come in?" Xil called.

I quickly jumped on the mattress - which erupted into fireworks. What the fuck. I gasped as colours spread over the black fabric where I'd touched it. It was like rainbows surrounding me, trapped in the material but close to bursting out of it. I'd never seen anything like it. This had to be some kind of technology, but the sheets were thin like silk, so how did it work? Where was the power source? Not that it mattered. I didn't really care how it did what it did. I slowly moved my hand over the bed and marvelled at the colours exploding into life. Sparks seemed to fly through the air, even though I knew they were inside the fabric. Beautiful.

I lay on my back, naked and surrounded by swirling colours, and told the guys to enter.

LESSON 7

BREEDING FOR ADVANCED BEGINNERS

My breath caught in my throat as I stepped into the room.

She was perfect.

Trish was spread out on the bed, her legs slightly parted, her nipples hard, her cheeks flushed. Her belly still wore the signs of our first mating: blue, yellow and green. She was ours. And she was ready to be bred.

I was rock hard already, and I hadn't even touched her yet. Luckily, the ceremonial breeding garment was designed with precisely that in mind. Instead of trousers, I wore a loose-fitting kilt. Beneath it, I was bare. My chest was covered in paint, the traditional symbols of my family and clan. Since we'd grown up in the same community, Xil and Havel had the same symbols except for two each that represented our parents. On our backs, we'd added our own sign, one we'd designed yesterday without Trish's knowledge. It would be our family's mark, to be passed through the generations from this point on.

"You look amazing," Trish gasped. "I never knew you guys had kilts. You look so Scottish, well, alien-Scottish."

I didn't ask her what that meant. The time for talking was over.

Before I joined her on the bed, I quickly looked around the room. She'd not removed anything. That meant she liked our arrangement. In the end, we'd decided to keep it simple, foregoing a lot of the ideas we'd had. It had felt wrong for Trish to know what we were planning, even though it had been helpful to have her mediate. We'd paired it all back to the bare essentials, making the room cosy, warm and comfortable. Since we'd only used a small part of our budget, Xil had splashed out on the most luxurious Lap'tan sheets. The expense had been worth it for seeing her on them. It was like she was lying on a galaxy.

She'd taken the fire stones and arranged them on the bed. Those had been my idea. We'd always had some of those in my family home and they reminded me of my childhood. I hadn't found any with the scents I was used to, but once we visited Kardar, I'd buy some of them She seemed to like the stones, or she wouldn't have put them next to her.

Xil cleared his throat, and I realised I'd not taken my place by his side. It was time to begin the ritual. Now that we'd built the nest, we had to turn it truly ours. Mark it with our scents and memories.

"We have built a nest to honour you," Xil began the speech that males had recited during the breeding ceremony for generations. "As our mate, you have secured your place in our hearts, in our minds and our home."

"You're in my heart, my mind, my home," Havel said solemnly before I repeated the same words.

"This nest is the symbol of what we pledge to you," Xil continued. "We shall keep you safe. We shall keep you warm. We shall keep you happy. And we shall keep you satisfied."

That was the signal to lift our kilts, revealing our erect cocks. I didn't have to look at Xil and Havel to know they were just as aroused as I was.

"Wow," Trish muttered before quickly covering her mouth with her hands.

Slowly, Xil unbuttoned his kilt and let it drop to the floor. "We shall provide you with our seed of life. We shall care for the offspring that we will create together. We pledge to keep harm from our family until the day we die."

"Until the day we die," Havel and I echoed solemnly.

"Will you accept this nest?" Xil asked and stepped forward until his legs touched the mattress. "Will you accept us as your mates?"

Trish nodded. "I do."

She bit her bottom lip the way she always did when she was nervous or unsure. I had to remind myself that she didn't know this ritual. She had no idea what would come next. There was no right or wrong for her parts of the ceremony, though. While the males' words were set and couldn't be changed, the female could reply with whatever she wanted. I thought it was intentional to give the female the power over this rite.

"Will you accept our seed as a symbol of our love?" Xil asked, his gaze locked on Trish. I was jealous it was him to ask her first. Before meeting her, I hadn't minded at all that he was the Captain of the ship. Now that we had a mate, I didn't always find it easy to watch Xil in charge.

Trish did a choked sort of sound, but then rose to her knees until her mouth was almost level with Xil's cocks.

She looked up at him with her beautiful wide eyes before taking his lower cock in her mouth. It wasn't part of the ritual, but it was perfect. My own cock ached, needing her touch. My tail wrapped around my thigh, even though it wanted to curl around Trish.

I almost drooled as I watched Trish take Xil's lower cock deep into her mouth while rubbing his upper cock with her nimble fingers. A thin line of drool ran down her chin, landing on her full breasts. I couldn't hold back any longer. I went on my knees next to Xil and gently put my hands on her hips, turning her ever so slightly towards me. I pulled her closer until I could kiss her naked belly. She gagged as Xil's cock pushed deeper into her throat, but the scent coming from between her legs made it very clear how much she was loving this.

I ran my tongue over her skin, slowly moving up until my head was between her breasts. Using my grip on her hips to keep her steady, I took one of her nipples into my mouth. It was hard and pebbled, perfect for suckling on. I sucked on her nipple as hard as I could without hurting her, relishing the way she moaned against Xil's cock. That was my doing, not his. I cupped her other breast with my hand and simply held it for a moment, admiring the weight. Her breasts were perfect. Everything about her was, but I could spend all day worshipping her boobs. I swirled my tongue around her nipple, causing her to arch her back and push against my face. She wanted more. Well, she only had to ask.

My tail uncurled from my leg and touched the inside of her thigh. With Xil's cocks blocking her view, she probably didn't know that it was my tail instead of my hand. I'd not dared introduce this to our mating until now, but today was special. Trish opened her legs, adjusting her position to give me access. Moisture glistened between her thighs, showing me exactly how ready she was for us. I'd enter her soon enough, but for now, my tail would give her the pleasure she deserved.

I moved it closer to her entrance, letting the tip run around her swollen sex, just about touching her. She quivered and tried to grind her hips against the tail, but I kept her locked in place, toying with her. I didn't give her the satisfaction of having my tail touch her where she really wanted to. I kept to the outer lips, smearing her juices all over her beautiful pussy, preparing her for me. For us. We were all going to take her, again and again. We wouldn't leave this nest until all four of us were sated, exhausted and carrying each other's scent. This breeding ceremony was the most important moment in a mate's relationship, and I was going to savour every single second.

Finally, I rubbed my tail's enlarged tip against her bud. She moaned against Xil's cock and her entire body shook. She was close to coming. I looked down at my own cock. So was I. If I drove into her now, there would be no holding back. But I was aware that Xil would be the first. Then Havel and I had to fight for second place. Where was that blue-skinned bastard? Without stopping my tail's slow circles around Trish's clit, I looked at my friend. He was still a few feet away from us, stroking his cock, his eyes glazed. He was enjoying the show. Good for him. I was more of a doer than a watcher.

"Please," Trish whimpered, breathing hard. "Fuck me."

"No," Xil growled. "I'm not going to fuck you. I'm going to *breed* you. I'm going to mark you. I'm going to fill you with my seed. And I'm going to make sure everyone knows you're mine."

A shiver ran down my back. That was hot.

"And then Matar and Havel are going to do the same. Breed you. Make you their mate. And once you've come again and again, milking our cocks, we're going to worship your body. We will show you how much we love and adore you."

I never knew he had it in him. That had been one poetic speech. Sexy. I was even hornier now, something I hadn't thought possible.

It was time to do something about that. Xil's would be the first cock to enter her, but nobody had mentioned anything about a tail. I flicked the tip of it against her clit one last time, then pushed into her in one hard stroke. She screamed in pleasure and bucked her hips against me. This time, I let her. I fucked her with my tail, wishing it was my cock. It wasn't quite as thick, but it was longer, and I could reach all the way into her depths.

"Klatting stop that," Xil snapped at me. "It's my turn."

With a whole load of regret, I pulled back and let go of Trish, joining Havel on the side-lines.

"Would you like one or both?" Xil asked our female. She didn't have to ask what he meant.

"Both."

Now I wished I'd prepared her little rosebud as well as her pussy. Too late. With Xil's large back hiding Trish from view, I couldn't see what he was doing, but I hoped he was using some of her moisture to get her ready for him. Xil's cocks were a little less thick than mine, but he had two of them to make up for that. Thankfully, this wasn't our first time with Trish, and she was used to our large alien cocks. She'd said that human males were less well endowed, which had flattered all three of us. We were above average for Kardarians as well, but it always felt good to be appreciated like that by a female.

With one hand, Xil positioned himself, then plunged into Trish with both cocks at once. She cried out and grabbed the bedsheet with her hands. Colours exploded all around her like fireworks as Xil started fucking her. It seemed the perfect metaphor for what was happening. Xil groaned in unison with Trish's moans, creating a song that I couldn't wait to join.

I stroked my cock, pretending my hand was Trish's tight pussy.

"Soon it's our turn," Havel whispered hoarsely. "You fuck her, I take her mouth?"

He surprised me, but I wouldn't turn down that offer. "Agreed. We shall fill her from all sides, in all her holes. She'll never want another mate ever again."

"I heard that!" Trish screamed. "And I will be yours, always."

I almost came at her words. I knew she meant it. She was ours. Our mate. To be loved, cherished and fucked.

Xil breathed hard as he pummelled into her. The sound of his balls slapping against her skin echoed through the room.

"I'm close," he groaned. The muscles in his arse were tight, and I knew I looked the same when I was on the last sprint, almost ready to spill myself within her.

"Then come in me," Trish begged. "I want to come with you."

"You shall." He reached around, probably to rub her clit while continuing to fuck her in deep, hard strokes. I had to admit, it was more than hot watching them from this perspective. Before, when we'd been with Trish all at once, we were usually on the bed, two of us caressing her while the third buried himself within her. Now, Havel and I weren't able to caress her skin. All we could do was watch as she exploded around Xil with a primal cry, at the same time as he pushed into her one last time, arching his back, filling her with his seed. A drop of precum dripped from my cock, landing on a random cushion. No matter. Soon, the entire nest would smell of our mating. That's what we'd built it for. And a proper breeding ceremony wasn't complete without our scent covering half the pillows.

Xil bent over Trish and kissed her. I gave my cock one last stroke, knowing it was my turn now. I waited until Xil pulled out of her and stepped aside, then there was no stopping me. Her pussy and arse were wide open, stretched by Xil's two cocks. Waiting for me.

I had no patience for foreplay. Been there, done that. I pressed my tail's tip against her tight arse and pushed against the resistance, snaking it into her dark tunnel. I twisted it from side to side, grinning with satisfaction when Trish's moans told me how much she enjoyed it. I'd never used my tail on other females in the past. It was something intimate, precious, and I'd waited for a mate like Trish to try it. The way my tail felt inside of her, the pressure her muscles put on me, it was a sensation unlike anything else. It was time to fuck her or I'd come before I'd even entered her.

"Ready?" I asked and met her beautiful eyes. She smiled at me, and that was all I needed.

I drove into her in one stroke. She was wet and eager, almost pulling me in. I bent over her until I could kiss her breasts, then sucked on one while slowly grating my hips against hers. I wanted it to last just a while longer. If I pummelled into her like Xil had, I'd come in an instant.

Her inner muscles seemed to milk my cock. I matched her rhythm with suckling on her nipple, giving it a gentle squeeze with my teeth every time I pushed into her arse and pussy. I let my tail fuck her hard, pulling out almost entirely before diving in again, making her squeal every time the tip pushed past her tight entrance.

"Do it," Trish moaned. "Come in me. Breed me. Be my mate."

There was no holding back. Not any longer. I stood up straight, lifted her legs until my thighs were pressed against hers, and fucked her harder than ever before. It seemed like both an instant and an eternity until I came, shooting my seed deep into her. I screamed at the same time as her, then kept her screaming by fucking her with my tail. I kept my cock inside her, still hard, enjoying the sensation of feeling my own tail through her inner walls. I'd only need a short break before I could do this again. And then again. She was mine.

"My turn," Havel said and put a hand on my shoulder. "I've changed my mind. I need to fuck her in her pussy first before taking her mouth."

As much as I wanted to stay in her warm, dark caves, I knew it was time to relinquish my position.

I pulled out of her, kissed the sole of her foot simply because it was at the same level as my mouth, then gently lowered her legs until they dangled over the side of the mattress again. Only when I stepped back, I realised how exhausted I was. I supposed it wasn't just from this mind-blowing sex with Trish. No, she'd also been abducted, and we'd been shopping. Both of those would have been enough to make any male tired.

I lay down on her other side and slid an arm around her shoulders, supporting her while Havel took his place at her feet. Instead of fucking her right away, he went on his knees and licked her entrance, cleaning her. Maybe he wanted his scent to be the only one he could smell on her beautiful pussy. I didn't care. I closed my eyes, snuggled against my mate and just enjoyed her closeness. Her moans grew louder and more frantic. I almost felt guilty for relaxing while she was still in the throes of another oncoming orgasm. Her skin was hot and sweaty, just like my own. We'd all need a shower after this. If Xil hadn't booked us a table at some fancy restaurant, I would have voted for staying in our nest for the next few days. We'd only leave for food and the occasional shower. With

Trish, of course. A shower without her pressed against my naked body wasn't worth it.

Just before Trish succumbed to Havel's skills with his tongue, he stood up. "I want you on all fours," he said hoarsely. "I want to take you from behind."

Trish shivered and her sweet aroma filled my nose. Her arousal was reaching new heights. She slowly turned onto her front and climbed to all fours. She had to be exhausted, but the thought of being taken by Havel like that seemed to be enough to give her new strength. Not that I knew what that felt like. I'd never been with a male.

Her breasts hung low, ripe for the picking. I twisted a little until I could reach her perfect nipples. Realising what I wanted, she lowered herself just enough until her breasts touched my lips. I waited for the moment Havel entered her, then opened my mouth and sucked in her hard nipple. I vaguely felt Xil doing the same on her other side. We were latched onto her, holding her in place like Kardarian nipple clamps, until Havel came with a triumphant cry.

We ended up in a huddle on the soft mattress. It had stopped its colourful display and was now showing large streaks of paint instead. Blue, yellow and green, just like the cum stains on Trish's skin. We hadn't added any new ones today, but this was only the beginning. One day, she'd be covered in our colours.

"I never got to give you my present," Xil muttered sleepily.

"What is it?"

He chuckled. "You'll find out the next time we're in this nest. I promise."

"I'll hold you to that." I heard her smile in her voice, and I had to grin myself. She had no idea what she was in for.

LESSON 8

HOW TO BEHAVE IN A FORMAL SETTING

I hadn't thought I'd want to set foot on Kitt-Y-6 again, but when Xil had suggested going to some fancy restaurant, I couldn't say no. A restaurant in space - I had to see that. Besides, Xil had looked so hopeful that it would have been cruel to deny him this pleasure.

After a quick shower, I met the guys by the airlock. They'd all dressed in their nicest clothes. Not all of them were to my taste. At some point, we'd need to have a chat about the state of their wardrobes. At least they hadn't cut holes into their trousers again. I chuckled to myself at the memory of their attempt at lingerie.

Since we'd never actually bought any clothes for me at that stall, I was in my usual attire, although I'd pinned up my hair with some chopsticks I'd found in the galley. Hopefully, the restaurant wasn't so posh that they'd not let us in. I assumed that every alien species had their own idea of what was formal and posh, so we could simply pretend that we were at the height of fashion.

"Our shuttle has arrived," Havel announced with a look at his communicator. "Right on time."

"Is it too far to walk?" I asked.

He laughed. "You couldn't walk there at all. The restaurant is in the outer ring that circles the main part of the space station. You only get there by shuttle or one of the service elevators, which we don't have access to."

I'd got a glimpse of the station's layout when we'd approached, but I'd still been nauseous after our bumpy ride and hadn't paid full attention to it. Two giant rings surrounded the long, oval station. I'd assumed they were just for keeping the station supplied with power or stuff like that. Never in a million years would I have expected a fancy restaurant to be in those rings.

Xil held out his arm. "According to the human videos we watched, you'll have to hold onto me," he explained. "You'll have to explain why, though. Are you unsteady on your feet before a *date?*"

He emphasised the last word as if it was something strange and peculiar to him.

I laughed. "You need to stop watching those videos. And no, I'm not unsteady. Look at my shoes. Do you see any high heels? No. So don't worry about that. But I'll take your arm anyway because I like touching you."

Xil wiggled his eyebrows. "I know. You did a lot of touching in our nest."

"So did you. All of you." I licked my lips. They still felt a little swollen.

"That was only the beginning," Matar whispered into my ear. His hot breath kissed my skin, and a pleasant shiver ran down my back, ending right between my legs. "When we're back, we'll return to our nest."

Havel stepped closer and ran his hand over my bum. "We hadn't even reached the main course yet, little human."

I shivered and suddenly I was glad for Xil's support.

"If you continue like that, we'll never get to the restaurant," I huffed, but it was a weak protest. I had no issue with them taking me right here, ripping off my clothes, fucking me against the wall.

What was going on with me? I'd never been this horny before I was abducted. Now, I was like a dog in heat, always ready for their cocks.

"Yes, we better go," Xil said. The door slid open, revealing a sleek silver ovoid parked next to the Jade. It looked like it had been taken right out of a science-fiction movie. I rolled my eyes at myself. I was in *space* surrounded by *aliens*. I better get used to it.

A round door opened in the shuttle's wall and we stepped inside. There was just about enough space for the four of us. Even another woman my size would have been a tight squeeze. The silver walls were lined with benches topped with red velvet pillows. It looked like velvet, anyway. When I sat down, a seat belt appeared out of nowhere and snaked around my waist. I pulled on it just to see if it would open, but it stayed tight. I wasn't sure if I liked that. Being strapped into a shuttle without a way to free myself seemed daunting, especially after my earlier abduction. If Professor Katila somehow took control of the shuttle, we'd be defenceless.

The guys didn't seem to have any issue, relaxing into their seats. The door closed without a sound, and we took off in one smooth motion. The walls that had been silver until now turned translucent, giving us a view of the spaceport.

The shuttle swerved around much larger ships, easily manoeuvring its way to the very top of the hangar. A hatch slid open, just big enough for the shuttle, and then we were back in the vacuum of space. There had to be some kind of invisible airlock to prevent the oxygen from escaping. Even though I'd seen lots of space in the Jade, being in such a tiny shuttle with windows all around me was different. This might be what it felt like to drift in the vast nothingness in just a spacesuit. I'd asked the guys about that, but they'd forbidden me from ever attempting that. They only ever went on a spacewalk for essential repairs, and all three of them hated it. Even lots of blowjobs wouldn't change their mind. And those worked to persuade them of almost anything.

The first ring came into view, slowly circling around the station. From up close, it was much bigger than it had seemed from the Jade. We flew alongside it, slowly and with occasional turns to let us see the ring from all sides. I was starting to suspect the shuttle was giving us a tour and not just a quick lift to the restaurant.

"The rings are quite an old-fashioned space station design," Matar said, breaking the silence. "Lots of station enthusiasts come here to see them up close."

Figured that there was an equivalent of railway fanatics.

"We should see the restaurant shortly."

I was glued to the windows, fascinated by the majestic turn of the rings. They reminded me of whales slowly moving through the depths of the ocean for some reason, not that it made any sense.

A neon sign attached to the outside of the ring caught my attention. Seriously? It looked like an American diner. That had to be the restaurant. I adjusted my expectations a little. Maybe not quite as posh as I'd imagined.

We landed just as smoothly as the take-off had been. The walls turned silver again before the door slid open.

"After you," Xil said, clearly trying out another line from some film. Goodness me, my aliens were adorable.

I climbed out of the shuttle, glad I didn't wear a skirt or dress.

A tall alien awaited us, towering even above my guys. I wasn't sure if they were male or female - they had a long beard decorated with tiny crystals as well as six teats on full display. The only clothing they wore was a flimsy loincloth. Their feet were furry and ended in thick black claws.

"Welcome to the Outer Ring Restaurant," they welcomed us in a deep voice that made me think of church bells ringing. "A reservation for four?"

"Yes, under the name of Xil of the Jade," the captain replied and held out his arm to me again.

I took it to keep him happy. The other two stood close to me, so close I felt their warmth.

"Follow me," the alien said and led us through an intricate metal gate, away from the shuttle and into the actual restaurant.

I gasped at the sight. Not a diner after all. Thousands of lights sparkled on the ceiling like stars, while every table had candles floating above it. The room was dark, but not gloomy, letting the candles and stars provide all the light. Small tables were scattered across the large room with enough space between them to give it an intimate feel. The floor was thick carpet that my feet seemed to sink into. And then there was the view. Windows reached all the way to the ceiling, offering us a breath-taking view of space to our left and the station to our right. The second ring, barely visible, rotated around the station. It seemed to move slower than this ring, but that may have been an optical illusion.

The waiter led us to a table on the left, hidden behind a wall of plants. It was the perfect spot. When I sat down, I couldn't see the rest of the restaurant, making it seem like we were alone with nothing but the vastness of space.

"This is amazing," I breathed, my heart beating faster. "I didn't think it would be this beautiful."

Havel pulled a chair out for me. I may have swooned a little. They were really trying to make this as perfect as possible. And as human. Next time, I'd ask them about Kardarian dating traditions, but for now, I'd just enjoy the evening.

"Menus will appear on your communicators," the waiter explained. "For now, here are some complimentary drinks, chosen by the AI cook based on your species, weight and pheromones."

My what?!

A tiny drone appeared above us, holding four glasses. What was the waiter for then? The menus and the food delivery was automatic, so why was there even a person?

The drone set the smallest glass in front of me, filled with what looked like apple juice. Or urine, but I didn't want to go there. The guys all had the same blue liquid in their glasses, but they varied in size. Matar had the biggest.

"I think there's a direct correlation between my glass and the size of my dick," he announced with a wide grin. "The AI seems to know its stuff."

Men. Always the same.

I held up my glass. "Cheers!"

The guys stared at me in confusion.

"Isn't cheers slang for 'thank you'?" Havel asked. "Are you thanking us for taking you here? Or the drone for delivering the drinks? Or the AI for choosing this drink?"

"No, I wasn't thanking anyone. It's what you say before you clink glasses."

"Clink?" Xil repeated. "I know Ankanis smash their glasses together after they're done with their meal and then use the shards to carve their names into the table. They're not allowed into some restaurants because of that. Do humans conduct a similar ritual?"

I laughed. "No. Let's just forget it. What drink did they give you?"

Matar took a sip and a dreamy expression crept across his face. "Bandulan liqueur. This AI is klatting amazing."

"Can I try?"

"Better not. This stuff is strong. Maybe before we leave, that way you won't be drunk during the meal."

I was getting used to that. The guys had some beer-like alcohol on the Jade that I wasn't allowed to drink. Well, technically I was, but after the first time and the worst hangover in the history of mankind, I'd decided to stick to non-alcoholic beverages.

I tried my own drink. It was sweet but nothing like apple juice. Maybe if you mixed mirabelle plums with quince and bananas, you might get something vaguely resembling this concoction. No, scratch that. It was too alien to compare it to Earth tastes. But it was amazing. I emptied half my glass before remembering that we were supposed to look at the menu.

I activated my communicator with a flick of my wrist, and a holographic menu appeared right in front of me. The text - in English - was written on three sheets that seemed to compete at grabbing my attention. They moved from side to side, changing position, pushing in front of each other.

"The AI is trying to decide what you might like," Havel explained with a laugh. "Here, press that button and they'll freeze."

I did as he showed me and the menu turned still, giving me the chance to actually read it. Not that any of the dishes made sense to me. Lopus steak with iask leaves and quagbu gratin. How was I supposed to know which of these dishes were good, let alone safe to eat for humans?

"Are any of these things poisonous?" I quietly asked the guys.

Xil roared with laughter as if I'd made the biggest joke of the galaxy. I kicked him beneath the table, but Matar's pained gasp told me I'd missed. Oops.

"The menu only contains dishes that are agreeable with your species," Havel explained. He didn't laugh, which made him my favourite mate at this moment. "Once you've read through them all, you can activate the AI again, and it'll rank them by what it thinks you'll enjoy most. Of course, you may be the first human ever to eat at this restaurant, so I don't know how accurate it'll be."

I skimmed the menu, but it was pointless. Even though some words were translated into English, most didn't make any sense at all. Luckily, I was pretty easy with food. Living the way I had before the guys had abducted me, I'd been glad for any food I could get my hands on. I could be choosy when it came to exotic meats, though, which made me ask Havel if I could sort the dishes to only show vegetarian ones.

"Are you sure?" Xil asked, still chuckling. "Goo'on fowl is a delicacy."

"Thanks, but I think I'll stick to something veggie myself and then try some of yours."

"You can taste mine any time you like, sweetheart," Xil said in a low, sultry voice.

I hated that his words made my pussy throb with need. As if we didn't just spend hours in our nest. I should concentrate on the food. On the restaurant. And not on the extremely hot and horny guys surrounding me.

The waiter reappeared, saving me from responding to Xil's flirting.

"Have you chosen your meal yet?" they asked pleasantly.

"If so, please press your choice on the menu and it will be brought to you momentarily."

They gave us a short bow and left without another word. Yeah, they were utterly useless. Nice, friendly, yes, but also not needed. Was this what Earth's restaurants would be like in the future? Automated except for a random waiter to greet you?

I didn't know if I'd ever find out. For now, returning to Earth wasn't on our agenda. There was nothing there for me, and I'd much rather explore other planets. Unless the IGU told my mates to return to Earth for some reason, I doubted we'd go back there again.

Havel helped me choose a vegetarian dish, then pressed a whole lot of things on his own menu. I'd not even considered having several courses. I'd grown up in poverty and wasn't used to splashing out food.

As soon as everyone had made their choice, the holo menus disappeared. I blinked, my eyes getting used to the dark again. The candles floating above us twinkled like stars, while also giving off a pleasant aroma.

"Do you like it here?" Matar asked me after a moment's silence.

"It's beautiful. Have you been here before?"

"Only me," Xil said. "With my father, when we still spoke to each other."

"He's loaded," Matar whispered. "One of the richest Kardarians out there."

"Doesn't matter," Xil said, steel in his voice. "Let's talk of better things. Like where we're going from here."

"Riva Four is beautiful at this time of year," Havel suggested. "The trees will be laden with fruit. As long as we don't expose ourselves to the locals, we could spend some time there. Our moon of honey."

It took me a moment to understand what he'd meant. "Honeymoon," I corrected him with a laugh. "And you only do that after you're married."

"Do you want to be?" Xil asked seriously. "Married? I've read about it. I thought mating would be enough, but we can do a marriage, too, if you'd like. And then we can go on the moo- honeymoon."

I thought about that for a moment. Did I want to get married? No, not really. I knew without a doubt that I loved my guys and that they loved me. They'd built me a nest, for fuck's sake, no sane person would do that unless they loved their mate. And we'd done their strange kilt ceremony. I licked my bottom lip. Those had been hot. I'd have to tell them to wear kilts more often. Like, all the time. With nothing underneath, obviously. I could educate them about the advantages of going commando, maybe even some practical exercises... they'd forget about Professor Katila very fast.

"No, we don't need to get married," I told them. "But you're right, that doesn't mean that we can't go on a honeymoon. Or simply go on holiday, all of us together. Our relationship is new. There haven't been humans with Kardarians before. We can pick and choose whatever traditions we want. So I say we take all the good stuff and ignore the boring or tedious customs."

"Cheers to that," Havel exclaimed and raised his glass just like I'd done earlier. He was a quick learner.

A buzzing sound made me look up to four approaching drones. This time, we had one each hovering above our heads before they slowly descended, setting their loads on the table. I waited before they'd buzzed off before inspecting my food. Well, I couldn't actually see any food. I'd been given an ovoid looking like a tiny version of the shuttle we'd arrived in.

"What is that?" I asked, staring at the metal pod. "Don't they have plates here?"

I'd assumed a plate was a universal thing. The guys had them on the Jade. Not round, square, but still the same concept as on Earth: a portable and washable surface for your food.

Xil laughed. "This place is too expensive for plates. Lay your hand on it and see what happens."

Luckily, Matar and Havel seemed just as confused.

With a shrug, I placed my hand on the ovoid, and it dissolved at the touch. Yes, it *dissolved*, raining down in tiny flecks, landing on my food. The bottom half of the pod stayed solid, now acting as a sort of bowl.

"Seasoning," Xil said as if that was entirely normal. "If you want more, just use your communicator to alert the waiter."

Okay then...

"What if I didn't want any seasoning?"

Immediately, all three guys looked at me with concern.

"You don't?" Xil asked. "We can get you a new portion without any."

"We'll complain to the cook," Havel added.

"They should never have done that without asking," Matar growled.

I couldn't help but laugh. And here I'd thought the tribitt was cute. My mates were on an entirely different level.

"Guys, it's alright, it was just a hypothetical question. Do we get cutlery or do we eat with our hands?"

Instead of a response, Xil pressed both his hands on the table, palms down. A strange light pulsed from underneath, then the metal surface began to boil. I blinked, trying to understand what was going on. A second later, a perfectly formed set of utensils lay next to Xil's hands. Not quite a knife and fork like we would have used on Earth, but quite similar.

"They're custom created for each guest," he explained. "You can take yours home with you after as a souvenir. Look, it's even got the restaurant's logo embossed."

I copied him, and to my relief, the metal didn't actually boil. The temperature stayed the same and within an instant, I had a fork and spoon. No knife. Finally looking at my food, I understood that I wouldn't need one. It was a sort of stew with green and blue bits floating in a dark liquid. And it was smoking. Not steaming like any sizzling dish would, but smoking as if it had just been on fire. I sneezed.

"That would be the burnt yaki roots," Havel said, already digging into his own meal which was smoking in the same way. "They don't taste like much raw or even boiled, but if you burn them, they release their flavour. Only the best cooks know how to infuse a dish with yaki root smoke. I've only had it once or twice before."

Okay then. This evening was becoming weirder and weirder. My food had been seasoned with smoke and tiny metal fragments. Normal. Totally normal.

My stomach growled, and I decided it was time to push all my questions aside. While the stew didn't look as appetising as I'd hoped, it smelled delicious.

And it tasted divine. My tongue may have had an orgasm after I swallowed the first spoonful.

Flavours exploded in my mouth, so full of depth that I was sure I'd never tasted anything this amazing before. Layers upon layers of taste overwhelmed my senses, but not too much so that I couldn't wolf down the stew.

We ate in silence, all of us completely occupied with our food. I even forgot that I'd wanted to try the guys' dishes. By the time I'd emptied my bowl, I was stuffed to the top and wouldn't have been able to even squeeze in a single scoop of ice cream. Which was almost unheard of. 'There's always space for ice cream because it melts and runs into all the little gaps', my grandma used to say. Alien stew had proven her wrong for the very first time.

I leaned back, sated and a little sleepy.

"Would anyone like dessert?" the waiter suddenly asked. I was in such a food coma that I hadn't even noticed them approach.

"No," we said as one.

Havel groaned a little. He had three empty bowls in front of him - no idea how he'd managed to eat all that.

"Do you require a private space to ruminate?" they asked.

I stared at them. "Ruminate? Like a cow?"

"Some species do that," Matar whispered. "Others will expel the food they've just eaten just so they can try more of the dishes on offer."

Like in Ancient Rome. Disgusting. And such a waste of food.

"Just the bill, please," Xil said with a wry smile. "And could you order us a shuttle?"

A strange pain suddenly erupted in my stomach, like I was being stabbed from within. I clutched my belly but tried not to let the guys notice.

"Where's the loo?" I asked the waiter and got to my feet.

"Follow me," they said, but as soon as I'd taken the first step, the pain exploded into agony and I collapsed to the floor, unable to even break my fall.

"Trish!"

"What's wrong?"

The pain was making it hard to breathe, hard to think. Blackness teetered at the edges of my vision as I curled into a ball, praying that this would be over soon.

LESSON 9

FIRST AID FOR PANICKED MALES

My mate was writhing in agony. Her face was deathly pale, the only colour her red-rimmed eyes. Tears ran down her cheeks as she screamed in pain.

"I'm not feeling too well," Havel suddenly groaned and then he went down, too. Klat, he was our medic, the male supposed to help Trish. Now he was on the floor, clutching his belly, clearly unable to help anyone, least of all himself.

"I'll get help," the waiter shouted and ran off.

I kneeled by Trish's side while Matar checked on Havel.

"It's going to be alright, love," I whispered and lay my hand on her hot forehead. She was burning up. "Help is coming. You'll be back to normal in no time. Just hold on, little human, hold on."

I didn't know what to say or do. I was helpless. It was the worst feeling in the universe. Trish was in pain, and there was no way I could make her better. If I could have taken her pain, I would have without hesitation. I was prepared to feel the burning whip of the Great A'Ta on my back if it meant Trish wasn't suffering. And I didn't even believe in A'Ta.

"He's running a fever," Matar reported. "His fangs are extended. Not sure what that means."

Trish didn't have fangs I could check to see if it was a shared symptom.

It took the waiter an eternity to return with four other beings, two of them wearing the same loincloth while the others' white suits identified them as medics.

"What happened?" one of the healers asked and pushed me aside. She was a petite Ankani, but the authority in her voice made me obey her immediately.

"She just collapsed, holding her stomach. A few minutes later, my friend did the same. They're both in agony. You'll have to give them something for the pain."

"I'll decide what to give them," she snapped. "Did they eat the same food?"

"No. She had a vegetable and root stew while he had a loomani sausage. You'll have to ask the waiter if any of the ingredients were the same."

"Yaki roots!" Matar exclaimed before the waiter had the chance to speak. "They both had yaki root smoke infused with their meals."

Klat. He was right. I'd never heard of yaki root being poisonous, but it wasn't my area of expertise.

"Peti'i, get me the antidote," the medic ordered the other healer while at the same time rummaging in her bag. She pulled out two syringes, stabbed one of them in Trish's upper arm, and then hurried over to Havel to give him the same injection. "That's going to stabilise them until we've got the antidote. Yaki root can be poisonous when burned for too short a period, but I wouldn't have expected this to happen in this restaurant."

"I'll... I'll tell the cook," the waiter stammered and ran off.

"Get the manager, too!" I shouted after him. "I've got a thing or two to say to them."

Fury raced through my veins, and I had a hard time not to attack the remaining two waiters standing in the background. This was a clear case of negligence. They could have killed my mate and my friend.

I growled.

"Xil?"

Trish opened her eyes and looked right at me. Some of the anger dissipated into relief.

"Are you still in pain?" I asked and stroked her forehead again.

"Of course she is," the medic admonished me. "Don't ask such stupid questions. I've given her some light pain killers, but I can't give them anything stronger until we have the antidote. The two drugs might interact, and I don't want to risk that."

"Hold my hand?" Trish asked weakly, and I was only too willing to oblige. She barely had to strength to return my grip on her hand. It scared me.

I looked over at Havel. He was no longer writhing in pain either, but his face was pale and his fangs were still extended. He tried to hide his pain, just like Trish, but it was clear that both of them were suffering. I was going to kill that cook. We'd come here to have a wonderful evening, to celebrate our completed nest. This was a disaster.

The other medic returned, holding a metal lockbox. I squeezed Trish's hand. "Not much longer now, little human. You're going to be fine."

"You might want to step back," the female medic warned me. "The antidote might induce vomiting, and you don't want to be in the line of fire."

I didn't move. "I don't mind. My mate needs me."

Matar didn't leave Havel's side either. I was proud of my friends, my family. We stood together even in the face of adversity and vomit.

Luckily, it never came to that. As soon as the medic had injected Trish and Havel with the antidote, colour returned to their faces.

"Wow, that worked fast," Trish said and sat up without needing help. I wrapped an arm around her shoulders to steady her, just in case - plus after almost losing her, I needed the physical contact. It took all my mental strength not to throw her over my shoulder, carry her to our ship and ravish her in the nest until we'd both forgotten about today's events.

"No nausea?" the medic asked but was interrupted by loud retching from Havel. One of the waiters handed him a bowl and my poor friend started filling it with the contents of his stomach.

The healer looked almost pleased. "Just like I said, the drug can cause vomiting. You'll both be fine. Don't eat anything today, but drink lots of fluids. Go to bed early and rest. Tomorrow you should be able to eat normally again, but maybe avoid yaki roots for a while."

"Never again," I growled.

I helped Trish to her feet but kept my arms around her. I wasn't going to let go of her any time soon.

"I'm fine," she muttered, but she didn't try to get out of my embrace. On the contrary, she leaned against my chest, just the way I liked it.

The waiter arrived with three other aliens in tow. The largest of them, a species I'd not encountered before, wore an apron covered with stains. The cook, I presumed. The other two were clad in business suits, a female with a bright green mane and a fellow Kardarian male.

He greeted me with the traditional fist-on-chest gesture, but I didn't return it. I wanted to greet him with fist-on-nose and fist-to-his-balls, but luckily I had my arms around Trish and attacking him would have meant letting go of her.

"I apologise on behalf of the entire Outer Ring Restaurant," the male said. "I can't explain how this happened. We've never had any issues like this before, but of course, our cook will be disciplined."

The flabby cook had the decency to look guilty. Maybe the punishment should be him ingesting poisonous yaki roots. That way he could feel the pain he'd inflicted on my family.

"We will, of course, compensate you for your troubles," the Kardarian continued. "We have a new restaurant that just opened on Labeari, the resort planet near the Kepler Two space station. How about two weeks all-inclusive at the resort with all expenses paid? Plus a generous stipend so you can enjoy all the pleasures Labeari has to offer?"

"Are you trying to bribe us?" I snarled. "I assume in return you don't want us to tell anyone about the poisonous yaki?"

The male took a step back, fear flashing across his face before he smoothed his expression. "Not at all. I just want to make sure you all have a relaxing time to recover from what happened. How about we throw in money for fuel and some delicacies to sustain you during your journey? Plus any salary you might miss out on during your holiday?"

"We'll take it," Trish said before I could attack the slimy Kardarian. He was a shame to our species, weaselling his way out of the situation. "But we want three weeks plus free food at all your restaurants for a whole year."

The male's eyes widened just a fraction before he nodded. "Agreed. And you won't tell the media about this, right?"

"Our ship could use an upgrade to our engine," Matar said from behind me. "We'd want to travel to Labeari as fast as possible."

"Obviously." The Kardarian sighed. "I'll make the necessary arrangements. Again, I apologise for the inconvenience."

He walked off, followed by everyone except the original waiter.

"I'm so sorry," they said, before also shuffling away.

Havel's laugh interrupted the moment of silence that echoed their departure. "We got a good deal. Might have been worth the pain." I turned just in time to see him bend over his bowl again.

Poor guy.

Professor Katila looked angrier than I'd ever seen before. I hadn't thought Karangi could get this furious. They were known for being benevolent, kind and intelligent, but right now, Katila didn't seem any of those. Her middle eye was blazing with anger as she stared us down through the video link.

"Say that again," she hissed.

"We quit," I said calmly for the third time in a row. "We'll no longer be part of your course. We don't care what grade you give us for the beginners' class. We don't care at all about you and the IGU. All we want is to be left in peace and spend time with our mate."

"You would never have found your mate without my course. I never expected you to be such ungrateful-"

"Ungrateful?" I repeated. "You basically blackmailed us into becoming part of your case study. You should be grateful that we agreed to that. And you've only got yourself to blame. If you hadn't kidnapped Trish, we might still be willing to cooperate with you."

"I didn't kidnap her," Katila seethed. "I only commissioned it."

"How is that any different," Trish demanded furiously. "Just because you didn't get your hands dirty doesn't mean you're innocent. Just accept it, we're quitting. We've got better things to do than dance to your tune."

"You'll regret this. All the time and resources I invested in you... you're going to pay for it. I will have to start my research from scratch. So many hours wasted... You better watch your back. Yaki roots aren't the only poisonous things out there."

She ended the transmission before I could reply. I turned to the others. Their shock mirrored my own.

"How did she know?" Havel asked. "We didn't tell anyone about the yaki. Do you think that was her doing, too?"

"I wouldn't put it past her," Trish said. "She doesn't seem to respect laws and ethics, so what would stop her from bribing the cook to poison us?"

"But to what end?" I questioned. "What good would that do? The kidnapping was a test to see how we'd react and if we'd manage to rescue you. As awful as it was, you were never in real danger. If we'd not saved you, they would have released you eventually. Poisoning you and Havel is an entirely different matter. You could have died. Why would Katila want that?"

"If I was gone, she could have made you abduct more humans. That's what she wanted from the start. It would have fit her course. It's called Alien Abduction for Beginners, after all, not Alien Mating With The Female You Abducted."

"I don't know. As much as I loathe her, I don't think she'd go that far. She's watching us, who knows, maybe she had a spy in that restaurant?"

Havel sighed. "It doesn't matter. We're free of her now, that's what counts. As much as I wanted to have that certificate to show our families that we're proper abductors, it's not worth the trouble."

Trish nodded. "It's the knowledge that counts, not the qualification. You know how abductions work - not that I'll ever let you abduct another female." She laughed. "I'm the only abductee in your life and that's what it'll stay like."

Matar pulled her onto his lap. "Yes. It's perfect. You, us, the Jade. And your little tribitt."

Her pet was sleeping in a basket by her feet. While the animal loved cuddles while it was awake, it preferred to sleep without being touched. It had actually growled at me earlier when I'd got too close to the basket. He had slept through our launch from the space station. I was glad he hadn't got scared, but we had yet to see how he would react when we encountered some space turbulence.

"That reminds me, he needs a name," Trish said. "And I don't want to decide that myself. I want it to be something meaningful for all of us."

"Is this what it's going to be like once we have offspring?" I asked with genuine curiosity.

"No offspring any time soon. But once we do get

pregnant, then yes, I'd like us all to come up with names together."

"*We* get pregnant?" Havel repeated. "I'm sorry to disappoint you, but Kardarian males don't have a uterus."

Trish laughed until tears appeared in her pretty eyes. "It's just an expression. I'm going to be the one carrying our baby, but it's something you will all be involved in."

"Of course. We'll watch over you every minute of the day," I told her. "We'll massage your feet, we'll cook your meals, we'll hold your boobs when they get too heavy."

Trish broke into laughter again. Her cheeks were bright red, and I was starting to get worried. "Uhm... no boob holding required. I've got a bra for that. Although... I won't say no to you doing that while we're in our nest."

"My hands are much warmer than your silly bras. I'm sure you'll change your mind once your breasts are full of milk for our hungry offspring. I remember my aunt sitting on my uncle's lap all day, him holding her breasts..."

I stopped because she was still laughing.

Havel looked at his communicator. "Careful, chicken, you're not getting enough oxygen."

That made her laugh even harder. Had we broken our human?

"What names were you thinking of?" I asked to distract her. I didn't want her to suffocate.

"Maybe something to do with his colour," she said, her voice now hoarse from all the laughing. "What's the Kardarian word for green?"

"Skweke," Havel replied.

"No, that's too hard to pronounce. We need something cuter. On Earth, we have a green plant that's considered lucky. Clover. Is there a translation for that?"

I shook my head. "Not that I know of. We don't have many green plants on Kardar."

She looked at me as if I was crazy. "Your plants aren't green? What about the grass?"

"Grass is a Peritus thing. Our planet's surface is covered in fur."

I didn't think her eyes could get any wider. "Fur? Like animal fur? You're kidding me, right?"

"No, not animal fur. Plant fur. It might be that your translator doesn't have an equivalent word for it. But anyway, we don't have that... clover."

The little tribitt raised his head as if he knew that we were talking about him. He squeaked, an adorable sound that immediately made me want to pick him up and cuddle him. I bet that was a trait designed by the pet breeders.

"So cute," Trish cooed. "How about squeak?"

"The translation for that would be boop," Matar said. "Not boob, like your beautiful boobs. Boop."

"Boop," our mate repeated as if tasting the word. "Boop. I like it. Boobieboop. Boopboop. Boooooooop."

"We've broken her," I whispered to the others. "Maybe it's an aftereffect of the poison?"

"Boop it is," Trish announced. "Lord Boop, since he's the first of all the pets we're going to have."

I exchanged a look with Havel and Matar. Giving her the tribitt had been a massive mistake.

TRISH

I was getting used to the nest. Lying on the exploding-colour-sheet with pillows surrounding me from all sides made me feel both comfortable and safe. Plus the three naked guys were a definite bonus. Havel was to my right, Matar to my left and I was spread across Xil. We'd ignored the doctor's advice to take it easy. I bet she wouldn't have been able to resist these males either.

It felt right. Our bodies touched, turning us into one being. We were not longer four separate people. In this nest, we were one.

"I never thought I could feel this happy," I whispered. "How is this even possible?"

"Only A'Ta knows," Matar replied solemnly. "He has led us together and blessed our mating."

"Or maybe it was destiny, not some deity's doing," Havel said, but there was no animosity in his tone. We both accepted Matar's beliefs, even though we didn't share them.

"However we got together, I'm never letting you go," I told them. "You're mine until the end of the universe."

"And you are ours," Xil whispered and kissed the nape of my neck. His hot breath made my skin tingle and heat spread through my body, pooling between my legs. As if I hadn't just fucked all three of them. We should probably sleep like that medic had recommended. I felt fine, but I wasn't sure about Havel. He'd been more affected by the antidote than I had. The poor guy.

I reached out to him and stroked his hard chest. The greenish freckles on his otherwise blue skin seemed to move beneath my touch. If I hadn't been so comfortable on top of Xil, I would have climbed on Havel and licked those spots. He loved that.

Matar's tail twitched where it was wrapped around my thigh, and I chuckled, starting to stroke his chest as well. He purred and grasped my hand, leading it down until my fingers touched his cock. He was hard again, rock hard and ready to plunge into my depths. Maybe sleep could wait...

Suddenly, all the lights in the room started flashing, and an ear-shattering siren made me sit up straight.

"What's happening?" I screamed against the noise.

The guys jumped up, and Xil pulled me to my feet. He grabbed my shoulders, his eyes wild with emotion.

"We're under attack!"

The siren stopped, and a very familiar voice echoed through the room.

"I decided not to wait. It's time for you to hand over the human." Professor Katila sounded genuinely deranged.

"I'll let you live if you do. You'll go back to working for me. If not..."

The Jade lurched to one side, and I would have fallen if Xil hadn't caught me just in time.

"You're all going to die."

PIKI CAKES RECIPE

For the first time ever, the Intaran Bakers' Association has given permission for a version of their famous piki cake recipe to be printed. Of course, some (or all) ingredients had to be replaced with Peritan equivalents. Actually, these might be nothing like the real piki cakes that the whole galaxy raves about, but it'll give you a general idea. Or not.

Bake at your own peril.

But seriously, they're delicious.

INGREDIENTS

- 50g butter at room temperature (or softened if you live in a cold place like space)
- ¼ cup brown sugar
- 50g plain yogurt
- 1 egg
- 1 cup self-raising flour
- ½ cup rye flour (or brown flour)
- 100g dark chocolate, chopped, or chocolate chips
- 1 ½ tablespoons cacao powder
- 1 cup cooked beetroot – about 140 grams

INSTRUCTIONS

1. Preheat the oven to 170C/340F, line a baking tray.

2. Grate or puree the beetroot.
3. Beat the butter, sugar and yogurt in a bowl until well combined. Add the egg.
4. Stir in the remaining ingredients, adding the beetroot last.
5. Shape the biscuits into small balls and place on the baking tray. If the dough is too moist, add some more flour.
6. Flatten the biscuits with the back of a spoon or your fingers.
7. Bake for 12-14 minutes.
8. Cool on a tray.
9. If desired, sprinkle with icing sugar or cocoa.
10. Devour.

PIKI CAKES RECIPE

For the first time ever, the Intaran Bakers' Association has given permission for a version of their famous piki cake recipe to be printed. Of course, some (or all) ingredients had to be replaced with Peritan equivalents. Actually, these might be nothing like the real piki cakes that the whole galaxy raves about, but it'll give you a general idea. Or not.

Bake at your own peril.

But seriously, they're delicious.

INGREDIENTS

- 50g butter at room temperature (or softened if you live in a cold place like space)
- ¼ cup brown sugar
- 50g plain yogurt
- 1 egg
- 1 cup self-raising flour

- ½ cup rye flour (or brown flour)
- 100g dark chocolate, chopped, or chocolate chips
- 1 ½ tablespoons cacao powder
- 1 cup cooked beetroot – about 140 grams

INSTRUCTIONS

1. Preheat the oven to 170C/340F, line a baking tray.
2. Grate or puree the beetroot.
3. Beat the butter, sugar and yogurt in a bowl until well combined. Add the egg.
4. Stir in the remaining ingredients, adding the beetroot last.
5. Shape the biscuits into small balls and place on the baking tray. If the dough is too moist, add some more flour.
6. Flatten the biscuits with the back of a spoon or your fingers.
7. Bake for 12-14 minutes.
8. Cool on a tray.
9. If desired, sprinkle with icing sugar or cocoa.
10. Devour.

ALIEN ABDUCTION FOR EXPERTS

THE INTERGALACTIC GUIDE TO HUMANS #3

BEFORE THE LESSON

Professor Katila wiped her three eyes before turning around. She wasn't someone used to crying, nor was she willing to show her emotion in public. Even though her boyfriends had certainly given her every reason to cry.

"You can't do this," she snapped, using anger to hide her despair. "You can't leave me."

Hex sighed but made no attempt to reach out for her like she'd hoped. "It's over, Kat. You know that. We all do. It's time to move on."

"It's not over. I refuse to let you go."

Hex pointed at the ship behind him. "You can't stop us. You had your chance, and you blew it. Once the waves settle, you're very welcome to visit us."

"But maybe wait a few IG months," Hix muttered, exchanging a look with his torso-brother.

Katila was tempted to stamp her feet, but she was a well-respected professor and there were students and teachers milling all around the spaceport. She couldn't lose her composure in front of them. Maybe that was the reason why Hex and Hix had refused to say goodbye at their apartment and insisted she come to the port instead. She wasn't going to make a scene here. Back home, it would have been an entirely different matter - which was the reason why her boyfriends were about to break up with her.

"If you go, I'll make sure to turn your lives into misery," Katila hissed. With her eyes blazing, she looked nothing like the gentle, benevolent beings Karangi were known to be. But she had always been different. She'd tried to fit in, pretending to be someone she wasn't, but now she was at the end of her tether. How dare they leave her. She was one of the richest females on the station. She was beautiful, intelligent, and excellent in bed. Multiple lovers had confirmed that over the years. So, she had cheated on her boyfriends, big deal. They knew how hot some of her students were, how irresistible. It was part of her research to discover the sexual practices of other species, especially those who might be suitable for future abduction experiments. Hix and Hex may be lovely, but they weren't as sexy as some of the other males she'd slept with.

"Goodbye, Kat," Hix said firmly. "We're going now."

They turned and walked up the ramp of their ship, swaying their hips. She loved the way they walked, so confident and alluring. Hix and Hex shared one torso, but they were two separate beings. If Katila wanted to keep the routine she was used to, she'd now have to find two boyfriends. If they didn't occupy the same body, she'd need more space in her apartment, an extra bed, more food. It would get complicated quickly. There weren't many Gemi'i left, so the chances of getting a new set of Gemi'i mates were slim.

Katila trembled with barely suppressed fury as the ramp ascended into the ship. Hix and Hex hadn't even waved to her one last time. They were on the way to a new life, leaving her in pieces.

She balled her long, thin fingers into fists. She'd find them. For now, she'd focus on her work, but one day, she'd take her revenge. They'd made the biggest mistake of their lives when they decided to leave her.

Slowly, she walked back to her apartment, which was going to look ever so empty now that her boyfriends' belongings had gone. She'd have to get used to being single. Maybe it was a good idea not to search for new partners right away. She'd have so much more time for her studies now that she didn't have to entertain her boyfriends in the evenings. She'd be able to take more students into her bed without having to hide it. Yes, maybe single life wasn't so bad after all.

But she wasn't going to forget about this insult. Hix and Hex had it coming.

PRACTICAL ASSIGNMENT

ESCAPING A TRICKY SITUATION

My ears hurt from the alarms blaring at me from all sides. I didn't get why the guys wouldn't turn them off. We all knew we were screwed; we didn't need a siren to remind us.

Our teacher was attacking us. Not something I could have predicted. It was even less likely than my own alien abduction a few weeks ago. Even though I hadn't believed in aliens when I still lived on Earth, it had still been something that *could* have happened. There were enough crackpot reports about strange lights in the sky, disappearing cattle and alien experimentation on naked humans. But a university professor firing at my spaceship trying to kill me and my mates? Nope, never imagined that to happen.

I wasn't sure how long the Jade's shields would hold. She wasn't a ship made for battle. I'd asked the guys once and they'd shown me the weapon system they'd installed as a defensive measure against space pirates. Matar was shooting back at the ship attacking us, but they kept returning fire. I assumed they had a ship made for this with proper guns and shields.

"What do you want?" I shouted at Professor Katila. She was still showing on our screen, seemingly completely relaxed. Bitch. I had no doubt that she'd let us die if we didn't do what she wanted.

The Professor smiled at me. Before all this, when I first met her, I would have taken it to be a friendly, indulgent smile. Now, I knew better. It was just a façade. Beneath all her beauty, she was rotten to the core.

"I want you to do something for me," she said sweetly, still sounding a little crazed. No surprise about that. "And you'll have to promise me you'll do it before I agree to cease the attack."

"Do what?" Xil growled.

"That I shall tell you after you agree to our deal."

"Not happening."

"Then I wish you a lovely death."

She turned away from the camera but didn't end the transmission. She was toying with us. She knew she had us exactly where she wanted. We didn't want to die and we stood no chance against our attackers, so our only option was to agree to her demands.

"Why us?" I asked her. "Can't you get someone else to be your lackeys?"

Without turning around, Katila said, "I need this to stay under the radar. No traces, no paperwork. And your males have proven themselves to be capable abductors."

"You're going to make us abduct someone again?" Xil asked. His face was contorted in anger and worry. He knew we didn't really have a choice. I wanted to reach out and hug him, but I was clinging to my chair. They were still shooting at us and the Jade shook and wobbled. Our poor ship.

"Two someones, actually, although they come in one handy package. Abduct them and bring them to me."

Xil turned to the other males who were frantically working on their consoles, trying to keep the ship flying. "What do you think? I'm not making this decision alone."

"It's not like we have a choice," Havel grunted without turning away from the displays flickering in all sorts of alarming colours.

Matar nodded. "He's right. I'm not prepared to die today, so the only option is to do what she wants."

I hated to hear the resignation in his voice.

Xil looked at me. "What about you?"

"I'd hate to be responsible for abducting someone, but as long as she doesn't insist on them becoming your mates as well, it's the best bad option we have."

"Agreed." Xil turned to the screen, squaring his shoulders. "We accept."

Professor Katila swirled around, a satisfied grin on her face. Her third eye was half-lidded, but I wasn't sure what that meant. "Wonderful. I've given the command to stop shooting at your ship. I'll send over the details of your abductees shortly, although I understand if you have to return to KITT-Y-6 for repairs before your mission."

She blinked out, leaving me seething with indignation. Us having to repair the Jade was her fault. That bitch was going to pay for it.

At least she'd been true to her word. The shakes stopped, as did the blaring sirens.

"They're retreating," Matar reported.

Xil got up and swept his gaze over the screens. "Status report."

"Shields are at thirty percent. The hull has been damaged at several places, but the emergency insulation has worked and we have no actual holes. Katila was right though, we need to have repairs done before we can safely fly to wherever she wants us to."

The captain growled. "I'm going to rip out her heart as soon as I get the chance."

"How long are we going to need to stay at the station?" I asked. KITT-Y-6 held nothing but bad memories for me, with the exception of the Piki cakes and my little tribitt, of course. I should really check on him. In the heat of the moment, I'd forgotten about Lord Boop, but he must have been scared.

"Four, maybe five IG hours," Matar said. "I'll try and get it done as quickly as possible. Luckily the restaurant owner already transferred us that compensation payment, so we've got enough funds to pay for the express service. You can go do some more shopping or exploring, if you want, although I assume you don't want to."

"You're right, I have no desire to step foot on that klatting station again."

The guys stared at me, then laughed.

Xil got up and lifted me from my seat, swirling me around. "I love you."

If I'd known using one of their Kardarian expletives would make them so happy, I'd have done it earlier. Klatting was a pretty good word. I still preferred fucking, but from now on, I'd change my vocabulary to match that of my mates. It was strange to think that we weren't talking the same language even though we were mates. My body was covered in their colours, signifying our close bond, yet I knew maybe a handful of Kardarian words. It would probably be a good idea to learn their language at some point. I didn't even want to imagine what would happen if our translators failed. We wouldn't be able to communicate at all. I pushed that idea further up my list of priorities.

Xil kissed me and I could almost taste his relief of having resolved the situation without anyone getting hurt. I wrapped my arms around him, holding him tight. I thought he needed comfort more than me at that moment. He'd almost lost his ship, his crew, his family, his life.

I kissed him back with renewed passion, pouring all my love into the kiss. He groaned and thrust his hips against mine, presenting his erection. Sadly, as much as I wanted some yay-we're-not-dead-sex, this wasn't the time. He knew that too. With one last brush of his tongue against mine, he let me go.

"I'll check on the tribitt," I muttered and left the bridge before I could change my mind and kiss them all.

To my surprise, Lord Boop was fast asleep. How did the little animal do that after we'd barely escaped certain death? My heart was still racing, and I couldn't imagine sleeping for the next few hours at the very least.

I gently stroked his fluffy forehead. His ears twitched, but he didn't wake up. I cooed over his cuteness, my heart filling with adoration. Slowly, the fear lessened and my breathing calmed. Pets really helped with stress, including alien ones.

I prepared some more food for him and left it in a bowl next to his bed, just in case he was peckish when he woke up. As much as I wanted to stay with the little space bunny for a while longer, the guys probably needed me. We had a lot to do in preparation for our upcoming abduction. A shudder ran down my back. I never thought I'd be involved in abducting someone. It had been done to me and even though everything turned out perfectly, I still didn't want another person to go through the same thing. I'd draw the line on probing this time. I wasn't going to let the guys probe some random alien. I was the only one they'd get to probe. Oh, the good old days...

Xil was alone on the bridge.

"Matar is checking on the engines and Havel is making sure our computer didn't miss any damage," he said before I could ask about the others. That's how attuned we were to each other. He answered my unspoken questions. No, I wouldn't let anyone else get into our perfect relationship.

"Have you looked at Professor Katila's files yet?" I asked. "Who are we going to abduct?"

He pressed a button on his wrist communicator and an image appeared on the large screen in front of us. A strange male creature seemed to be looking down on us. Its two heads were almost identical, although the one on the right had slightly larger nostrils. Yes, just nostrils, because they didn't have any noses, nor ears, for that matter. Their eyes were almost human in shape and size, but their mouths were too wide and their lips strangely patterned, almost as if they had scales. Below the shoulders, they resembled my males. Humanoid, two legs, two arms, the same proportions I was used to. Their skin was covered in a thin layer of white down, reminding me of a freshly hatched bird. Weird.

"Is that one or two people?" I was a bit embarrassed to have to pose that question, but to be fair, I didn't want to assume that this male was like Siamese twins back on Earth. It could have been just a guy with two heads, sharing the same mind.

"Two," Xil confirmed. "Hix and Hex."

"Their mother clearly wasn't very creative," I muttered.

"Gemi'i don't have mothers. Well, they do, but they don't grow up with their parents after they hatch from their eggs. The mother lays the eggs in the desert region of their planet, then moves on, letting the sun do the job of incubating the eggs. The hatchlings are born with the ability to walk, but only a handful survive the journey out of the desert and into one of the habitable areas. It's why the Gemi'i that survive are known to be hardy and able to survive almost anything."

"Are they going to be hard to abduct?"

Xil patted his lap, and I took the invitation without a second thought, sitting down on his thick thighs. He wrapped his arms around my waist, and I leaned against his chest, enjoying his warmth. Half an hour ago, I wasn't sure if we'd make it. Feeling him like this was reassuring. We were alive and we were going to stay that way.

"I'm not sure. I've never met one of their kind, but I doubt it'll be easy. Katila wouldn't have given us this job if anyone could do it. No, she chose us because we've taken her course and we know what we're doing." He chuckled. "Mostly, anyways."

"What do you need me to do?" I asked.

"Maybe you could look into their species, research their planet. Defences, weaknesses, habits. I'll dig into Hex and Hix's background, see if I can find out more about who they are and why Katila wants them."

"Aye, aye, Captain," I said with a grin. Now that the main danger was over, it felt good to smile.

LESSON 1

RESEARCHING YOUR ENEMY

I used my new wrist communicator to dive into the IGU database. It was surprisingly easy. Matar had given me access to the ship's AI as well as all the Alien Abduction for Beginners material, and the system was similar to that of Earth computers. Much more sophisticated, of course, and the content was shown to me in holographic 3D, but still, the basic concept was the same.

It didn't take me long to find the entry on Gemi'i.

Instead of reading the various documents, I had a look at the pictures first. Both drawings and photographs showed males and females. There was a 3D model that I was able to move around with my hands, zooming in wherever I wanted. Just like Hix and Hex, all of the Gemi'i were two-headed. Or one-bodied, depending on how you looked at it. I took a closer peek at the male model's crotch. Only one dick. Surprising, really. I would have assumed they'd want one each, but I supposed nobody was in charge of nature.

Once I'd taken in the strange sight, I opened the first document and scanned the text. I didn't want to become an expert in Gemi'i. It was enough to know the basics that would help us with the abduction.

Gemi'i lived on three different planets in the same solar system. They'd also colonised two moons, but those were mostly used for mining. It was unlikely our targets lived there. Still, that left three entire planets to search. Their kind were ruled by the Hydrapta, what sounded like a Queen. I scrolled down to find a picture of her. Wow. She had three heads, four arms and what looked like more than just two breasts squeezed into her ample bosom.

Impressive. She also stared at the camera with so much distaste that I instantly decided I didn't want to meet her.

Most of the information in the database wouldn't assist us in abducting our targets. I didn't care what they ate (omnivores), how long they lived (around two hundred IG years) or how they procreated (eggs). They seemed to be a peaceful species who preferred to be among their own kind. I supposed three planets was plenty for a population of only a billion. I imagined what it would be like if we had three Earths. Wow. Maybe we wouldn't have destroyed our planet and each other if we'd had that much space. But then, maybe not. Humans loved killing each other. It was a miracle we'd made it this long.

"Anything interesting yet?" Xil asked, looking up from his own research.

"No, nothing. Unless you want to know that they like to eat some sort of leaf wrapped in animal dung."

"No, thanks. I didn't need to know that. Shall I make you a cup of tea?"

"I'd love that. Are there any piki cakes left?"

Xil chuckled. "Half a storage hangar full. You can have more than one, but I doubt you'll manage to eat that."

He was right. As delicious as piki cakes were, they were also incredibly filling. Besides, my stomach was still a little queasy after our near-death experience.

While he left the bridge, I continued scrolling through the files. It was interesting, but not what I was looking for. This wasn't just me trying to learn about a different species. It was research that might keep us alive. If we failed, who knew what Professor Katila would do to us. I doubted she'd let us fly away into a happy ever after.

Finally, just when Xil returned with a small tray, I stumbled across the perfect snippet of information.

"Gemi'i have one weakness in particular," I read out to Xil. "They can be easily knocked out by a hit to the fleshy part where their two heads diverge. It will render them unconscious for at least ten IG minutes. In battle, Gemi'i wear specialised armour that covers this intersection."

"But not if they're unaware of being our targets," Xil said cheerily. "Well done. Havel is going to look at their physiology as well, see if our standard tranquilisers would work on them, but if not, we now have another strategy."

"Did you know they live on three different planets?" I asked. "Katila didn't give us coordinates, did she?"

"She didn't. I don't think she'd take kindly to us asking, so we will have to take a different approach. Once we're closer to their solar system, we might be able to intercept their media and intra-planet-communications. If we're lucky, we'll be able to find something about them."

I took the cup of tea he offered and breathed in the smoky scent of his favourite tea. Havel preferred something much sweeter, while Matar wasn't much of a fan of tea in general. The smoky, strong taste matched Xil well, I thought.

"I came across all sorts of names while reading," I told him. "Not a single one of them ended with X. Hix and Hex might be unusual enough names for us to find them in their databases."

Xil smiled. "Handy. I assume they must be special in some way since Professor Katila wouldn't do this for just anyone. Klat, she tried to kill us. I highly doubt they're just some students or even friends of hers."

"You think she has friends?" I asked drily.

"You're right. Unlikely. It would really help to know what they are to her. I might go through the IGU records, see if they're listed as students or staff somewhere. That would give us a clue to their importance."

He handed me half a piki cake before turning back to his own communicator. He swished through the information much faster than me, but he'd probably grown up with this technology. Earth was so far behind all this. I felt a bit like a cave woman coming into a modern city.

While nibbling on the cake, I continued my search. It was hard work, mostly because so much of the information was repeated or irrelevant. At some point, Xil showed me how to make notes so I could keep track of what I'd found. We worked in silence. I kind of wished I had the little tribitt on my lap, but I couldn't be bothered to get up. If I stopped reading now, it would take forever to get back into the swing.

"Look!" Xil suddenly exclaimed and pushed a holographic image to the main screen.

I stared at it in shock. "It can't be," I muttered after a moment.

It was a video recording of Professor Katila walking arm in arm with Hix and Hex. They were on some kind of space station with bright corridors full of people. Katila and the males were pressed against each other, closer than friends would be. We couldn't hear what they were saying, but Katila was clearly happy and laughing. One of the males - I didn't know which head belonged to which male - bent to the side a little and kissed her.

"Mates," Xil said, looking at me with the same confused expression that likely displayed on my face. "Klatting mates."

MATAR

It had taken forever to order all the parts we needed to repair the ship. The Jade had taken more damage than I'd first thought, but at least the vital systems were all intact. Thanks to our newfound wealth, I'd splashed out on the fastest delivery and repair service available.

I met Havel on the way to the bridge. He was covered in soot and dirt.

"Did you crawl through the pipes?" I asked with a smirk. I'd managed to keep the stains to my overalls, leaving my handsome face clean for Trish to admire. Havel, on the other hand, had black dust all around his cheeks. If I had to decide who to kiss, I'd definitely choose me.

"Very funny. The med bay has taken some damage and I tried to fix one of the devices. It exploded in my face before almost setting the ship on fire. I'm lucky to get away with only some soot as the only damage."

"I never heard a fire alarm," I said, taken aback.

"That's because it's not working. Didn't you check the alarm systems? They're offline."

I stopped in my tracks and pulled up a system status overview on my wrist communicator. The alarms showed as functioning. Strange.

"They're online," I said, showing it to Havel. "They should have worked."

"They klatting didn't. Suppose it was better this way, I wouldn't want to have scared Trish unnecessarily, but we need to get them working again."

"I agree. I'll handle it. The first delivery should get here in a moment, can you go to the airlock and sign for it?"

He huffed as if he wanted to complain, but then nodded and walked away in the opposite direction. I continued to the bridge. I wanted to check the screens there, maybe they would divulge why our alarm system wasn't working. It was urgent. If another fire broke out due to the damage, we wouldn't know until it was too late.

I found Xil and Trish laughing hysterically. Trish had tears in her eyes while Xil's yellow cheeks had turned ochre.

"By the Great and Terrifying A'Ta, what is going on?" I demanded. "Are you on some kind of drugs?"

In response, the captain simply pointed at the main viewscreen. I looked, blinked, looked again, then understood why they were laughing.

Professor Katila was snogging the aliens we were supposed to abduct. She kept alternating between them, leaving wet traces all over their faces. Their down-covered arms were around her, massaging her bum. I gaped at the video, unable to believe what I was seeing.

Trish turned to me, giggling when she saw my expression. "We think they broke up with her. That's why she wants us to abduct them."

I didn't have the words to reply to that. Klatting professor. She was getting us involved in her personal life? That was wrong on so many levels. If they'd left her, they had a good reason for it, and after she'd attacked our spaceship, I could imagine a whole range of reasons.

"Does that change things?" I asked Xil. "Can we do this if they're unwilling to be with her?"

He growled; his laughter gone in an instant. "Klat her. She put us into an impossible situation. If we don't do what she asked, she's going to try and kill us again. If we do, then we might condemn two beings to slavery or whatever else Katila has planned for them. I doubt she's going to let them go if they tell her they don't want to be with her."

"Could we report her to the university?" Trish asked. "Surely what she's doing is illegal."

Xil sighed. "We can try, but I bet she's prepared for that eventuality. She might tell them we're lying, and I bet she has evidence to back her up."

"Still, we should try," our human insisted. "What's the worst that could happen?"

. . .

We found out an IG hour later. I was working on the engines, fixing some of the damage. Havel was by my side, holding one of the parts I was about to solder to a broken pipe, when Xil roared through the comms system.

"Guys, come to the bridge now!" he yelled.

Havel dropped the metal part and ran. I followed him as fast as I could, my mind spinning with possibilities of what had happened. Was Trish alright? Had she been injured somehow? Xil had sounded both furious and scared.

I almost bumped into Havel when we entered the bridge. I realised why he'd stopped to stare. Xil was on the floor, cradling Trish in his arms. She was pale, shivering as if she was cold. Tears were running down her face. That sight alone would have made me want to murder whoever had caused her to cry, but what was much worse was the blood seeping from her right ear.

"Fix her," Xil said in a choked voice.

Havel straightened his shoulders, and I knew he was trying to push away his emotions, focus on being a medic. He kneeled by their side and pulled the med scanner from his belt.

"What happened?" he asked gently.

"Katila," Xil spat. "She appeared on the screen, told us she knew we'd complained, and next thing I know Trish is screaming in pain, clutching her head. Then she started bleeding and mumbling nonsense. I've not been able to get her to tell me where she's hurting."

Havel put a hand on Trish's shoulder and gently made her look at him. "Deep breaths, sweetie. It's going to be fine. Where does it hurt? Just the ear or somewhere else? Your head?"

She looked at him with wide eyes, then made some strange guttural sounds. Had Katila messed up our mate's brain?

LESSON 2

DEALING WITH UNFORESEEN EMERGENCIES

I got up and pointed the scanner at Matar, who was hovering right behind me. Klat. His slug's microchip had been fried, although the slug itself was still alive. Already suspecting the outcome, I scanned Havel's and my own chips. Same result. For some reason, our brain slugs had survived while Trish's had died in the process.

I explained the situation to the others. Trish looked at me in confusion, pointing at her ears. I wished she'd be able to read Kardarian, or that I could write her Peritan language. But it was no use. I only knew one English word: fuck. She'd used that a lot.

"It must have been Katila," Xil growled. "She gave us the slugs at the start of the course. She must have installed some kind of failsafe that would give her control over them. What are we going to do now? Do we have any other slugs on board?"

I shook my head. "No. We can see if we can get any from the station, but it might take some time to install her language on them. It's not like a lot of humans ever leave their planet. It's a rare language that not every shop will have in stock."

I opened the station's shopping inventory on my comms device and scrolled through the translation options on offer. Klat. They did have brain slugs, but only the most basic versions. Their other devices might offer English, but I doubted they'd been tested on humans. It might be unsafe to implant one in Trish. At least we could get them and understand her. It wouldn't be ideal, but better than nothing.

"I'm going to kill that klatting bitch," Matar snarled. "By A'Tar, she will be dead, I swear it."

Trish said something, not that I understood a word of it. She ended with, "Klat". Despite the seriousness of the situation, I couldn't help but grin. It said a lot about us that we'd learned each other's swear words but nothing else. We'd relied on the translator slugs too much.

"As soon as we've got this all sorted, we're going to take English lessons," I announced. Xil frowned at me, probably annoyed that I was giving orders as if I was the captain, but then he nodded.

"Agreed. And we'll teach her some Kardarian. If we ever go home to Kardar, she needs to be able to communicate with our relatives who don't have translation implants."

I took an antiseptic wipe from my medical kit and gently cleaned Trish's ear. "It's all fine," I told her, hoping she'd recognise the soothing tone I was using even though she couldn't understand the words. "Your brain is intact, it's just the slug that's died. I'll pull it out now, I don't want it to get infected. You'll have to hold still for me. Xil, can you hold her head in place? I don't want to hurt her."

He gently placed his hands on either side of her head. She looked at me in confusion, but she trusted us enough not to struggle. Good girl. I pulled out some old-fashioned tweezers, wishing I had something more sophisticated to impress her. It was the best tool for the job, but I wanted something bigger, shinier. Oh well, size wasn't everything.

Trish said something, the guttural sounds harsh and unfamiliar. She clearly wasn't happy about me going near her ear with tweezers, but a look at Xil reassured me that he had her firmly secured. I stroked her hair, both for her and my own reassurance, then got to work. The slug had embedded herself deep within her ear channel, but now that it was dead it wasn't able to struggle against my grip on it. I pulled it out as gently as I could, but Trish still winced in pain.

"Be careful," Matar hissed from behind me. "If you hurt her, I'm going to klatting break your bones."

"Easy, he's doing his best." Xil's voice was deceptively calm.

The slug exited her ear with a plopping sound, and I let it drop to the floor. Just because we all used them didn't mean that I found them anything but disgusting. Whoever had come up with the idea of embedding slugs near our brain was one crazy person. The IGU provided them as part of their eco-friendly policies, preferring to use organic over artificial matter. I doubted they'd asked the slugs if they wanted to be used for this purpose instead of happily slugging away in their natural habitat.

"Ahaahu allsl gisy otfff," Trish exclaimed and pointed at the slug. Or something along those lines. I couldn't make sense of the sounds tumbling from her lips. They didn't seem to exist in our alphabet, and I doubted I'd be able to replicate them.

"It's dead," I explained again. "That's why you can't understand us."

"Do we need to remove ours as well?" Xil asked.

"We need to remove them when we replace the microchips, but I think for now it's best to keep them in so they can continue to feed on soundwaves. I'm not sure if they'd wither and die outside of our ears."

Xil grimaced but didn't argue. Both him and Matar accepted my medical authority. Mostly without question.

Trish reached out and poked the dead slug with a finger. She laughed when it wobbled beneath her touch. At least her laugh was still recognisable.

The Captain let go of her head and put his hands on her shoulders instead, starting to massage them. She loved having her back kneaded, so this was a good way to keep her calm despite everything.

"Havel, go and find us some way to communicate with her. Matar, continue your work on the engines. Have the repair supplies arrived yet?"

"Aye, they got here just when we got your call for help. I'll need a bit longer to fix everything if I don't have Havel to help me, but we'll get out of here in a couple of IG hours."

Xil sighed. "I'll continue the research on our targets. I'll take Trish to spend some time with the tribitt, that might occupy her mind."

"Wait, we're idiots!" I shouted in an eureka moment. "Her wrist comms is set to English, that's how she's been helping with your research. We can send her a message via that."

While speaking, I already typed a quick 'Trish, can you read this?' into my own comms device.

Her bracelet vibrated and my heart filled with hope as her eyes lit up in surprise. She opened the message, grinned and gave me a thumbs up. I was glad she'd taught us that gesture at the very beginning, otherwise it may have confused us even more.

She typed something and it appeared on all our comms. I was proud how she'd already understood the device's system even though she'd only just got it. Our mate was clever, and I loved her for it. Not that I wouldn't have loved her if she'd been a little less clever.

"What is going on?" Matar read out her message.

I was the fastest typist, so I started the conversation, explaining to Trish what had happened to her brain slug. Matar left the bridge to continue his repairs. Xil was still on the floor, holding Trish, making me rather jealous. I wanted to be the one to have her in my arms. In fact, that's exactly what I was going to do. I reached out and took her hands, pulling her to her feet.

"I'm going to check her over in the med bay," I told Xil and gently guided Trish out of the room before Xil could protest. "Have fun with your research."

His snarling response was cut off by the doors sliding closed behind us. I'd forgotten to tell Trish where I was taking her, but she followed me without question, fully trusting me.

In the med bay, she hopped onto the table in the centre. My cock hardened when I thought of the first time we'd had her in here. The probing had been delicious. The way she'd squirmed beneath my touch...

My comms beeped and I read Trish's message. "One day you need to probe me again."

I looked at her in surprise, then grinned. *It will be my pleasure,* I typed. My erection pressed against the tight fabric of my trousers and I wished I was wearing something looser. Or nothing at all, preferably. I wanted to bend her over right now and fuck her from behind. She was so tight when I did that, so amazingly tight.

"I'm going to check you over," I said at the same time as typing it. "Just in case the slug left any parts of it behind."

She pulled a face, then took off her shirt. She wasn't wearing a bra and her full breasts invited me to play. To squeeze, to suckle, to cherish.

Sadly, this wasn't the time. That's what my brain was saying. My cock had other opinions, firmly supported by my aching balls. My heart stood behind the two, but for once, my brain won. We needed to focus. Repair the ship, re-establish communication with Trish, then fly to the Gemi'i star system and abduct the torso-brothers for Professor Katila. Then drop them off at the IGU space station and hopefully kill our teacher. She deserved it for not just threatening us, but harming our mate. She'd made Trish bleed. She'd abducted her. She'd frightened her. That was unforgiveable. I may be a medic rather than a soldier like Matar and Xil had been, but inside of me slumbered a warrior who was ready to surface in order to protect Trish.

With a deep sigh of regret, I typed a message for her, again saying it out loud to make it less awkward. "I'm sorry, not now. I promise I'll do a proper probing on you once we're done with our mission. I'm going to do a quick scan on you, then I need to see if I can get you a translator here at the station."

Trish nodded to confirm she'd understood and put her shirt back on, looking just as regretful as I felt. My cock was still hard, especially once I saw her nipples push against her shirt. Klat. I had to concentrate.

I bid her to lie down on the bed and pulled the large med scanner over her body. It was more accurate than the handheld one and I wouldn't be reassured that she was completely healthy until I got the all clear from the machine.

She reached out for my hand and I took it in mine, gently squeezing it in reassurance. She smiled at me, then looked at the scanner and rolled her eyes. I didn't need a brain slug to understand the meaning of that. She thought I was being overprotective.

While the scanner was doing its work, I logged into the station's shopping system again. Maybe I'd overlooked something. There had to be something that was compatible with human physiology. What was the closest species to humans? Ferven perhaps? They were larger and the males had horns, but otherwise they were very similar. I checked the IGU database. Close enough. If I could find a device that was approved for Ferven, it might be suitable for Trish.

Just when the scanner finally finished and retracted back into the ceiling, I found the entry I was looking for. It wasn't an implant like I'd hoped for, but a tiny headset worn on both ears. It was ugly as klat, but it would do for now. Once we got to the IGU with our abductees, we'd be able to get new brain slugs. This time with no link to Professor Katila.

I ordered four of the devices to be delivered to the Jade as soon as possible. I could have got something fancier for the guys and me, but I didn't want to risk them being incompatible with Trish's old-fashioned device.

Now, we just had to wait and hope that they would work, and we could talk to our mate again.

LESSON 3

ALIEN ABDUCTION FOR PROFESSIONALS

The Gemi'i star system finally appeared on the viewscreen. Five planets circling one sun, three of them inhabited by the Gemi'i race, the others too close and too far from the sun. My research had narrowed down our targets' location to G-3. It was the most likely location, anyway. We had no guarantee they'd be there. And even so, we had an entire planet to search.

At least we'd be able to log into their interplanetary network once we got a little closer. I was hopeful that I'd be able to find the two males mentioned somewhere. Their names were somewhat unique and the good thing about Gemi'i were that they always appeared in pairs. What were the chances of finding another duo called Hix and Hex?

Trish stared at the screen. I realised this was going to be her first alien planet. She'd been to a space station but hadn't set foot on a different planet yet. I wished I could make it more special for her. We were supposed to go on honeymoon, not hunt down and abduct two alien males for our crazy professor.

"It's beautiful," she sighed. Her voice sounded strange through the new translators, but at least we could understand her now. I couldn't wait to have new brain slugs, though. Her accent was jarring, and she'd said that we didn't sound very nice to her either. I wondered if she would have fallen in love with us if we'd only had these antique translators. She didn't sound sexy at all, but then, her body was the epitome of sexy. She was our beautiful mate and I'd love her forever, strange voice or not.

"That one to the right is G-3," Havel explained. "It's the smallest of the three planets, but also the one we're going to approach first."

Trish was right, the Gemi'i system really was beautiful. A dark green haze surrounded G-3, making it seem mysterious and somewhat magical. Their sun was larger than that Trish was used to, but a little smaller than the one Kardar circled.

"We should get access to their network in a few seconds...got it," Matar announced. "I'll log your comms into the network, that way we can all research at the same time. The connection will get faster once we get closer to G-3."

"This is nothing like the Earth internet," Trish muttered while staring at her holographic comms screen. "I have no idea how to even enter a search term."

Matar reached over and started entering some code into her device. "I'll give it a different skin, making it appear like the system you're used to. It won't be quite the same, but easier for you to navigate."

I left them to it and started diving into the Gemi'i network. I began with searching their news for any mention of Hix and Hex. The second search result gave me the first lead. They'd been given an award for educational services to the people of G-2. It had been three IG years ago, but it might help narrow down their location further. I added other parameters to the search, concentrating on anything to do with education. More and more interesting results popped up, but I stopped when I came across a biography on a local university's network presence.

"Guys, look at this," I said and pushed the information to the main screen for them to see. "This is from last year. They started a job at the Pontrin University on G-2. That must have been after they left the IGU. There's no note that they left, so let's hope they still work there."

I instantly changed the Jade's course from G-3 to G-2. Pontrin was a small town near the planet's south pole and should be easy to find.

"There's a space port we can land at," Matar announced, also looking at the navigational data. "Unless you want to do the tractor beam method this time?"

I shook my head. "No, if they're at a university, they'll be surrounded by people. We don't want their abduction to be public. We'll do some reconnaissance first. Find out where they live, how they commute between their home and the university. Find a spot where we can abduct them without anyone else seeing us."

"Won't we stand out?" Trish asked. "I was the only human on the space station and that one was full of aliens from all over the galaxy. I doubt there are any more humans and even Kardarians on G-2."

I smiled at her, proud at her sharp intelligence. "You are right, mate. We will put on costumes to hide our identity."

She didn't look convinced. "Costumes? Like for Halloween? Are you going to dress as a giant yellow banana?"

I didn't know what a banana was, but if she wanted me to dress as one, I would.

"Is that some kind of Peritan warrior?" I asked curiously.

She broke into laughter. "Not quite. But seriously, unless you have some kind of invisibility suits, I doubt we'll be able to avoid attention."

She was right. I searched through the documents on my comms device until I found the Alien Abduction for Beginners folder. There had to be some information in the course that would help us disguise ourselves. I didn't like having to draw on resources created by the female who'd forced us to do this abduction, but it was our best chance to be successful.

"You were traders before you abducted me, right?" Trish asked and I nodded.

"Yes, but we'd always wanted to be full-time abductors. Trading was just something to carry us over until we'd succeeded at our first proper abduction. But now that we have you, we won't be abducting anyone else, so I suppose we need to return to trading once we've dealt with Professor Katila."

"Could you pretend to deliver an order to the university? I'm sure they get sciency things from all across the galaxy. I can stay here and coordinate the abduction from afar."

"They do have a department of intergalactic genetics," Havel said. "That could work. We can pretend to have samples from Kardar for them."

I thought about Trish's plan. It was good and had a high chance of success. I didn't like the idea of leaving her all alone on the Jade, however. Not after we'd almost lost her.

"I will stay with you," I decided. "Havel knows most about genetics, so he'll be the expert, while Matar can be the one negotiating prices. Not that you'll actually sell anything. Your task is to find Hix and Hex, and shadow them until you see an opportunity for the abduction to begin. Trish and I will then fly the ship to your location and either pull them up with the tractor beam or wait for you to sedate them and bring them to us. Agreed?"

The guys nodded their assent, while Trish smiled at me.

"This is so exciting! I can't believe I'm actually getting involved in a proper alien abduction!"

I grinned at her enthusiasm. Despite the severity of the situation, she was right, it was a great opportunity to hone our abduction skills.

HAVEL

We took a shuttle from the space port to the university. We weren't the only non-Gemi'i, which was reassuring. We wouldn't stand out too much. I hadn't spotted any other Kardarians, but several other species from neighbouring systems. I was sure they'd seen my kind here before.

The university was a in a sleek, spheric building that glinted in the sun. Glass covered all surfaces, giving us a view of the inside. I wasn't sure I'd like being watched like that if I was one of their teachers or students, but that didn't matter.

I was carrying a large case with the letters SAMPLE on it in several languages. It had been Matar's idea, making it extra obvious why we were at the university. The entrance had a simple scanner to detect weapons, but we walked through it without being stopped. Not that we had any weapons on us, that would have been silly. We didn't want to get into trouble, we just wanted to stalk out our target.

Matar headed right to the reception desk staffed by two Gemi'i males. No, wait, one of them had a male and a female head. Interesting, I hadn't realised that was possible. The scientist in me wanted more information, maybe even a sample - how ironic - but this wasn't the time or place.

"We've got a delivery for Hix and Hex," Matar told them. "Can you point us in the right direction?"

The double-male Gemi'i smiled pleasantly, making his wide mouth seem even larger, and looked at a screen. "Third floor. They're not teaching just now, so you might find them in their office. Shall I announce you?"

"No," I said quickly. "I'll have to use the washroom first, it's been a long journey."

The head on the right gave me a sympathetic smile. "Just down this corridor. There are cubicles adapted for various species, but let us know if you need any special arrangements."

To keep up appearances, we headed into the direction he'd pointed at. As soon as we were out of eyesight, we took an elevator up to the third floor. Compared to the bright, inviting reception area, this was just a boring corridor with doors on both sides. Offices, most likely.

We split up, Matar turning right, me left. Luckily, all the doors had name signs written in IG Standard. Our translators weren't fancy ones that had a link to our visual cortex, able to translate writing. Usually, we didn't have a use for that, but thankfully, this university was used to having students and teachers from other parts of the galaxy.

I finally found their office at the end of the corridor and used my wrist comms to call Matar. I didn't want to shout and draw attention.

"What now?" he whispered as soon as he'd joined me. "Do we knock?"

I shook my head. "We don't want to attract their attention. I can hear movement inside, so how about we mark this office on a map and then go outside and watch them from there? We can try flying a drone close to their office window or use binoculars."

"Good idea. Thank A'Ta that they have those glass fronts. Very suitable for reconnaissance."

We made our way back to the ground floor. Just before stepping through the scanner, someone called from behind, "Didn't you find them?"

It was the Gemi'i at the reception. They both looked at the sample box I was still carrying. Klat.

"We found them, and they gave us some new samples in return," I said with a reassuring smile. "Thanks for your help."

"Have a safe journey, then. Come visit us again."

I exchanged a look with Matar, glad that we'd dealt with that little problem. Professor Katila would have been proud - before she turned into a bloodthirsty maniac.

We walked around the building until we got to below Hix and Hex's office. I called Xil back on the Jade.

"Captain, can you dispatch a drone to our location? As small as possible."

"On it. Is everything going to plan?"

"Yes, we've located the targets and will now try and spy on them from afar until they leave the campus."

I felt like a professional abductor, giving him a report like that. Maybe we shouldn't stop abducting altogether. We wouldn't keep our abductees on our ship, but we could deliver them to other people who'd pay us for them. Not slaves, obviously, but there had to be a way to continue doing alien abductions without taking them on as additional mates. Trish wouldn't be happy with that, and to be honest, neither would I. One little human was enough for us.

The drone arrived only a few IG minutes later. I let Matar take control of it, since his comms implant let him have the most precise control of the device. He flew it close to their window and let it hover in the air. Sudden movements would attract attention, but the drone was small enough to not be noticed as long as it stayed in one place.

"I'll transmit the video feed to your comms as well," he announced, and I pressed a button to accept it.

Our targets sat in their office, reading an old-fashioned paper book. Did they have the same reading speed or did one always have to wait for the other to finish a page? I decided that once we'd abducted them, I'd do some more research on Gemi'i. They were fascinating.

We stood there for ages, before I had the idea to go into a restaurant we'd seen on the way from the spaceport. We could monitor the drone from that distance. The menu was a selection of supposedly Gemi'i delicacies. I'd never heard of any of them, even though the menu was in IG standard, so I randomly pointed on one dish. The waiters looked at me with a smirk but didn't comment. Matar on the other hand ordered a portion of crackers. That seemed a little too safe to me, although it didn't say what kind of crackers they were.

Our drinks arrived first, bubbling and steaming blue concoctions. I'd thought I'd ordered tea, but this was nothing like what I imagined when I thought of tea. That implied hot liquid being poured over some sort of plants, but this drink was cold and seemed to have a life of its own. I gave it a sniff. Sweet, not too bad. It tingled on my tongue when I took a hesitant sip and felt sticky in my throat. The taste wasn't awful, but I didn't like the feel of it.

"Delicious," Matar sighed. "I don't know what it is, but I want more of it."

I pushed my glass over to him. "Take mine."

Checking my comms, I was reassured that Hix and Hex were still reading their book. What a nice job that enabled them to read while being paid for it.

The dish I'd ordered turned out to be a heap of what looked like bright pink worms. Maybe it was pasta, like the spa-ghetto Trish liked. I poked at it with the strange instrument they'd given me. The worms wriggled and moved. They were klatting alive.

Matar laughed and handed me a cracker. They were blue and green, not exactly appetising, but tasted good enough. Bland yet with a hint of spice. As if the cook had been extremely hesitant with adding flavour. Oh well, we weren't here for the Gemi'i cuisine. That made me think, though.

"Do we need to stock up on food for our abductee?" I asked in hushed tones so that the nearby waiters wouldn't hear us. "Will they be able to eat what we have on board?"

"You're the medic. That's your job to figure out."

I growled at Matar. Some help he was. Our fabricator should be able to create the nutrients our Gemi'i abductees would need, but there was a big difference between adequate nutrients and food that you actually wanted to eat. Yes, we were going to take them against their will, but that didn't mean we had to treat them like prisoners. We were only doing this to keep our mate safe from Professor Katila.

I waved over the waiters. "Can you wrap this and prepare a selection of your favourite dishes to take away? We'd like to give our crew a taste of Gemi'i cuisine."

Delighted, the waiters hurried away.

"Did you see the prices in this place?" Matar hissed. "This will be crazy expensive."

"I don't want them to be unhappy. They won't be once they reach Professor Katila, but let's make their abduction experience as positive as it can possibly be."

Matar stared at me, then sighed. "You're right. Maybe we should sedate them before using the tractor beam. That will lessen any stress and anxiety."

"First, we need to find out where they live and where best to abduct them."

I checked my screen again. They'd put away their book and were now getting dressed in a long, black coat.

Matar got up. "You wait here for the food and have it sent to the Jade. I'll follow them."

Klat. That plan had backfired. Now I was going to sit here doing nothing while Matar had all the fun.

LESSON 4
ALIEN ABDUCTION
FOR EXPERTS

I wanted popcorn. Watching the Gemi'i torso-brothers was boring. All they did was read in their office. They had a comfy sofa that I wanted to abduct and bring here onto the bridge. The chair I sat on was getting uncomfortable. I could have moved onto Xil's lap, but then that would have ended in sex and we needed to stay focused.

"What do you think they're reading?" I asked Xil. "A textbook? Fantasy? An alien abduction novel?"

He snorted. "I really want it to be the latter, but I assume it's something to do with the course they teach. From my research, they're diligent and hard-working, so I doubt they'd read fiction while on the job."

Boring.

I continued dreaming of buttery popcorn until they finally got up and left their office. The drone whizzed around the building and hovered near the main entrance. Hopefully, they'd use that to exit the university and not some other doors.

"What now?" I asked Xil.

"Now we continue to follow them until Matar and Havel tell us it's time to abduct. I've requested permission to take off at will and the spaceport has confirmed that. We won't have to wait and mess with bureaucracy once it's time to begin the abduction."

To my relief, Hix and Hex appeared on the screen again, walking away from the university building and towards a shuttle station. I kind of wished I was out there with them. The shuttles were sleek, semi-translucent pods that reminded me of gelatine pills. They flew at breakneck speeds, bringing people from A to B much faster than even planes back on Earth would have managed. I wanted to fly in one of them and see what it would feel like.

"Can the drone keep up with the shuttle?" I asked.

"We'll find out, but I'm not sure." Xil opened a channel to Matar. "Can you somehow get a tracker on them? We don't want to lose them in case you don't get into the same shuttle with them."

"On it."

We watched as Matar caught up with our target and *accidentally* bumped against them. A blinking dot appeared on the map of Pontrin that Xil had pulled up on the main screen.

"Nice work," the Captain praised. "Where's Havel?"

"Getting food for our abductees." Matar sounded amused. "He's having it sent to the Jade, so be prepared to take a delivery soon."

Xil looked at me. "Food? Why?"

"No idea. Do Gemi'i need a special diet?"

"If they do then my research didn't show it. Havel must know what he's doing, though, he's an excellent medic."

Talking about the fabricator gave me an idea. "Do you

think your magic food machine can make me popcorn?" I asked Xil.

He gave me a strange look. "Pop-corn? I recently read that pop is another word for sex. What are you implying, little human?"

I laughed. "No, it's a snack. You heat up corn kernels and they pop into big, fluffy popcorn goodness. Then you add sugar or salt or butter or toffee..." My mouth was starting to water at the thought. I'd once come across an ancient bag of caramel popcorn in an abandoned building. It had been soft and stale, but the taste had still been magnificent.

"When we abducted you, we programmed the fabricator with a range of Peritan recipes. Go have a look, maybe this popping corn is one of them."

I almost ran to the galley. It still boggled my mind that this machine could create most foods I desired from just a supply of base materials. I didn't really want to know what it used to make the meals I ordered, but so far, they'd all been delicious. It wasn't very good at replicating fruit and vegetables, but the lasagne I'd had just before we reached Kitt-Y-6 had been amazing.

I scrolled through the menu. No popcorn. Figured. There was however a recipe for brownies. Better than nothing. I needed sugar to survive this tiresome abduction. I'd never thought that I'd get bored during an alien abduction, but just sitting here on the Jade, watching from afar, wasn't as excited as I'd imagined. I wanted to be part of the action, but it had been my own idea to stay behind. Silly past-Trish. That had been a bad decision.

I returned to the bridge with a plate of brownies. They smelled delicious, even though they lacked the crispy crust I loved. The space port back home had an amazing cafe and diner. Not that I'd been able to afford to eat there, but one of the assistant chefs had once exchanged some brownies for a kiss. I shuddered at the wet, disgusting experience that kiss had been. Nothing compared to the kisses I got from my hot, alien males. They couldn't even be called the same thing.

"That smells good," Xil remarked as soon as I joined him. He grabbed two brownies at once and stuffed them into his mouth. One day, we'd need to have a chat about table manners. They may look like massive brutes, but they didn't have to behave like it.

"Did anything happen while I was gone?"

"Matar didn't manage to get onto the same shuttle as our targets, so it's good he tagged them with a tracker. Havel is now on following them, too. The food he ordered should arrive here any minute now.

I nibbled on a brownie, savouring every tiny bite, while watching the drone's camera feed. It was whizzing behind the shuttle, but it wasn't keeping up. The shuttle was getting smaller and smaller, and it would soon lose sight of it.

I checked the map for the blinking tracking dot. They'd slowed down. Ah, yes, the shuttle had stopped, giving the drone the chance to catch up. Hix and Hex got out of the shuttle and started walking slowly along a road leading to a residential area. High tower blocks rose into the sky as if trying to tickle the pink clouds above them. This really looked like a different planet. Futuristic, alien, strange. And beautiful. I didn't know what materials the towers were made from, but it was nothing like I'd ever seen before. Shiny, sleek, but with a slightly organic look. It was hard to describe.

"Do you think they live in one of those?" I asked Xil. "It'll be hard to abduct them from such an enormous building."

"We'll see. You should make more of these cakes in the meantime." The plate was empty with only crumbs left. That glutton. I'd only had one while he'd devoured nine brownies. Urgh. Men.

"Make your own. I'm not your cook."

He raised an eyebrow. "You're not? I thought that was the reason we abducted you. Our own little human maid."

I looked around for something to throw at him but came up empty. I'd take my revenge later, when I didn't let him fuck me. He'd get to watch while the others got the pleasure they deserved. Not Xil though, no, not after eating my brownies.

"Look, they're taking a path away from the skyscrapers," Xil suddenly said, eyes fixed on the screen. The drone had now fully caught up with them, flying at a safe distance so not to be spotted. "Matar, where are you?"

"Just got off the shuttle," his reply came in an instant. "Havel got here before me, he took a faster one."

"I can see them," Havel said, having listened to our transmission. "I'm just behind the drone, which is why you didn't spot me."

Xil made the drone turn around, giving us a view of Havel. He waved and grinned at the camera, before continuing to walk at a fast pace to keep up with the Gemi'i. Even though they shared the same body, they didn't seem to have any coordination issues. I wondered if they controlled one leg and one arm each or if one of them had full control over the body and the other was just a passenger. That would suck in the long run. What happened if they fell in love with two different people? Would they have to make a schedule to spend time with them? Or become some sort of triad?

Not that it mattered. They were our targets, to be abducted and brought to Professor Katila so we'd stay safe. I should stop thinking about them. It would only make it harder to turn them over to that crazed bitch.

"Get the Jade ready," Havel ordered. I knew Xil would be grumpy about that. He hated it whenever one of the other guys told him what to do. On one hand, he always insisted that they were a family, but on the other hand, he loved being in charge.

"There's a park behind this building and it might be a good place to abduct them. Matar, hurry up so we can sedate them together."

Now that action was finally happening, I sat on the edge of my seat, every fibre of my body filled with tension. This was exciting.

"Was this what it felt like when you abducted me?"

Xil chuckled. "That was very different. Remember, we found you by the side of the road, barely conscious. There was no drone involved, no pursuit, no stalking. You made it much easier for us."

"I shouldn't have," I grumbled. "I should have fought."

"No, it was perfect that way. Our first proper abduction. We were so proud."

I laughed. My mates were adorable when it came to abductions. But now that I was part of one, I kind of understood why they'd wanted to become professional abductors. This was fun.

The drone turned around a corner and we saw the park Havel had mentioned. It was a wide open space with a few gnarled purple trees dotted around the landscape. Such a stark contrast to the modern buildings right next to it. Hix and Hex took a winding path through the park. Darkness was slowly setting and not many other people were around. If Havel and Matar did their job right, nobody would notice the abduction.

Though as much as I loved my aliens, I somehow doubted they'd get this done without mistakes.

Xil started the Jade and we took off from the space port. Because of flight zone restrictions, we had to ascend quite a distance until the city below us was just a flickering of lights and colours. It made sense that we weren't allowed to be any lower or the shuttles may have collided with us.

He gently steered us towards the park and hovered high above. I doubted we were visible from the ground, not now that it was almost dark. And even so, people here were used to seeing spaceships all the time, so close to a major space port.

On the screen, I watched as Matar joined Havel and they now walked together.

"Maybe they should hold hands, pretend they're a couple," I joked, but Xil took me seriously.

"Do what Trish said. Maybe kiss."

"Klat you," Matar hissed. "I won't kiss Havel. Not even if I pretend that he's Trish." I was almost a little disappointed. It would have been hot to watch. Not that this was the time or the place.

"Should we get closer to them and hit them with a tranquiliser?" Havel asked. "Or do you want them conscious?"

"Sedate them," Xil ordered. "It'll make things easier. We don't want them to scream and attract attention. Split up. Havel, you hide near that little copse of trees. Matar, involve them in a conversation, ask them for help with... something that makes them go there."

"An escaped puppy," I suggested. "A tribitt in distress."

Xil shot me a look, rolling his eyes to show me what he thought of that idea.

"Excellent idea," Matar said, and I grinned at Xil in triumph.

I wished I had more brownies as we watched the abduction take on shape. Havel hid in the shadows, hopefully with his prepared syringe in his hand, ready to take out the Gemi'i. Matar ran towards them, waving his hands in distress. He was a surprisingly good actor.

"Please, help me, my offspring has got stuck in a tree!"

We couldn't hear their response, but the Gemi'i followed Matar towards the copse of trees. Perfect. So far, everything was going to plan. The drone had trouble piercing the darkness, so all we could see were shadows. The sounds coming through the speakers sounded promising, though.

"They're out cold. Engage the tractor beam," Matar announced.

Xil didn't move. "Please."

"What?"

"Say please. You're not the Captain, you can't give orders. Turn it into a request."

Matar huffed but complied. "*Please*, engage the tractor beam, oh wise and wonderful Captain."

I snorted at the sarcasm dripping from his every syllable, but Xil was mollified and fiddled around with the controls.

"You may want to go to the med bay," he suggested to me. "I'll join you as soon as I've got the Jade back in orbit and on autopilot."

"Aye, aye, Captain." I gave him a mock salute and ran from the bridge before he could react. I loved teasing him.

Matar

I looked at them with pride. Hix and Hex were on a bed in the med bay, sedated yet about to wake up. A few small feathers drifted to the floor, part of their white fluffy down. Havel had run a quick scan of them to make sure they were alright. This had been an extremely successful abduction.

"Should we cuff them?" the medic asked. "I'm sure we can subdue them if they fight, but I don't want them to damage anything."

I shrugged. "If you want. Maybe we should probe them while we're at it. Improve our probing skills."

"You will do no such thing!"

I turned to find Trish standing in the doorway, her hands on her hips.

"Probing is reserved for me. They're our guests, not our experimental subjects. Understood?"

My heart was close to exploding with pride for our wonderful female. She was so clever, so confident. We'd done well in choosing her.

"Understood," I confirmed with a smile. "We'll be sure to probe you at the earliest opportunity."

Her cheeks turned dark pink, my new favourite colour. She was adorable.

"I've already thought of some new instruments I could build," Havel said." And this time, I won't forget to attach some sensors or a camera to the probe."

I cringed at the memory of our botched first probing. Not that it hadn't been fun and educational. And *hot*. But we had indeed forgotten the whole point of probing, which was to gather data on our abductee.

Hix and Hex just about fit onto the bed. They were narrow up until their chest, but then turned wide with their two heads. Havel was in medic paradise, taking a lot more scans of them than were necessary. I could already see him getting all sad once we delivered them to the IGU and he'd be no longer able to study them.

One of the Gemi'i torso-brothers groaned.

"Are they waking up?" Trish asked.

"Last chance to tie them up," Havel warned, checking his instruments.

"I'm not into that kind of thing." The left head was awake, a smirk on his lips. He didn't look scared at all, just tired. "Hey, Hix, wake up, we've been abducted by aliens."

"So cool," Hix yawned without opening his eyes. "Just five more minutes."

I stared at them in disbelief. Abductees weren't supposed to behave like this. How were they so calm?

"I'm assuming Kat sent you?" Hex asked. "Come on, Hix, help me sit up or hand over the reins. I want to look our abductors in the eye, not lie here like a lump sack of coal."

The other head yawned again. "You have control."

So that's how it worked. One of them steered their body at a time, giving the other a break to just ride along. I imagined how nice this would be on long, boring walks. I could just snooze away while my torso-brother did all the work. But then, did I want to be trapped in the same body with another male? Share the same cock? No klatting way.

Trish stepped forward. "Let me do this, boys." She winked at me. "Welcome to the Jade. Yes, you have been abducted, but do not fear, we're going to take good care of you."

"A human, how curious." Hix stared at her with unabashed curiosity. "We've never been abducted by a human before."

I frowned at him. "Have you been abducted a lot?"

"Yes, for research purposes. It's never a good idea to teach a subject without having personal experience in it."

With the way he was grinning widely, I had a hard time deciding if he was serious or making this up. His torso-brother seemed to have gone back to sleep, not caring at all that they were on a spaceship far from home.

"What does she have on you?" Hix asked.

"Why do you think we're not doing this voluntarily?" Trish shot back. "This could be our assignment."

"Sure, it could be. In a parallel universe where logic and madness have been reversed. No, Kat put you up to this and since you look like decent folk and not hardened criminals, I assume she's forcing you to do it. It's something she'd do."

Trish turned to me. "I'm kind of sad they don't think we're criminals. I was enjoying this rogue, pirate kind of feeling."

"We can do some pirating once we're done with this," I promised her. "Maybe one the way to Labeari, once we finally get to have our honeymoon."

"Honeymoon?" Hix looked from her to me. "Are you mates?"

"They're mine," Trish confirmed with a proud smile. "All of them."

I didn't like the dismissive glances Hix took at Havel and me.

"Is there another one?" the Gemi'i asked. "Someone a little more impressive?"

A growl broke from my throat and my tail slapped against the floor. "Maybe we should tie them up after all."

Havel flashed his fangs. "Maybe we should. And then do some very intimate probing."

Hix laughed. "Alright, now I see what you like about them."

"Stop talking," Hex muttered groggily. "How far are we from the IGU station?"

"Two IG days," Trish said before I could. I was impressed, she was really getting the hang of calculating time in the intergalactic standard way.

Hix sat up - it was clearly him controlling their body - and Hex let out an annoyed groan.

"Then we have some time to come up with a plan."

LESSON 5

ASSISTING YOUR ABDUCTEES

Once I was sure the Jade was on the right course and everything was running smoothly, including the machinery that had been damaged during the attack near Kitt-Y-6, I joined the others in the galley. I'd watched their first encounter with Hix and Hex from the bridge and had been very proud of how Trish had taken the lead. Maybe we should have a chat during our honeymoon, see if she'd be interested to do abductions with us full time. I was enjoying the rush of excitement this challenge had caused.

Our Gemi'i abductees sat on the small bench on one side of the room, which gave them enough space to sit comfortably. They had a drink in each hand so that they didn't have to share a glass.

That reminded me of something. "Klat, I forgot about the food."

Havel looked up at me. "I thought it had been delivered to the Jade?"

"It was, but I never went outside to bring it in. We had to take off to get to you in time for the abduction... it's still at the spaceport."

"I paid a lot of credits for that," Havel hissed, his fangs visible. "And now you klatting joke of a Captain tells me that you forgot it?"

I roared at him. I wouldn't tolerate insubordination. I'd admitted my mistake and that was it, everyone should just forget about it. Time to move on. We had more important issues than a basket full of very expensive Gemi'i food.

"I'm sure your replicator will do just fine," Hex said with a shy smile. "We're used to that. There was no source of good Gemi'i dishes on the IGU station either."

"Such a waste," Havel grumbled under his breath and it took all my will power to ignore him. I should throw him out of the air lock for that. I was his klatting Captain and he ought to respect me.

Matar cleared his throat. "Hix and Hex want to discuss our next steps with us. They know we're not doing this because we want to, but because Professor Katila isn't giving us another choice." He turned to the torso-brothers. "If we don't deliver you to her, she's going to attack us again. She has resources at her disposal, and I don't think she'll hold back. She had our mate kidnapped, then our ship shot at. I have no doubts that she'll try and kill us if we don't comply."

The Gemi'i nodded, their expressions sombre. "You are right," Hex said. "Kat is not to be trifled with, not when she gets into one of her rages. She's probably stopped taking her medication again."

"Medication?" Havel asked, curiosity piqued.

"When she gets into her bi-yearly mating cycle, her emotions became extremely unstable. Karangi usually spend this time with their mates, who emit a pheromone that counteracts the effects. Since we weren't Karangi, she was taking medication during these cycles."

"Or maybe she just went crazy for good," Hix mused. "She's always been teetering at the edge. Her work - and us, back then - stopped her from stepping over the line, but I knew that us leaving made it likely that she'd go mad."

His brother nodded. "It was a calculated risk."

"Why did you leave her?" Trish asked. "Besides her being a psychotic bitch, obviously."

Hix smiled, a dreamy expression transforming his face into someone a lot younger. "When we first met her as students, she was wonderful. Clever, sharp as a Ferven blade, witty, beautiful. Both of us fell in love with her right away."

"And neither of us had expected that," Hex added. "Back then, we were very different and were going through a bit of a personality crisis, like most Gemi'i do at some point. Even though our species has always been this way, interacting with aliens who don't share a body can create jealousy and unrest."

I could imagine that. Being stuck with a second male within me? No way. We'd probably be dead by now, having killed each other.

"When we met Kat, it was just what we needed," Hix continued. "Both of us loved her. It gave us a common purpose and connected us again, turned us from enemies into brothers once more. It was good for her, too, I believe. She was a workaholic, never spending any time outside her office, so having us to distract her from work was important. It was very cliché, falling in love with your teacher, but she never made it feel awkward."

I couldn't imagine Professor Katila in love. Workaholic, yes. Everything else, no.

"Why did you break up?" I asked.

The two males looked at each other as if to decide how much information to give us.

"It was no longer working," Hex said after a pause. "She was becoming erratic, jealous, emotional. She didn't want us to leave our dwelling. She didn't want us to be alone with female students. And she wanted..."

He sighed, letting his torso-brother continue.

"Offspring. She wanted offspring." Hix sighed deeply. "But our species aren't compatible. Gemi'i lay eggs, but Karangi give birth. Like you humans, I believe. We may have been willing to adopt, but that's when her behaviour was getting more and more unpredictable. We didn't want to bring a youngling into that kind of volatile environment. When we refused, she threatened to get some of her scientist friends involved who'd take our seed by force. She was obsessed by the idea that through science, she could carry our offspring. And the one thing you need to know about her is that once she's come up with a plan, she won't veer off that path. She'd decided she wanted younglings with us and that was it. She didn't care about our opinion on the matter."

"We tried to reason with her," Hex continued when his brother fell silent. "We distracted her with presents, asked for help from her university superiors, but nothing worked. She got worse. One day, we woke handcuffed to the bed. She'd gone to work and left us there. That was the moment we agreed to leave."

I was stunned by their story. Force them to give her their seed? What kind of person would do that, no matter the gender? Katila was even crazier than I'd thought.

"There's no way we're going to return you to her," Tricia said with determination. She stared at me, as if expecting me to protest, but I had already come to the same conclusion. Handing them over to that crazed female was as bad as abusing them ourselves.

"That's very kind of you, human," Hex said and shot her a warm look. "But we always knew this moment would come. We've been waiting for it. And we've not been sitting around idle while back on our home planet. We came up with a plan long ago. Now we just need your help to put it into action."

"What plan?" I asked, reminding them that I was the one they had to convince.

"What matters most to Kat - besides her offspring fantasy - is her work. Without it, she's nothing. No influence, no power, no purpose. So, we're going to take it all away from her."

"We already tried reporting her to the IGU authorities. In return, she destroyed our brain slugs, making us unable to communicate with our mate for a while," I said, my heart sinking at how useless their plan was. I'd expected something more from these two clearly intelligent academics. They'd had time to come up with a really good plan and all they had was the idea to destroy Katila's klatting reputation? Bah.

"We have evidence," Hix grinned slyly. "We've got enough to get her in front of a tribunal. Maybe even a criminal trial, if we send this to the right people. She's bent a lot of rules over the years. Ignored student welfare. Even endangered her students."

"You could say that" Matar interrupted. "She klatting shot at us."

Hex nodded, which looked a little weird considering that Hix's head stayed in the same position. "We can add your recordings of that to our files. That will make it even more damning. The juiciest bit however is that we were her students when she first started having sexual relations with us. Of course, we were willing and over age, but the IGU strictly forbids relationships between staff and students. Add to that the fact that she handcuffed us to a bed, robbing us of our freedom, plus threatening to physically harm us... it's not looking good for her. Especially because we filmed it all."

Trish gasped. "You've got it on camera?"

The torso-brothers grinned. "We knew she was going to cross a line," Hix explained. "So, we installed a hidden camera in our bedroom. To be honest, we'd assumed she'd try and do worse than just handcuff us. Still, it was a good decision. We recorded some of her craziest outbursts, ready to be sent to Professor Z, the IGU headmaster. Once he sees that, she'll be without a job."

I shook my head. "That doesn't sound like a good plan to me at all. So what, she'll be out of work. What will stop her from coming after us, after you? I bet she had a good salary and has saved enough to pay for some space pirates to attack the Jade."

Hex wasn't dismayed by my scepticism. "There's a paragraph in the IGU contract which states that whoever will fall foul of the University's rules and regulations forfeits any salary paid to them in the past, as well as assigned accommodation. Her bank account will be empty. She won't have the means to take revenge. She'll be powerless."

"I say we kill her," Matar muttered. I was tempted to agree with him, as tasteless as that option was. Neither of us were murderers, but we'd do whatever we had to in order to keep our mate safe. Trish was our priority.

Hix and Hex looked shocked at the idea. "We loved her, once," Hix said, putting a lot of emphasis on the l-word. "She did horrible things, but we could never kill her. That's not our way."

"No killing," Trish confirmed.

"No killing," I repeated as the responsible, dutiful Captain I was. "But let's not make it too easy on her. We need to thoroughly destroy her until she regrets all she's done."

"I want her to beg us to take her in," Hix said darkly. "I want her to repent and apologise."

Trish laughed. "I can't see her apologising for anything. She's not that kind of person."

"You're right," Hex confirmed. "It will be a new learning experience for her. Apologising 101."

LESSON 6

APOLOGIES FOR ARSEHOLES

The closer we got to the IGU station, the more worried I became. What if our plan failed? What if Professor Katila knew what we were up to, what if she shot at us again? I wasn't so much scared for me as I was for my guys. I couldn't lose them. Our translator problems had shown me how much I needed them in my life. Their voices, their minds, their bodies. Definitely their cocks.

Having Hix and Hex on board left us little privacy. The Jade wasn't built for six people, even though two of them shared a body. Yes, there was a lot of storage in the cargo hold, but that area was kept too cold to live in. Luckily, I didn't mind sharing a cabin with the guys...although we didn't get to spend as much time in our nest as I wanted to. We were kept busy with making plans, alternative plans and then backup plans for the alternative plans. Finally, on the day we got close enough to see the IGU station on our sensors, everyone was satisfied that we'd done enough preparation. The data package was ready to be sent, full of evidence of Professor Katila's misdemeanours and crimes. Matar had cut together footage of the attack on the Jade, highlighting the intensity of the assault and how crazy the Professor had sounded. How it had been completely unprovoked. I'd only been able to watch that video once before I felt sick. We'd almost died. It had been a little too close for my liking. Now, we were walking right into the cave of the lioness, who likely wasn't as unprepared as we were hoping. She had to know that Hix and Hex might turn us. That we wouldn't just hand them over like she wanted. Despite her madness, she was an intelligent female. She wouldn't have made it all the way to Head of Department if she wasn't clever.

The IGU station was larger than Kitt-Y-6, the size of several cities. The Gemi'i had explained that all the faculty members lived here, unless they were on research assignments. The IGU offered thousands of classes and had over ten thousand teachers and professors. I'd barely believed that until they'd started talking about all the individual languages spoken in the Galaxy. That made it more tangible, thinking that each language would need several teachers, support staff, and so on.

Many students moved to the station too to take lessons in person, sometimes bringing their families. Add to that staff to keep the whole thing running and you ended up with a space station of massive proportions.

"We're close enough now," Matar announced. "We're only an hour away from docking. Shall I transmit the data now?"

"Check the identification keys one last time," Havel said, earning himself an annoyed look. Matar had checked and re-checked everything all morning. I put a hand on his shoulder, and he smiled up at me. The guys were in their chairs on the bridge, but the Gemi'i torso-brothers and I were standing in the centre, watching the station getting bigger on the view screen. I'd forgotten whose lap I'd sat on the day before yesterday, which meant I didn't know who to choose today. I'd been strict with making sure each of my three males got to spend some quality lap time with me. I knew I was teasing them, especially when I wriggled around, pushing down against their cocks, but they loved it. Once we were done with this mission, we'd finally get to go to the resort planet for our honeymoon and have as much sex as we wanted. I couldn't wait.

"Do it," Hix and Hex said as one. It was creepy when they did that, synchronising their voices as if they were one person. They kept insisting that they were two very separate individuals, but this eroded that argument.

Matar turned around on his swivel chair. "You two should press the send button. It's your plan, your data."

The torso-brothers exchanged a look, then nodded. They reached over and pressed the big red button on Matar's console. I was pretty sure that hadn't been there earlier, but it seemed fitting. Big red buttons were fabulous.

"Aaaaaand...sent." Matar said. "That's it arrived in the inboxes of Professor Z, the Dean, the IGU Council and various other people who have the power to stop Katila. Now we just have to wait."

"Can we see who's read the message?" I asked.

"Yes, I've programmed it so we get a notification on the screen. Want to bet who reads it first?"

"Aye," Xil chuckled. "And I know what the prize for the winner will be." He gave me a meaningful look that made me panties wet in an instant. "With an alternative prize for Hix and Hex."

Phew. Not that I thought Xil was going to pimp me out to the Gemi'i brothers, but I didn't want them to get any wrong ideas. We'd become friends, but nothing more. I felt no attraction towards them and besides, three males were plenty. Especially if one of them had two cocks and another a tail. I was running out of holes for them to fill.

"I vote for the Dean," I said without really knowing who that was. "I assume Professor Z is too busy to read every message immediately."

As soon as I'd spoken the last word, Professor Z's name popped up on the screen. Klat. We hadn't even started our bet and I'd already lost.

Matar pulled me down onto his lap. "I have some plans for you," he whispered, his voice oozing seduction and promises. His cock grew hard against my arse. If we'd been in a different situation, I'd begged him to take me right here, right now.

We waited in silence for the IGU's Headmaster to react. Would he send a message? Call us? Invite us to a meeting?

The minutes passed slowly. The Dean's name finally appeared on the screen, followed by those of some Council members. Hix and Hex had explained that an elected Council decided day-to-day matters of the university. It was split into three parts responsible for student, staff and faculty wellbeing. We'd sent our message to all three since this issue affected everyone.

I hated how we couldn't do anything but wait. I wanted to call the headmaster, shout at him to hurry up, but I doubted that would help our cause. No, we had to be patient, no matter how impatient as was.

"What do you think he's doing?" Havel muttered almost to himself. "Is he calling his staff? Ordering her to be arrested?"

"As much as I want you to be right, I doubt it," Hex said with a sigh.

"The IGU's wheels turn very slowly," Hix added. "They will talk about it, start an inquiry, talk about it even more. They won't arrest her until they're sure there won't be repercussions. The IGU's reputation is everything. But they will put her on a leave of absence, I hope. That will be the first punch, creating the first cracks in her self-confidence. She perceives herself to be powerful, safe from repercussions, so let's watch her fall, even if it's a slow fall."

"We should have killed her," Matar growled. "So much quicker." His tail banged against the floor like it always did when he was nervous or agitated.

"There was no lesson for Killing for Beginners," Havel quipped. "We may have messed it up."

I rolled my eyes. My mates were adorable in their belief in education. They'd be the ideal targets for scammers offering them a quick '100 Ways to Get Rich Fast' course, taught by a Nigerian prince. I had to make sure they didn't spend any more money on IGU courses. The abduction one had been simply ridiculous. Probing, nest building, going shopping... I doubted many true abductors actually did that. Not that I was complaining about the shopping trip. It had resulted in my little tribitt, Lord Boop, who was happily snoozing in his basket last time I checked. He slept a lot, but in the cutest way, with his tiny green front paws covering his face as if he wanted to shut out the world. I totally understood the feeling.

Finally, a notification sounded. A call from the IGU. Xil pushed the incoming transmission onto the main screen so we could all watch, but only he was being seen by the other side. He had his shoulders pushed back, his chin up, his brows furrowed. His shirt had a wide neckline, exposing his scales. He looked kind of scary, a predator waiting for his prey. Definitely like someone you'd want to listen to.

The being who appeared on the screen was nothing like I'd ever seen before. It reminded me of a giant shrimp, with bulbous white eyes on stalks, shimmering chitin plates covering its body and long pale-blue appendages that sprouted from where its cheeks would have been in a humanoid. It was strangely beautiful, in a creepy way. The background behind it was a simple white wall, so there was nothing to give away its size. It could have been a five-inch shrimp or a five-metre monster.

Only it's head and upper torso was visible, so whether it had multiple legs, a tail, or other shrimpish features was left to the imagination. Its eyes were fixed on Xil, but they seemed to be able to move independently from each other. The right eye stalk quivered every few seconds, but I had no idea what that could mean.

"Professor Z, thank you for contacting us," Xil said when the giant shrimp didn't take the first step.

Wait, this was Professor Z, the headmaster of the IGU? It had to be a joke. Right? I'd expected someone at least vaguely humanoid, wearing a robe like Professor Katila, sitting behind a desk, but instead we were faced with a crustacean.

This galaxy was strange as fuck.

"You have sent me some very disturbing information." The Professor's scratchy voice came through the speakers, but his mouth wasn't moving. Well, if I interpreted the location of his mouth correctly. Who knew, it may have been on a different part of his body. Nobody said the eyes had to be near the mouth, right?

"Are you sure of the validity of the accusation? Is the proof verifiable?"

Spoken like a true academic.

"Of course. We have credible witnesses, but we were also attacked ourselves. We have a video recording of Professor Katila admitting that she was the one ordering the unprovoked assault on our ship. It's in the files."

"Yes, yes, I've watched it. I also looked up your student records. You barely made it through the Alien Abduction for Beginners course. It could suggest that this is a simple revenge for your bad grades."

Xil huffed. "Trust me, we wouldn't travel all this way just because of some low marks. Besides, in my book, the abduction was a full success. Our abductee is still with us and has become our mate."

"Is that so..." Two hair-covered appendages appeared from the bottom of the screen and wiped across the Headmaster's eyes. I shuddered, a little creeped out. I really should get used to not everyone looking like my mates and I, but still... this was very different.

I stepped in front of Xil's chair to face Professor Z. "He speaks the truth. They abducted me, but they did an excellent job, which is why I stayed. Professor Katila graded them poorly on some aspects of the abduction, but that wasn't relevant to the overall success. They - we - didn't have any grudge with her until she had me kidnapped, attacked our ship, and forced us to abduct two of her former students."

I purposely didn't call Hix and Hex her lovers or mates. I wanted to highlight how she'd broken the rules by starting a relationship with them while she'd been their teacher.

"These are some graves accusations. I shall investigate them further. But first, you say she forced you to abduct two beings. Obviously, that is highly irregular. How did she force you? What were her threats?"

Xil gently wrapped his large hands around my waist and moved me to the left so that he could look straight at the Professor again.

"She made the demands while she was shooting at our ship. We didn't have a choice. Our vessel isn't made for battles and our shields were close to failing. If we'd not agreed, she would have killed us."

"Maybe she was bluffing?" the Headmaster questioned. "How do you know that she truly would have destroyed your ship and killed you?"

"I had no doubt about her sincerity. She seemed fanatic, crazed almost, and I swear she was about to kill us. Not just us, our mate, too. Please, watch the video again, you'll see the way she acted. Those weren't the actions of a sane person who can be reasoned with."

One of Z's eyes turned backwards, looking at something we couldn't see. I bet those rotatable eyes came in handy during lessons when a teacher had to prevent his students from cheating.

"I will take necessary steps," he announced after a moment. "My secretary will schedule a meeting with you for later today. Please don't be late."

With that, he disappeared. I chortled. Don't be late? There was no way we'd miss this for the world.

The IGU station's space port wasn't much different than that we'd arrived at on Kitt-Y-6. Sleek metal walls, a ceiling so high it was barely visible, hundreds of vessels in all shapes and sizes. The ship next to the Jade had an organic look, like jelly wrapped around a metal cocoon, that made me want to touch it to see if it would react. I knew better than that, though. Space was a dangerous place for those who liked to poke unknown objects.

A little green alien greeted us. She looked like I'd always imagined aliens. Bright green, two antennae on her head, otherwise fairly humanoid features. She looked almost too much like an extra in some sci-fi film.

"Welcome to the Intergalactic University," she said in a pleasant voice. "Professor Z has asked me to accompany you to his private conference room."

"I'd hoped there would be guards," Hix muttered from behind me.

He sounded a little scared. I would be, too, knowing that Professor Katila wasn't far. To be fair, I was afraid of what she might do. Had she been told yet that we'd complained about her? I assumed she knew. She'd known almost immediately when we'd tried this before. I rubbed my right ear. As disgusting as the thought of a brain slug was, it had been more comfortable than our current translator solution. Havel was going to procure us some more slugs while we were here, but first, we had to see the Headmaster. I was looking forward to seeing the rest of his body and finding out if he really did look like a giant mantis shrimp.

The six of us - five if you only counted the pairs of legs - followed the green female out of the busy space port and into a lift. Again, just like at Kitt-Y-6. She pressed her hand against a sensor and the elevator moved. Not up. To our right. I quickly reached out to the handrail and held on to steady myself. Did you still call this a lift if it didn't go upwards?

"I should say, it's unprecedented for Professor Z to clear his calendar like this," the alien chirped. "You must be very important guests."

She was clearly fishing for information. Xil must have come to the same conclusion, for he simply said, "We are."

She stayed quiet after that. I wished the lift - or whatever it was - had windows so I could see where we were going. The holo display above the doors showed strange symbols I didn't recognise. I supposed that if this didn't go up and down, floor numbers wouldn't make sense.

Finally, the lift came to a stop with a slight shudder. I waited a moment before letting go of the handrail, just in case it decided to move again.

The female beckoned us to follow her. "He's meeting you in his favourite meeting room. Again, very out of the ordinary."

The corridor we stepped into was brightly lit, almost too much so. I squinted to take in the curved walls and colourful art covering them. It was a welcoming space, if a little bright. There were no doors that I could see, so I gasped when our guide suddenly veered to the right and walked right through the painting of an alien landscape.

"What the fuck!"

Xil chuckled. "Intelligent walls. They change on an atomic level whenever needed, like when someone wants to go through them."

"We're going to walk through walls," I muttered. "Like ghosts."

"No, like IGU employees." Matar laughed. "I regret not coming here to our induction ceremony now. This place is cool."

He drawled out the *cool*, showing me just how proud he was of having learned that use of the word. He hadn't quite understood why it was hip to be cold, but he loved to impress me with his Earthisms.

Before stepping through the wall myself, I lay my hands against the surface. It wasn't as cold as metal should be, but I also didn't sink in like I'd expected.

A head - the green alien's head - poked through the wall. Without the rest of her body, she looked like one of those stag trophies hunters had mounted to their walls. Except that she was very much alive, with a slightly annoyed expression that made me step back.

"Are you coming?"

I nodded and took a deep breath before stepping through the wall. For a moment, it felt like walking through warm water, but then cool air hit me, dispelling the feeling. We found ourselves in a large meeting room that didn't look like the rest of the IGU station at all. Plants were everywhere. They hung from the ceiling, they covered the walls, they were in large pots in the corners. Very few of them were green, with most displaying yellow and orange shades. Only a single one was a flower, the one on the table in the centre of the room. Its sunflower-yellow petals were as large as my palm and curled inwards at the tips.

A strange mixture of scents assaulted my senses, and I couldn't help but sneeze.

"Our mate is allergic," Havel snarled at the green alien. "Remove these plants immediately."

I held up my hand. "I'm not allergic. At least, I don't think I am. It's just a sneeze."

He gave me a sceptical look, but at least he didn't pull out his medical scanner like he usually did when he thought something was wrong with me. Which happened a lot. He'd read way too much about human diseases and constantly imagined me suffering from at least two or three of them. What did you call it when not you, but your mate was a hypochondriac on your behalf?

"Please, be seated," our guide said pleasantly, ignoring our little mini medical drama. "Can I get you some refreshments?"

"That would be lovely," I replied before the guys could say no. I was thirsty. Hopefully, they add human appropriate food on the station.

She disappeared through the wall again. Again, I was tempted to touch it, see if it would react, but I just about managed to restrain myself.

Around the table were four chairs, one for each of us. Well, with Hix and Hex sharing one, obviously, because they only had one bum. Was Professor Z going to stand? Or was he too large for a chair?

"I don't trust this," Hix said after they'd sat down. "It's going too smoothly. We didn't think we'd get to talk to the Headmaster right away. What if this is a trap? What if Kat manipulated him?"

"I've thought the same, but we don't have a choice," Xil admitted. "The alternative is leaving without a resolution. I don't want to look over my shoulder for the rest of my life, worrying that she might try to kill us after all. Do you?"

"Obviously not." Hex sighed and exchanged a look with his torso-brother.

While the guys sat at the table, waiting in silence, I explored the exotic plants littering the room. Some of them were downright ugly, especially the phallus-shaped orange bulb at the end of a long trunk. A girl could come up with all sorts of ways to use that plant... and not as decoration.

I stopped by a three-pronged cactus with spikes that were secreting some kind of purple liquid. Poison? Perfume? I wasn't quite brave enough to find out.

A knock on the door made me turn away from the weird and wonderful plants. The little green alien entered again, carrying a tray with a large carafe and a plate of cakes almost the same colour as her. At least I thought it was cakes.

"Professor Z will join you in just a moment. For now, please help yourself to refreshments."

I pointed at the grass green cakes. "What's that?"

"A delicacy from my home planet. You'll love it."

She left before I could ask her to expand on that vague reply. I gave the guys a questioning look, but they shrugged.

"Let me scan it," Havel said. "I want to make sure it's edible for both humans and Kardarians."

I gave one of them a sniff. Delicious. Notes of cinnamon blended with something similar to chocolate. As soon as Havel gave me the all clear, I took a bite. Flavour exploded in my mouth and I gasped. The cake may have looked dry, but inside it was moist. I moaned a little. Best cake ever. Maybe with the exception of Piki cakes.

"They're okay," Xil munched, chewing with his mouth open. I still had to teach them some table manners. "Nothing special."

"Nothing special? They're amazing!"

Oh well, more for me. Havel and Matar didn't look impressed either. Those guys were lacking some taste buds for sure.

The door slid open without a knock to warn us. The green female entered, this time carrying a glass container, no, an aquarium. Why on Earth was she doing that?

She sat it down on the table and arranged a tiny speaker next to it.

"Thank you, Myla."

Professor Z's voice came through the speakers and my eyes widened when I realised what that meant. I leaned a little closer and there he was, three inches long, sitting in the centre of the aquarium. He looked like a shrimp, just a bit more alien. His colours were so bright they seemed unnatural. He turned to me, looking at me from his white eye stalks. Somehow, I felt his humour. I bet he was used to this reaction.

But seriously, the headmaster of the IGU was a three-inch shrimp? How was that even possible? How was such a tiny brain capable of being intelligent enough to rise to this position?

Myla left the room, and the sound of the door closing gave me a good excuse to look away from the shrimp, I mean, Professor Z. I exchanged a look with Havel opposite me.

He was just as shocked. I wondered if this was known on campus or a secret. It had to be difficult for Professor Z to establish his authority when he had to be carried everywhere.

"I appreciate you taking the time to see us," Hex said, gathering his wits faster than me and the guys. "Have you taken any steps about Professor Katila yet?"

The headmaster swam over to the other side of the aquarium to look at the Gemi'i. Now that I could see his back, I gaped at the stinger at the end of his tail. It looked poisonous and deadly. Maybe he wasn't all that harmless after all.

"I have asked my assistants to go through the evidence you provided and gather some of our own as well. It's already been confirmed that you spoke the truth about the attack near Kitt-Y-6. That on its own is a grave crime that will be punished. I have ordered for Professor Katila to be taken into custody until we establish how to proceed. Of course, we have to be discreet. She's one of our highest-ranking members of staff and I don't want this to have any effect on the IGU's reputation."

"We understand," Hix said. "Will we be able to see her?"

"You want to visit her? After what you allege she did to you?" Professor Z's surprise was evident from his voice. I really wanted to know if this was his actual voice or if the device was more than just mere speakers and somehow translated his brain waves into sound.

Hix and Hex nodded emphatically. "We want to give her the chance to apologise. And to say goodbye. It will be good to draw a line under it all. Finish this chapter to start completely afresh."

Professor Z wiggled his appendages. "I will grant you ten IG minutes with her. But you have to be quick. She-"

The door burst open and Myla stormed in. "Sir, we're under attack!"

LESSON 7

REBELLIONS FOR IDIOTS

I jumped to my feet and pushed in front of Trish, hiding her behind me. The alarm and fright in the assistant's expression were real.

"What do you mean, under attack?" Professor Z asked calmly.

"A rebellion, no, a mutiny! They're on their way here, they want to unseat you and put someone else in charge of the university."

Z laughed. "They can try. Who's leading them?"

"Members of various faculties, mostly intermediate and support staff. I only saw a few professors. But one of them, Sir, it's-"

"Katila," he sighed.

"Yes. I don't know how she got out but she's free, leading them like some kind of revolutionary."

The headmaster's body turned bright red and his stinger lifted. "I will make her regret this. Summon the guards. And activate security protocol beta four."

She nodded, her eyes still wide with fear, then ran off.

"I apologise for the interruption," Professor Z said, as if this had been a mere inconvenience. "You may want to return to your ship until I tell you it's safe."

"No," Xil growled. "This is our fight, too. Katila has wronged us. We will make sure she gets her punishment.

If she takes over the IGU, that would be a death sentence to us."

"And to us," Hix muttered sadly. "We won't retreat either. We'll fight."

To be honest, the Gemi'i looked even less threatening than the tiny headmaster - he at least had a poisonous stinger - but I appreciated their enthusiasm.

"What is that security protocol you initiated?" I asked Professor Z.

"All guards will come to this building, securing the administrative areas as well as the Council and other leadership personnel. Then the doors and windows will be locked, and we'll wait for the guards outside to deal with the mob. We've got drones too, but I don't like to employ them unless it's a real emergency." I certainly classed this as a real emergency, but maybe he'd lived through worse things. With Professor Katila as one of his employees, he probably had.

"Do you have weapons here?" I asked him. We'd had to leave ours on the Jade. Not that we even had a lot of weapons, mostly what we'd kept after discharging from the Kardarian military. Still, once you knew how to fight and shoot, you'd never forget. It was like flying a spaceship.

The headmaster tapped the glass wall of his container and a screen appeared. Clever. He tapped his various appendages on it, navigating the IGU system far faster than I would have been able to with only two hands.

"They'll be delivered momentarily. There's also a ray gun in the cupboard to your right. The code is 6666."

I raised an eyebrow at that but didn't comment. I was the closest, so I got the gun. It was heavy and an older model than what I was used to, almost an antique. Hopefully, I wouldn't have to use it. I didn't want Trish anywhere near a battle. She was too precious to risk.

We waited in nervous silence. Xil had his arms wrapped around Trish. I wished our places were reversed. I'd much rather have her than the gun. But I was going to protect her no matter the cost. I'd die for her, no doubt about that. She was my mate and would be mine until the day I died, whether that was today or in a hundred IG years.

"Is it weird that I want to eat another cake?" Trish whispered.

Havel snorted. "Go ahead. I doubt we'll get the chance to eat something else anytime soon."

I watched her with fascination as she bit into the cake, her eyes fluttering shut, her expression relaxing into blissed out happiness. She was special, our little human.

Finally, after way too many IG minutes, the door opened to reveal six armour-clad guards. One moved to the table right away and picked up the aquarium, not surprised at all about the headmaster's tiny size.

"We've prepared the safe room," he said. "Will your guests join you?"

"Yes. Unless they've decided to return to their ship after all?"

Xil growled as if he'd been offended by that question. Trish put a hand on his arm to calm him down. "We'll stay."

The guard let his gaze wonder over us, then saluted the headmaster. "Follow me."

The safe room was larger than the conference room we'd been in. Screens covered all four walls, showing live feeds from various cameras across the station. Professor Z used his own container screen to control the big ones, enlarging one feed showing a group of about fifty people walking down a corridor. Most were armed, although some looked entirely out of place. Academics who'd never touched a weapon in their life. I scoffed. They weren't going to be much of a threat. At the head of the group, next to an old Ferven, was Professor Katila, her head held high, her steps filled with energy. I stared at her with hate, wishing I could reach her through the screen. The others should have listened to me. We should have killed her instead of doing this klatting diplomacy. Now she was loose, freed by some of her followers, and on the way to take on Professor Z.

"Maybe I'll employ drones after all," he muttered almost to himself. "They are better equipped than I expected. Hwar, I need you to look into how they were able to procure these weapons. Once we're safe."

"Yes, sir," one of the guards said. Four of them had stayed in the safe room with us, while the others were stationed outside the door. More were visible on the screens, running through the corridors on their way to confront the mob.

Luckily, this building was devoid of students who may have got involved in the fray. It was mostly admin staff here who'd now fled to safety.

One of the other guards, a female with a cleavage I would have salivated over before we abducted Trish, handed Xil a large box. "Weapons for you and your companions. You know how to use them?"

Xil chuckled. "I was the leader of a battalion in the Kardarian army. Yes, I know how to handle a gun."

Trish looked at him curiously. "I never knew that."

"It was a long time ago. I decided it wasn't what I wanted to do for the rest of my life. I'd only joined the army to please my father."

"You can tell me all about it later, once we're back on the Jade and Katila is in prison."

I leant over to her. "I know something much better we can do on our ship."

I let my gaze flick to her boobs, then her crotch, just to make it very clear what I was talking about.

A blush reddened her cheeks. Klat, how I loved that blush. Her change of colour wasn't as extreme as that of Professor Z, who still glowed bright red, but infinitely more adorable. I wanted to kiss her right now.

Xil handed weapons to Havel and the Gemi'i torso-brothers. They held it in a way that told they'd clearly never shot anything before, but I didn't comment. It might give them reassurance. As long as they didn't shoot anyone friendly by accident.

"Sir, we've formed a barricade near the toilets. They'll have to come that way if they want to get to your office," Hwar reported.

Of course, we could see exactly that on the screens. About twenty guards had blocked off one corridor using a portable force field. Unless the rebels had high calibre weapons, they wouldn't get through there.

"Good. Have some others circle around so they'll cut them off from behind."

"Yes, sir."

Myla, who'd already been in the safe room when we'd arrived, sprinkled a blue powder on the aquarium's water. Food?

"Thank you, my dear," the headmaster said, a smile in his voice. Not that you could tell that from his appearance. He floated upwards until he reached the lowest blue particles slowly sinking down the tank. His appendages moved, revealing something like a mouth opening. As soon as he sucked in some of the food, his colour turned from red to a dazzling array of blue and purple shades. Gorgeous. Maybe we could teach Trish to turn her cheeks blue, too. It would go well with her dark hair.

As soon as the mob turned the corner and saw the barricade, they went mental. Katila stepped aside, letting those with guns take the lead. They started firing on the force field, seemingly not caring at all that guards were behind it. I hoped they knew that the force field would hold and weren't intending to brutally kill the guards. This was a revolution of academics, not freedom fighters.

After a couple of IG minutes, they realised that they weren't going to get through that force field with fire power alone. Katila and some of the other ring leaders huddled together, discussing their next steps. We couldn't hear what they were saying, but the Professor looked disappointed. Had she imagined she could simply walk in here and take what she wanted? Maybe she'd become even crazier since we'd last talked to her. She might be so deluded that her intelligence had fled to safety.

The other guards sneaked up on them from behind and set up another force field just before the rebels even noticed their presence. Now they were trapped. And all without a single drop of blood shed.

"Good work," Xil praised.

"Thank you, sir," Hwar said with a respectful salute. He must have heard Xil talk about his military career earlier. I rolled my eyes at Xil's posturing. He was enjoying this. I supposed going from being in control of an entire battalion to a crew of two must have been hard for him. I never really thought about it. I was glad to be out of the army and happy to be on a ship with Xil and Havel, having grown up with them. The military had always been just a steppingstone for me. I'd got my engineering training there for free, but I hadn't planned to stay beyond that.

"Is that it?" Trish asked. "Are you going to arrest them all?"

"Eventually," Professor Z's voice came through the speakers. "I'm sure several of them will be willing to testify against their colleagues if that means a more lenient sentence. Now we have all the more reason to put Professor Katila on trial. Everyone has seen what she's done. That's enough to convict her and have her removed from the IGU, but the evidence you presented might herald criminal charges. We'll see. For now, you can leave safe in the knowledge that she's no longer a problem."

Hix and Hex stared at the screen. They must have been wondering whether it would still be possible to visit Katila in jail, but neither said anything.

"It's been a pleasure meeting you," Professor Z said to us. "Since you've been so helpful and have proved your skills, I've decided to award you honorary degrees of the Intergalactic University."

Havel gasped while I stared at him in shock. Us? Honorary degrees? We'd barely passed Alien Abduction for Beginners and now he was going to bestow us with such a merit? I didn't know what to say.

"T-thank you," Xil stammered, the first time I'd seen him lost for words. "It's an honour."

"And you two, would you like to return to the IGU as teaching staff?" the headmaster asked the Gemi'i. "I know you have a post at your home world, but I'd be happy to arrange a secondment, if you'd like to work here."

Their faces brightened as they finally turned away from watching Katila being arrested by guards.

I tuned them out and focused on Trish. "Are you alright?"

"Couldn't be better. Is it time for our honeymoon? And can we get the recipe for these cakes?"

I pulled her out of Xil's arms and into my own, hugging her tight. I breathed in her sweet scent, causing my cock to twitch. We had to get back to the Jade quickly so I could plunge into her. This moment of danger had made me horny.

I kissed her, tasting the spicy cake on her lips. It was a lot better mixed with her own special taste. I let myself go, drowning in our kiss, ignoring everything around us. She was mine, she was safe and she tasted delicious.

LESSON 8

COOKING FOR CULINARY CHALLENGED MALES

It was strange not to have Hix and Hex with us anymore. They'd decided to stay, although they'd promised to meet us again. Trish had been close to tears when we'd said goodbye. I hadn't realised just how much she'd grown to like the Gemi'i. Maybe it was good to have them gone. I didn't want any competition and would have hated to have to kill them. Trish was mine.

Xil had set course for Labeari, the resort planet we'd won a holiday on. I didn't like to remember the reason - Trish had got poisoned on Kitt-Y-6 - but I looked forward to relaxing, klatting by the beach, klatting in our hotel room, and even more klatting everywhere else.

Trish had explained that a honeymoon was all about getting to know each other. We already knew her, of course, but maybe there was a tiny part left of her body that I hadn't kissed, licked or touched yet. I'd have to make sure by worshipping her every minute of the day. She'd be sore and tired by the end of the honeymoon, but it would be worth it.

"Where's Trish?" I asked Xil. We were alone on the bridge. Havel had stocked up on medical supplies at the IGU station and was rearranging his med bay. He'd bought four new brain slugs and had inserted them as soon as we'd left. I rubbed my right ear. After having it gone for a while, that tiny pressure was going to take some getting used to again. At least Trish's voice sounded all normal now. No more old-fashioned translator tech needed to communicate with our mate. Brain slugs for the win.

"She's playing with her pet. Lord...you know what."

Just like Xil, I couldn't bring myself to call her fluffball by the name she'd chosen. It was a ridiculous name and I wouldn't support that.

"Good. I'm going to make a surprise for her. I got the recipe for those green cakes from the headmaster's assistant. I think we have all the ingredients and if not, I'll use the fabricator. Can you make sure she won't go into the galley for the next hour?"

Xil grinned at me. "You are going to bake? You? I doubt you even know how to use the heating compartment."

I punched him. Lightly. Very lightly. I didn't want to start a mutiny. "I know exactly how to use it. I just choose not to."

"Sure. Say what you want. I'll inform Havel to get some antidotes ready in case you poison yourself. Maybe some burn salves too."

I shot him a glare and headed to the galley. It was true that I didn't spend much time there. I knew how to use the fabricator and that was enough to make food that was filling and moderately tasty. But I wanted to show Trish that I could do this. Make something nice for her. And then she'd take me to our nest and klat me all night.

The easiest part was to find the ingredients. We didn't have quite the same flour as it said in the recipe, but flour was flour, right? There couldn't be much of a difference as long as it was powdery. The green plants the original recipe used for the cake's bright colour wasn't in our storage either, nor in the replicator's database, so I went for some Earth plants called matcha. Maybe it would make Trish happy to have some familiar tastes added to the cake.

Myla, the green alien, had only given me a list of ingredients without telling me how to actually mix them. She must have thought that I knew how to bake. Hah! That meant a true baker was slumbering within me and she'd recognised that. I'd make the best cake ever and Trish would love me for it.

With no clue about the right order, I simply dropped all the ingredients in a bowl and used a metal tool - no idea what it was called but it looked professional - to mix them. It took a lot of muscle power but eventually, all clumps disappeared, and the dough turned into something smooth and beautifully green. It looked right to me. I dipped a finger into the dough to taste it. Not too bad. Since I hadn't really enjoyed the actual cakes, I wasn't sure if this was what it was supposed to taste like, but it wasn't disgusting so that was a good thing.

I poured the dough into a metal container that looked like it wouldn't leak and put it in the heating compartment. Without any information on what temperature to use or for how long to keep it in there, I chose a medium temperature, one my wrist communicator said was good for roasting meat, and sat down in front of the heating compartment, watching the cake through the small window.

It was kind of calming to simply sit and wait for the cake to be ready. How many hours did a cake take? I imagined it would be quite a while. Luckily, Trish always spent a long time with her pet, so she wouldn't come here for the next few hours. Unless she got peckish.

"Xil, make sure Trish is well fed so she doesn't come to the galley," I said into my wrist communicator.

The Captain chuckled. "How's the baking going?"

"Excellent. The cake is in the baking process and hasn't burned yet."

"Yet." He laughed again. "Good luck, Matar. I shall make sure Trish doesn't go anywhere near the galley. Maybe I'll take her into our nest. That will keep her occupied for the rest of the day."

He ended the transmission before I could protest. That klatting bastard. Taking advantage of the situation. I hoped Trish would be too busy caring for her pet. I didn't want Xil to be the one to sate her needs before I could present my cake to her.

The cake was slowly rising in its metal container. That had to be the chemicals I had the replicator create. Would they also increase the size of other things? I adjusted myself, thinking of how good it would feel to fill Trish's tight holes with an even larger cock. I wasn't small by any means and barely fit into her, but one should always aim for more.

A whiff of something burning caught my nose and I jumped up in alarm. Surely the cake couldn't be done yet? It still looked green, not brown, and it wasn't on fire. Maybe just some leftovers in the heating compartment. I should have checked if anything else was in there before turning it on. Ah, yes, a tiny container was on the bottom rack. I recognised it as one of the bowls Trish used for her Peritan dishes. Whenever she got homesick, she got the replicator to make something called la-sah-na, but insisted it needed to go into the heating compartment even though the replicator cooked it perfectly. Apparently, it was all about the crust on top. I shrugged. Peritans were strange.

When the cake rose above the edge of its container, I started to get nervous. Was that supposed to happen? Would it grow even larger until it filled the entire compartment? What if it wanted to infiltrate the ship? What if I'd created a living organism ready to take over?

A shudder ran down my back. I may have doomed us all.

"Something's burning, did you know?" Havel strode into the galley, looking around for the source of the smell.

"I know," I snarled. "We should get our weapons. I think I've created a monster."

Havel cocked his head. "What?"

"Look at how this cake is growing in size. Soon it will fill the entire heating compartment. What if it will expand further? What if it needs all our space?"

The medic stared at me for a moment, then burst into laughter. He laughed so hard that he bent over, slapping his thighs. "You've really never baked before, have you? This is supposed to happen but don't worry, the rising agent will stop working at some point. Unless you used too much."

"I followed the recipe," I muttered, not telling him that I'd had to adapt most parts of it.

"Then everything will be alright. It does look quite similar to the cake we had at the station. If it tastes the same,

Trish will be all over you." He looked a little jealous. "Maybe I can say that I helped you?"

I growled. "No way. This is my cake and I will take full credit for it. You get some other surprise for her."

"Oh, I fully intend to. I'm already working on it."

With that mysterious remark, he left, still chuckling to himself. I glared at the empty doorway. He wasn't going to destroy this for me. Victory was going to be mine.

LESSON 9

SEX TOYS 101

I was going to cheat. Not just that. I was going to steal from the Captain. Xil wasn't going to be happy. He might throw me in the brig for a few days, but ultimately, I knew it would be worth it. I'd hacked into security and broken into his cabin. Nowadays, we all slept in the nest with Trish, but we still had our old cabins where we kept our belongings.

I rummaged around his sparse, boring possessions until I found what I was looking for. Perfect. Trish would love it. I grabbed it and sneaked out of the cabin, resetting the lock so that Xil wouldn't know I'd been in here. He'd figure it out soon enough, but I wasn't going to make it easy for him.

I pulled up a map of the Jade using my implanted communicator and located Trish. She was still with the tribitt. That gave me some time to set the scene. I hurried to our nest room, undressed and readied her surprise.

Only once I was fully prepared, I pinged her, asking her to come to the nest immediately.

"On my way."

My cock grew hard in anticipation. Every second that passed made my cock swell until finally, the doors slid open to reveal Trish. She was still fully clothed - of course, since she'd been cuddling with her pet instead of her mates - but we'd soon fix that.

Her eyes widened as she took in my naked body. "What's

that?" She pointed at the surprise I'd fixed around the base of my cock.

I grinned. "I'll tell you once you've got rid of those clothes."

She giggled and got out of them in record time. A drop of pre-cum glistened on my cock as I watched her strip. She was so gorgeous. She may not have had features like fangs, tails or scales like a Kardarian female, but she was drop-dead gorgeous. Our colours - blue, green and yellow - stained her abdomen and thighs, proof that she was ours. Mine. The prettiest human we could have ever kidnapped. We were so blessed to have her.

"Now tell me," she demanded. "Is that a cock ring?"

"Something like that. I bought it at Kitt-Y-6 and was waiting for the perfect moment." Lie. Xil bought it. I'd chickened out and bought her Piki cakes instead.

"And now is the perfect moment?" "We've accomplished our mission. We're safe. Xil is on the bridge, Matar in the galley. We've got the nest all to ourselves."

To make extra sure that we'd stay uninterrupted, I locked the door behind her with a quick command to my communicator. Now, that was much nicer. Xil wouldn't be able to stop me until I'd completed the mating. I smirked. It felt good to be a rebel.

Trish kneeled by my side, her nipples hard, her breasts perfect mounds. I reached out to squeeze them gently. One day, she'd told us, milk would squirt from those nipples. Once she was carrying our offspring. I couldn't wait for the moment when I could suckle on her, drinking her milk just like she drank the milk spurting from my cock. Scratch that thought. It wasn't actual milk.

"I'm still not sure what it is," she muttered and ran a finger over the toy. My cock twitched as if she'd touched it. I didn't know quite how this knotting ring worked, but it transmitted her touch to my skin. I couldn't wait to see what it would feel like to have it expand inside of her.

"The seller promised us endless pleasure," I reassured her. "It will make us feel even more connected. Come, let's try this."

I sat up so I could touch her pussy. She was wet already. As much as I liked to prepare her properly, spend some time on foreplay, I was too impatient today. Luckily, her lubrication was excellent. I'd done some research on it and discovered that her rates of lubrication were above average. Perfect for having three horny alien mates.

She straddled me and positioned her dripping cunt above my cock. I shuddered. So close. It took all my self-control not to grab her, throw her on her back and klat her like there was no tomorrow. Not today. Not now. I wanted to experiment with our new toy and that was best done slowly so we could truly savour every moment.

With a long, drawn-out moan, Trish sank on my cock, sliding all the way down until I was fully embedded in her. The ring was tight against the base of my enlarged cock, adding to the blissful sensation. Without warning, it started to vibrate.

"That feels amazing," Trish gasped. "Wow, if it continues to do that, I'll come in no time at all."

I had no idea how to change the settings of the toy. I didn't want her to find her release just yet. I was close myself, all the anticipation had affected me, but there was still research to do. At heart, I was a scientist and I was going to figure out how this toy worked and how I could improve it. I wanted to give Trish the best orgasm she'd ever had. Not that she'd ever complained that they weren't good enough, on the contrary, but I strived for perfection. Trish was going to be with us for the rest of our lives and I never wanted it to get boring in our nest. We'd have to find new ways to keep her satisfied. Our little female may have looked innocent on the outside, but inside she was a horny bitch in heat.

Trish began to ride me while I stayed still, simply enjoying the sensation of her tightness and the vibrations of the toy.

It was unlike anything I'd ever felt during klatting and it was delicious. I groaned as she slowly moved up and down my shaft, moaning every time her clit touched the vibrating ring. My self-control was waning fast. This was good, amazing, but I wanted more. I wanted it fast, hard and dirty. And I knew Trish loved that.

Decision made, I grabbed her hips and flipped us over so fast that I stayed embedded within her tight depths. She gasped, then grinned at me.

"Perfect. Now I can kiss you."

And she did. Her lips were so soft, so supple against mine as I claimed her mouth, plunging my tongue into her. She matched my pace, her tongue dancing with my own, our wild noises mixing into one loud groan. I started klatting her in earnest, pumping into her, using every muscle in my body. The ring was getting almost too tight around the base of my cock, but somehow, that slight pain was just what I needed. It made everything more intense. My dick had never felt this big.

I rammed into her as hard as I could, revelling into the gasps and moans that tumbled from her lips. I was getting close and I was sure that so was she. Was the toy going to engage automatically or did I have to do something?

I didn't care. I let go of all thoughts and questions. Trish was all I could feel, see, smell. She was my life, my entire universe. With one more strong stroke I came. My seed shot into her depths while her inner muscles milked me. She came with a cry, clinging to me so hard that her nails dug into my skin. She wrapped her legs around me as if she didn't want to let go. She didn't need to fear that. I was never going to let her leave. She was mine.

With that thought, the ring moved. I wasn't sure what it was doing, but it felt like it was sliding up my cock, further into Trish's pussy. She moaned, clinging to me even tighter.

"What are you doing?" she gasped, her eyelids flickering shut. Her cheeks were a beautiful pink while her skin was glowing with sweat.

"That's the surprise," I breathed, barely able to speak. The way the ring pushed along my cock felt like it was milking me, making sure every single drop of my cum was squeezed into her. I didn't have words for what I was experiencing. It was like nothing I'd ever felt. The closest thing to it would be Trish giving me a blow job while at the same time grasping the base of my cock with a firm grip, but no, that wasn't it.

"It's like you're growing," Trish moaned. "You're so big. How are you doing this?"

"This toy is going to connect us," I explained, remembering what the seller at the market stall had said. "It's locking me inside of you, making me unable to pull out. We're as one now, locked together. Some alien species do this naturally, it's called knotting. It's a mechanism evolved to make sure that the female absorbs all of a male's sperm, increasing the chance of her falling pregnant. It-"

Her eyes flew open. "You're trying to get me pregnant?" She pushed her hands against my chest, but I didn't budge.

"No, my sweet chicken, I'm not. I simply wanted to experience the intimacy of knotting. Since our Kardarian cocks don't have this feature, I had to resort to a toy. Don't you like it?"

She licked her lips. "I love it. It feels so full, like you're part of me, like our bodies have merged. How long is it going to stay like that?"

"Uhm...I don't know," I admitted.

To my surprise, she laughed. "That's so you! Does this mean we might be here for hours? Days?"

A strange hope rose in me. Being locked inside her for days? Yes, please. I couldn't imagine anything better. The ring was keeping me rock hard and even though I couldn't move to come again, I was sure that if I stimulated her clit enough, her inner muscles would squeeze me enough to help with that. I had no doubt that if she didn't have a contraception implant, I'd sire offspring today. I still felt my warm seed around the tip of my cock and imagined it being slowly absorbed by her, travelling all the way up to her eggs.

It had confused me greatly to learn that human females had eggs but didn't lay them. Not like chickens, the birds Trish had told me about, who also built nests just like the one we'd made for our mate.

I shifted a little and Trish moaned in response. "Do that again. Sooooo good."

I grinned and slowly rotated my hips, feeding on the blissed-out expression on her gorgeous face. I reached between us and gently rubbed her clit. Her legs tightened around me, encouraging me to continue. Her sounds became guttural, almost feral, as I helped her reach oblivion once more. She screamed as she came, convulsing around me, and that was enough to push me over the edge. I roared, my cock seemingly bursting within her. I felt more cum flooding her cave, stopped from escaping by my cock. And yes, it was still hard. I groaned. I had a feeling that I'd come more often today than I had ever before.

LESSON 10

THE SECRET TO A SUCCESSFUL HONEYMOON

"Captain, you better come to the nest."

Matar sounded upset, so as soon as I'd checked that the autopilot was still on, I ran from the bridge towards our living quarters. Was something wrong with Trish? Was she injured?

My heart raced and not from the running. I slid to a stop in front of Matar, who was waiting outside the nest room.

"What's going on?"

He was trembling with suppressed anger. "See for yourself. But before you go in...don't try and separate them. It'll hurt Trish."

I stormed into the room without delay. Havel and Trish were in the nest, naked, their bodies entwined. As much as I wanted to be in Havel's position, I didn't see anything wrong with that. They'd mated, so what. I was planning to do the same thing later. I might even join them now, since Trish was already naked and had been readied by Havel.

The medic shot me a guilty look. "Sorry."

"What are you sorry for? What have you done?"

Trish laughed. "Don't punish him. It's amazing."

I ran a hand over my head, trying not to lose my temper. By the great and terrifying Black Oboto, what was going on?

"Step apart," I ordered. "Trish, I want to talk to Havel alone."

Again, she chuckled. "I'm sorry, that won't be possible."

Her gaze wandered to her pussy, where Havel was still deeply embedded. They lay on their side, spooning, looking way too exhausted. Not that I blamed Trish. It was Havel's fault. But if he tired her out and she'd refuse me, I was going to punish him. Severely. I was the Captain; I was supposed to be the first to get to klat her. And the last. And in between, too.

"He's come five times," Trish whispered completely in awe. "I never thought that was possible."

Five times? How long had they been here? It couldn't have been more than one IG hour since I last checked on her. She'd been with her pet then. Five times in less than an hour? That shouldn't be possible, not even for me, and I was a virile Kardarian male in his prime.

I glared at Havel. "Explain. Now. Or I'll have you disciplined."

He didn't meet my gaze. "I...took your ring. The toy you bought at Kitt-Y-6."

Fury rose in me and it was barely possible to stay where I was and not launch my fists into his face. His guilty expression only fuelled my anger. How dare he! I'd bought that toy for me to use on Trish. I'd been waiting for the perfect time to use it, probably during our honeymoon when we had lots of time and wouldn't be disturbed. He'd taken that away from me.

I growled. If he hadn't been my friend and Trish's mate, I'd have thrown him off the ship. Without docking somewhere first. See how often he'd come without oxygen.

Now I knew why Matar had warned me not to separate them. If the salesperson had been right, they might be locked together for hours. I balled my hands into fists. Hours of him in her. How much of his seed had he already pumped into her? Was she already stained blue inside? Our mating fluid had only coloured her skin the very first time, but with this amount, who was to say it wouldn't stain her? A blue pussy to remind me every time of the humiliation...

I couldn't hold back any longer. I threw myself at him, being careful not to touch Trish. He moved away from her as much as he could with his measly dick still inside of her. I'd cut it off. That was it. Then he'd never get to do this again. He'd have to satisfy her with his fingers and tongue alone, while never able to experience the joys of a true orgasm again.

"Matar, get me a knife," I growled.

Havel's eyes widened in fear. Good. Now he was listening.

"Xil, stop it," Trish said firmly and put her hands on my back. She moved them in soothing circles, somehow erasing some of my anger even though I didn't want that. My fury was righteous. Havel had wronged me and I was going to take revenge.

"He just tested the toy for you, for us," she said, her voice sweet and enticing. "Now that we know how it works, the two of us can enjoy it again and again. Maybe without being locked together for hours. I'm starting to need the loo."

Havel looked even more scared now. Was he afraid to have her pee on him? I supposed that could be arranged.

"I'll make it up to you," he promised, and I knew he meant it. I could always tell if my friends were telling the truth, especially Havel. "I promise."

"As soon as we can move again, you can fuck me," Trish added. "Although I might need a shower first." She laughed softly. That sound took away the last sharp edges of my anger.

I got up and turned away from them. I didn't want to see their union any longer. "When we get to Labeari, you're going to be mine for the entire first day."

"Deal!" she shouted after me, but I didn't turn back. I was going to my cabin and wank to the image of me being the one inside of her instead of Havel.

Matar's cake was cold by the time they finally joined us. I ignored Havel but did give Trish a good look from top to bottom, making sure she was alright. She seemed tired, but otherwise fine. Klat, she was glowing with post-sex happiness.

"I made you some cake," Matar said as soon as she'd sat down. "It's no longer warm, but it might actually be better that way. The cakes at the IGU were cold too. And it's not the right green but-"

"Stop babbling," I barked, although I was secretly amused at how serious he was taking that cake.

I waited until he'd given Trish a piece, then grabbed a slice for myself. To me, it smelled just as bland as the one at the IGU, but I watched Trish with interest as she took her time inhaling the cake's scent.

"It smells delicious," she said, smiling at Matar.

Yes, I was definitely going to need at least an entire day with her. Alone. Without those two idiots. I was going to show her that I was the best of us. I'd make her forget them.

I watched her closely as she took the first bite. Havel did the same, clutching his med scanner. Seemed neither of us trusted Matar's baking skills. She smiled while chewing. It wasn't quite the orgasmic expression she'd had while eating the original cakes, but it didn't look like she was pretending to enjoy it.

"Those are good," she said, causing Matar to beam with pride. "They taste a little different from the ones at the station, but not in a bad way. What did you use to make them green?"

"Matcha tea," he replied proudly. "It's a Peritan ingredient so I thought it would remind you of home."

"To be honest, I've never heard of Matcha, but maybe it was something humans ate before the world went to pieces. It's not like we had a lot of exotic foods where I grew up."

Matar's smile wavered a little. "I can make you some of that tea later so you can try it."

"I'd like that."

"You can make it for all of us," I barged in, finding this conversation a little too Matar-and-Trish-sided. "Now that you've proven that you can cook, you'll be making a lot more meals for us."

I laughed mentally at his disgruntled expression. He'd not expected that. But if Trish liked his baking, then he'd have to do more of it. We wanted a happy mate.

"What kind of food will they have at the resort planet?" Trish asked while eyeing the cake, clearly tempted to take another piece. I picked one up and held it to her lips. With a grin, she took a bite while looking right into my eyes. They positively twinkled with temptation. If she didn't look so exhausted, I'd bend her over right now and klat her from behind while she was eating that cake. My cocks ached. Soon.

"All sorts," I replied, pushing away the thoughts of ravishing her. "Both local and interplanetary delicacies. We've got an all-inclusive package, so we can try all the restaurants we want. I've read there's room service too." I gave her a wink. "We'll make use of that for sure."

She took my thumb into her lush mouth and sucked it. Gah. Was she trying to make me lose control?

"I'm looking forward to that," she purred and gently nibbled on my thumb.

From above, Labeari didn't look very special. Lots of pink and purple. As a circumbinary planet, it had two suns, one of them currently blinding me through the windows of the shuttle. Labeari had been chosen as a resort planet for this reason - among others, like having no major predators that could attack tourists - because it meant it was always day on one part of the planet and always night on another. Perfect for species who needed one or the other, or for people who simply wanted to party in the dark thirty IG hours a day.

We'd parked the Jade at one of the seven space stations orbiting Labeari and had stepped onto one of the first-class shuttles reserved for all-inclusive guests like us.

We had the shuttle all for ourselves, with one attendant for the four of us. He was taller than me and had to slouch slightly to not hit the ceiling. His uniform didn't leave much to the imagination and I hated to think that all the staff on Labeari were dressed like that. I'd have to blindfold Trish to keep my jealousy in check. Or simply not leave our hotel.

I took a sip from my cocktail. Delicious. I'd have to find out the name of it so I could order more in the future. The alcohol content was just right for a Kardarian, while it would be way too strong for Trish. She's been given a different drink that was hopefully more appropriate for delicate humans. As fun as it was to get her drunk, I wanted her to experience the joys of the resort planet with a sober head.

"Landing in five IG minutes, please take a seat and strap in." The pilot's voice came through the intercom with a crackle. It was a universal fact that intercoms across the galaxy distorted the voice and came with unwanted noise. It wasn't any different for the comms system on the Jade.

Trish took my free hand. "I'm so excited. What do you think the sea will be like? Does purple water feel the same as that on Earth?"

"We fill find out," I said calmly, although her excitement was contagious. After all the troubles of the past weeks, it was a relief to have nothing but relaxation to look forward to. Lots of food, sun and sex. That's what a honeymoon was all about, after all.

"It will do wonders for your skin," the attendant said, smiling at Trish. "You'll look less pale in no time."

Trish glared at him. "Are you saying I need a tan?"

The attendant looked taken aback. "No, I meant to be more colourful like your mates. If you spend long enough in the sea of Labeari, your skin will turn purple. It's not permanent, of course, unless you want it to be. There are certain drugs you can take while here to make sure the pigments will stick. I know someone you can get them from, if you're interested."

"We're not," I growled. "Trish is beautiful the way she is." Besides, it might wash away our mating marks on her belly and thighs. No way. It showed the universe that she was ours and prevented anyone else from trying to claim her.

"Thanks, darling." Trish smiled at me. "Although it will be fun to see what I look like in purple. Will my hair change colour too?"

The attendant nodded. "Your hair is too dark to become fully purple, but it will certainly get a purple sheen, maybe some highlights."

Trish laughed. "I've always wanted to dye my hair, but it was too expensive. Such a nice, unexpected benefit."

I didn't mention that I liked her hair how it was. It reminded me of the colour of haram bark, the most resilient material on Kardar. Just like her. Resilient, strong, yet also supple and flexible when needed.

"You better hand me those glasses," the attendant said. "And then enjoy the view. We're landing at the main airport and the approach is simply spectacular."

I didn't look at the outside. My gaze was fixed on Trish, watching as she turned to stare through the windows, her lips slightly parted, her cheeks pink, her eyes wide with anticipation and excitement. I loved her so much it hurt.

TRISH

The first thing I noticed was the smell. Roses mixed with vanilla. I breathed in deep. Delicious. That scent made me hungry. Luckily, several small buffet tables lined the entrance hall of the space port. I grabbed a handful of what looked like nuts and hurried after the guys. Our baggage would be brought straight to our hotel. It was so weird to have people around to do stuff like that for us. We were being catered for front and centre and would be for the next three weeks. I'd leave Labeari as a spoilt princess who needed her own set of servants. I chuckled at the thought of turning the Jade into a version of this colourful, exuberant place. Not happening.

When we stepped outside the spaceport building, I couldn't help but stop and stare. A stone-paved avenue led towards the sea. Small market stalls were set up at both sides with vendors shouting their offerings. I'd thought I'd seen a lot of different species at Kitt-Y-6, but that had been nothing compared to the variety here.

"Make way for King Bloob," someone called from behind us. Four vaguely humanoids carried a ginormous square glass tank filled with bright green goo. Five dark eyes stared at me from within it, seemingly unconnected to a body. I stepped out of the way, bumping into Matar.

He slid an arm around my waist and pulled me further away from whatever strange gelatine royalty was passing us.

"Wait!" someone shouted from behind us, and I swirled around. It was the attendant from the shuttle, waving his hands in agitation. "Why did you leave? I've got a caddy ready for you to be taken to your final destination. It's too far to walk."

I glanced at Xil. I'd been following him; he'd looked like he knew where he was going.

"I was in the mood to stretch my legs," he muttered. Silly man. That guy really didn't know how to show weakness.

We followed the alien back to the space port. Around the corner from the entrance sat a row of hovering pods that looked like tiny versions of the shuttle we'd taken to the planet's surface. The attendant led us to one of them.

"This will take you to your lodge and will stay there as your designated vehicle. It has full voice control in all IG-recognised languages as well as a state-of-the-art entertainment system. There's also a mini bar that will be restocked automatically. Should you need any assistance, simply press that big purple button with the Labeari logo and someone will help you right away. Any questions?"

"Yes, can those windows be turned opaque?" I knew exactly why Xil was asking that and rolled my eyes. Did he ever not think with his dick?

"Of course, just use voice commands. Now I wish you a wonderful time on Labeari and please give my service five stars when you're sent a survey at the end of today."

The shuttle was snug for four people - mostly because my males were so big, it would have been spacious for four humans - but that was the perfect excuse for Xil to pull me onto his lap. He was rock hard. I was starting to doubt we'd make it to our hotel before he ended up between my legs.

His hands found their way to my boobs and he squeezed them until I couldn't repress a moan.

"What are you doing?" I sighed, pretending to be exasperated but actually wanting him to continue. I had to keep up appearances. I didn't want them to think that I was constantly ready to be fucked, even though I was. They were doing things to me, to my brain, to my ovaries. My sex drive had never been higher.

"Making you feel good," he purred in his most seductive voice, the kind that made me hot in all the wrong places. "I want you to know what this honeymoon will be like. We're going to make sure you're happy every single hour of the day. We're going to worship your body and mind.

We'll make sure you'll want for nothing. We may not be the ones paying for this holiday, but we'll provide you with all the care you could ever need."

Havel reached out and took my hand, giving it a loving squeeze. "We're yours, chicken."

"Computer, how long until we get to our lodge?" Xil asked.

"Approximately thirty IG clicks."

That was about twenty Earth minutes.

Xil nuzzled my neck, kissing me ever so gently at the same time as Matar's hand squeezed my thigh. "That's long enough to make you forget all that's happened," he whispered. "Let go of the past, little human. Our future is bright and it begins today."

And then they made sure to show me exactly how amazing my future would look like.

EPILOGUE

GRADUATION

A cocktail in one hand, a cone with non-dripping ice cream in the other, I was truly enjoying life. In fact, I'd never been happier. The suns were warm yet not too hot, while a gentle breeze was enough to keep me from sweating. I was naked, baring my skin which now had a purple tint to it. I loved it. I looked like I wasn't quite human anymore. And to be honest, that's what I felt like inside. After all I'd experienced, Earth seemed a very long way away. It was crazy to think that a few months ago, I still lived in a leaky hut, running errands for Chadra, trying to survive. Now I was relaxing at a resort planet halfway across the galaxy, surrounded by my three mates, sipping on a cocktail without a care in the world. Or in the universe.

Yesterday, we'd got a call from Hix and Hex. They'd jointly taken on the role as heads of the IGU's Alien Abduction department and had even invited us as guest lecturers for the upcoming term. Xil wasn't convinced that was a good idea yet, but it would be a good way to earn some money. Now that our honeymoon was coming to an end, we had to decide what to do next. We still had a nice amount of money left from what that restaurant owner at Kitt-Y-6 had given us, plus we'd be able to eat at his restaurants for free for the rest of the year, but at some point, those credits would run out. Hix and Hex had mentioned that we might be eligible for compensation money from the IGU, since Professor Katila had been their responsibility when she'd attacked us, but we didn't have any details on that yet. It would be a while until all that was going to be settled. Katila was in custody and a trial date had been set, but just like on Earth, intergalactic bureaucracy was a nightmare. Slow and frustrating.

I'd suggested that we could visit the guys' homeworld and find jobs there, but they weren't very keen on that. One day, they'd introduce me to their families, but they loved the freedom they had in space and had no intentions of settling down. I understood that completely. I'd never felt this free and happy in my life. Every day was a new adventure, whether it was cuddling with Lord Boop and his new girlfriend - they had fluffy animals jumping all around the beach and one of them had taken a shining to my tribitt, so I'd kind of adopted her as well - or exploring the beauty that was Labeari. Long walks along beaches where the sand varied from bright pink to dark purple, the high-tech equivalent of snorkelling in the sea, taking a panoramic flight to a restaurant perched on the edge of a mountain cliff...there was so much to see and do here that three weeks had passed in a flash.

Later today, we had a booking at the bubble bath swimming pool, followed by a massage and a candle-lit dinner, but tomorrow, we'd have to leave. It would be weird to be back on the Jade. I'd fallen in love with that ship, but she was small and I was now used to space, fresh air and swimming in the sea several times a day. I loved the sea. I'd grown up far away from any ocean and had ever only seen it on pictures. Of course, the sea here was very different, not just because of how it had turned me purple. Without a moon, there were no tides, but the water's colour changed depending on the time of day. In the morning, it was a pale lavender, slowly turning into a deep wine purple in the evening. The suns never set where our lodge was located, but the windows turned dark at night and stars were projected all over the walls. It almost felt like sleeping under the open sky.

Yes, I would totally miss this.

"Could we get a job here?" I asked, more thinking aloud than actually meaning it.

Matar sat up on his sun lounger. The silver specks on his skin twinkled in the sun like stars strewn all over his body. He was beautiful. In the artificial light of the Jade, I'd never really noticed them much, but here, they turned him into a sparkling god of sexy.

"As what?" he asked. "Don't get me wrong, I love it here, but I also don't fancy becoming an attendant. Have you seen what klatting nonsense they have to put up with? I wouldn't have the patience."

Yeah, that was a very valid point. I had no qualifications to speak of. The guys had certificates in alien abduction, but that wouldn't help them here. They also had experience in trading and the military, but again, unless they wanted jobs as low-paid guards, that was irrelevant.

"I saw a poster earlier that made me think the same," Havel said, also sitting up. A row of empty cocktail glasses lined the sand next to his lounger. I'd discovered that Havel had a seemingly limitless tolerance to alcohol. He downed that stuff like it was juice, while a single one of those would have made me drunk as fuck. I tried it in my first week here. The hangover had been spectacular, although at least it had resulted in foot massages from the guys. Almost worth it.

"What poster?" Xil asked without opening his eyes. Just like the rest of us, he was naked, his two cocks proudly on display. My core still ached from the pounding he'd given me earlier, before we'd had a swim in the sea and then retreated to the sun loungers.

"The IGU is setting up an outpost on Labeari," Havel explained. "They're going to offer courses for both the resort guests and staff. Some people like that Lurian triad next door have bought their own holiday lodges here and spend most of the year on Labeari. I assume they might get bored after a couple of months of having their brains fried by the sun and want an intellectual challenge."

The wheels in my head started spinning at breakneck speed. The guys had been given honorary degrees and asked to be guest lecturers in the future. Plus, Professor Z still kind of owed us for exposing Katila. This could be the opportunity we'd been looking for.

"Do you think they'll have an Alien Abduction department?" I asked, excitement bubbling up in me. "We could do mock assignments. I can be the helpless little human that they have to abduct. We-"

"No," Xil growled. "You're not getting abducted by anyone that isn't us."

"Then we can re-enact our own abduction. Show them how it's done. Come on, this might work." I jumped to my feet, bursting with energy. "Let's call Professor Z."

Havel chuckled. "Maybe put some clothes on first."

I looked down at my bare body, purple except for the blue, green and yellow mating marks that had stayed unaffected by the sea's pigments. "That's acceptable. Although maybe one of you should do the call. I didn't get an honorary degree."

It still annoyed me a little. I'd been the perfect abductee so I should get a certificate for that too, right? I didn't fight them nearly as much as I could have. I didn't take an escape pod like one of their previous abductees had. I'd even let them dress in *lingerie,* and I really should get a prize for enduring that whole nest building exercise. Yes, I deserved a degree for all that. And he hadn't taken our abduction of Hix and Hex into account at all.

I ran up a pink dune to our lodge and slipped into a simple blue dress that we'd bought at one of the many markets nearby. No need for panties since I was going to take off the dress as soon as I'd spoken to the IGU headmaster. After a quick do-my-nipples-show-check I asked the AI to call Hix and Hex. I didn't have the Professor's direct number and I doubted he would take my call without warning. He was a busy shrimp.

They answered almost immediately, dressed in an elegant suit with a tie each around their necks. As Alien Abduction teachers, they'd started the tradition of wearing a different planet's fashion each week, starting with Earth. They'd worn exactly the same thing yesterday. The sight of their feathery bodies stuffed into tight black suits made me laugh, but I tried to stay serious.

"To what do we owe the pleasure?" Hix asked with a wide smile. "I didn't think we'd hear from you again so quickly."

"I need to talk to Professor Z," I burst out. "Do you have his number, or can you transfer my call?"

They exchanged a look. "Is it urgent?"

"Very." For me, it was. Yes, it wasn't life threatening, but I really didn't want to leave this paradise.

"I've messaged him," Hex said. Ah, I forgot, they had communicator implants like Havel. "While we wait, what's this about?"

"Did you hear they're starting an IGU outpost on Labeari?"

Again, they looked at each other. "We did," Hix said with a wry smile. "Are you about to ruin our surprise?"

"Surprise?"

"If this is what I think it is, you won't need to talk to Professor Z. So, tell me, what do you want to see him about?"

"We want to stay here," I admitted. "And I thought, well, Havel thought that we could somehow work for the IGU. We're good at abductions, as you guys know by experience. And I guess I could teach about life on Earth, maybe English language lessons, and-"

Myla appeared in a separate window on the screen.

"We won't need to talk to the Headmaster after all,' Hix said before she could even say hello. "Sorry about the interruption."

"But...wait, this is about what we discussed?"

It seemed everyone was in on this except for me and the guys.

"Yes," Hex confirmed. "No need to bother Z."

"Alright. Bye, sweeties!"

Her image disappeared and I stared at the Gemi'i. "Sweeties?!"

Hix's feathers fluffed up, but Hex stayed calm. "A new development. Now that we no longer have to fear that Katila could come after us, we can finally start our lives again. That includes dating." He grinned, clearly pleased with himself. "Isn't she lovely?"

"She is. Does she make cake for you?"

Hix's downs became even fluffier. Was that the Gemi'i equivalent of bluffing?

"That...and other things." Hex laughed. "But let's talk about you. We had planned it as a surprise, but I guess we'll have to tell you now. Tomorrow morning, Professor Z is going to call you with a job offer. We knew you didn't quite know what to do next and after you gushed about Labeari yesterday, we pulled some strings. I feel like I shouldn't tell you yet. The Headmaster is going to be disappointed if it's no surprise."

"I need to know, but I can keep the guys in the dark. They're outside, they're not listening. Then it's still a surprise for them."

"I suppose that's an acceptable solution," Hix said. His feathers were slowly going back to their original position, but he still had a bit of a flustered look. If I hadn't been so keen to find out more about the IGU jobs, I would have teased him about it. "Alright, the quick version is that all four of you can be employed by the IGU. We'll have some permanent staff on Labeari with regular guest lecturers from across the galaxy. There won't be an entire Alien Abduction department, but we managed to arrange two full-time staff positions for that course. Plus, the outpost needs a medic, so we thought of Havel."

"And what about me?"

They both grinned, making their large mouths appear even wider. "That's the best bit. You're the only person who's been both an abductor and an abductee. Plus, you've got experience in handling three aliens that aren't your own species. We'd like you to be the deputy head of the outpost."

I stared at them. "You want me to be in charge? Me?"

"Don't worry, you'll get training and support," Hex added quickly. "And you will have a boss to go to for guidance. But they won't always be on the planet, so most of the time, it'll be you in charge."

I didn't know what to say. This was crazy. I'd thought of maybe teaching a lecture or two, talking about my own experiences and what I'd learned by reading the guys' course materials, but actually leading this outpost? Wow. I'd not expected that in a million years. My first instinct was to say no, that I wasn't qualified, but this was our chance.

"You'll get housing provided by the IGU," Hix said, likely seeing how torn I was. "And the same all-inclusive food and entertainment access you have just now. We're still haggling over your salary, but don't worry, we'll get you something good. We're in your debt, after all."

"Anyone would have done the same," I said automatically. This wasn't the first time we'd had this discussion. They truly felt that they owed us for not handing them over to Katila. As if that had ever been a choice, not after we found out what she'd done to them.

"They wouldn't have, so let us pay you back in kind. You have until tomorrow to decide. Please try and act surprised when Professor Z calls you or he'll be disappointed. But we know you'll say yes. And guess who will have to come to Labeari regularly to check on the outpost? And who will bring their new date along with an entire case full of favourite cake?"

They grinned again, clearly pleased with themselves.

They'd had me at cake.

The guys looked at me expectantly once I re-joined them on the beach.

"I can't tell you, but you're going to be happy," I said as vaguely as possible.

"I'm already happy." Matar smiled and got up, taking me into his arms. I snuggled into his embrace. His touch felt *right*, proving that we were meant for each other. The other two joined us without a word until I was surrounded by my mates, touched from all sides, breathing in their scents.

"I'm happy, too," Xil said and cupped my face. I opened my lips just in time for his mouth to crash against mine. Xil didn't do gentle kisses. He claimed like the Captain he was.

Havel ran a hand over my belly and even though I didn't look down, I knew he was tracing the mating marks on my skin. "And me. As long as we're together, we're always going to be happy."

So cheesy. I'd never been able to explain that word to the guys since they didn't know what cheese was, but they excelled at being adorable. And slightly cringey.

I broke the kiss to speak. This moment felt important somehow. Like we were about to flip a page of our life together.

"I'm so glad you abducted me. You changed my life in the best way possible. Everything that we've been through only made us stronger. And now look at us, together like we were meant to be. I love you. Xil, Havel, Matar, I love you all so much."

I melted when I looked up, seeing them burn with desire and love.

"Together," I said one more time before kissing them one by one, showing them exactly how much I'd meant my words.

They may have abducted me, but I'd stolen their hearts.

THE END

Want to know what they got up to on their honeymoon?
You can read an exclusive bonus scene here:
skyemackinnon.com/downloads

And of course, there's a recipe for the green cake included in this book, just flip the page.

This may be the end of Trish's story, but not that of the Intergalactic University nor the Starlight Universe.
Get the next three books in The Intergalactic Guide to Humans Vol. 2 *box set! Or flick the page for a list of all of Skye's books.*

Subscribe to Skye's newsletter for all the latest books and updates:
skyemackinnon.com/newsletter

MYLA'S GREEN CAKE RECIPE
(MATAR'S VERSION)

After Matar had his go at Myla's original recipe, don't expect this to taste like the real thing – but it's still delicious! In case your spaceship doesn't have a heating compartment, use your microwave to make this a fast and yummy treat.

INGREDIENTS

- 4 tbsp all-purpose flour
- 1 tsp matcha powder (the better quality, the more intense will the colour be)
- 1/4 tsp baking powder
- 1 1/2 tbsp sugar
- 3 tbsp milk
- 1/2 tbsp vegetable oil
- Optional: chocolate chips; frosting or icing

HOW TO DO IT

1. Mix the dry ingredients in a large mug.
2. Slowly add the milk and oil, whisk until the dough is nicely blended and a beautiful green.
3. Cook in your microwave at full power for about a minute. Check if the cake is fully baked (it can still be a little squishy) and wait a few minutes before tucking in. You can also cover it in frosting or icing, but Matar doesn't have the patience for that.
4. Share it with your favourite alien.

You can download a printable version of this recipe at skyemackinnon.com/downloads.

THE STARLIGHT UNIVERSE

This book is part of the Starlight Universe, an entire galaxy filled with hunky aliens, exotic planets, and the human women ready to find love among the stars.

Starlight Highlanders Mail Order Brides

Alien Highlanders in kilts come to Earth in search of brides... and take them to planet Albya. Three m/f standalones full of humour, action and steamy romance. Part of the Intergalactic Dating Agency.

The Intergalactic Guide to Humans

A humorous take on alien abductions, probing and other shenanigans. One reverse harem trilogy about clueless aliens and the human woman they abducted, followed by several standalone romances with various pairings (m/f, f/m/f and m/m). If you want light entertainment filled with unicorns, fabulous misunderstandings and unusual body parts, this is the series for you.

Starlight Vikings

Set on Earth and on the spaceship Valkyr, this trilogy of m/f standalones is all about hunky alien Vikings in need of females. Part of the Intergalactic Dating Agency.

Starlight Monsters

These aliens are not your usual humanoids... they have claws, fangs, tails, scales, knotty dicks and will growl at you. Interconnected m/f standalones with lots of action, steam and fated mates.

ABOUT THE AUTHOR

Skye MacKinnon is a Scottish romance author who was raised by elves in the mystical Highlands and calls the Loch Ness monster her friend. Her bestselling books weave together romance with action, suspense and whimsical humour, creating page-turners filled with strong heroines, alpha heroes and loveable monsters.

Whether she's writing about aliens in kilts, hunky Vikings or cat shifter assassins, Skye likes to put a new spin on familiar tropes. Some of her heroines don't have to choose, some fall in love with other women, and others get abducted by clueless aliens.

Skye lives with her bossy cat on the west coast of Scotland and uses the dramatic views from her office as an inspiration, no matter whether she writes fantasy, paranormal or science fiction romance. Until she gets abducted by aliens, that is.

Subscribe to her newsletter:
skyemackinnon.com/newsletter

Find all of Skye's books on her website, skyemackinnon.com, where you can also order signed paperbacks and swag. Many of her books are available as audiobooks.

PARANORMAL & FANTASY ROMANCE

- **Claiming Her Bears** (post-apocalyptic shifter reverse harem)
- **Daughter of Winter** (fantasy reverse harem)
- **Catnip Assassins** (urban fantasy reverse harem)
- **Infernal Descent** (paranormal reverse harem based on Dante's Inferno, co-written with Bea Paige)
- **Seven Wardens** (fantasy reverse harem co-written with Laura Greenwood)
- **The Lost Siren** (post-apocalyptic, paranormal reverse harem co-written with Liza Street)

SCIENCE FICTION ROMANCE

- **Starlight Highlanders Mail Order Brides** (sci-fi m/f romance, part of the Intergalactic Dating Agency)

- **Starlight Vikings** (sci-fi m/f romance, part of the Intergalactic Dating Agency)
- **Starlight Monsters** (m/f romance)
- **The Intergalactic Guide to Humans** (sci-fi romance with various pairings)
- **Between Rebels** (sci-fi reverse harem set in the Planet Athion shared world)
- **The Mars Diaries** (sci-fi reverse harem)
- **Through the Gates** (dystopian reverse harem co-written with Rebecca Royce)
- **Aliens and Animals** (f/f sci-fi romance co-written with Arizona Tape)

OTHER SERIES

- **Academy of Time** (time travel academy standalones, reverse harem and m/f)
- **Defiance** (contemporary reverse harem with a hint of thriller/suspense)

STANDALONES

- Song of Souls – m/f fantasy romance, fairy tale retelling
- Wings of Time and Fate - YA fantasy
- Their Hybrid – steampunk reverse harem
- Partridge in the P.E.A.R. - sci-fi reverse harem co-written with Arizona Tape
- Highland Butterflies – lesbian romance

BOX SETS

- Daggers & Destiny – a Skye MacKinnon starter library

- Stars & Seduction - a Sci-Fi Romance starter library